Steam Tinker

by

Laura Strickland

A Buffalo Steampunk Adventure,
Book 8

Steam Tinker

Cover Art by *Diana Carlile*

The Wild Rose Press, Inc.
PO Box 708
Adams Basin, NY 14410-0708
Visit us at www.thewildrosepress.com

Publishing History
First Edition, 2021
Trade Paperback ISBN 978-1-5092-3609-1
Digital ISBN 978-1-5092-3610-7

A Buffalo Steampunk Adventure, Book 8
Published in the United States of America

Women rarely came to Lionel's door, no. They certainly never begged. The fact that this woman had beautiful, expressive eyes that displayed her every emotion, that he could catch the scent of her sweet perfume as it competed with the smell of the rain, and that she had an endearing accent notwithstanding, Lionel could not allow himself to be seduced.

Slowly and carefully, he examined the unit on the cart once more before shaking his head.

"She may be past reanimation."

"She can't be." Miss Gregory's fingers tightened. "Anyway, I've heard you can perform miracles."

Lionel attempted to withdraw his arm from her grasp. She refused to release him; their joined limbs extended above the mess on the cart.

"He sure can," Sammy piped up. "Why, he resurrected Mordred here, and he was a right rusty mess when he got here."

"Mordred?" Miss Gregory looked startled, as well she might.

The battered unit rumbled forward. Lionel had done his best with him, polished his outer skin to a dull silver and replaced the worst of his battered parts. In truth, the unit had been put back together from a score of others that would never run again. A more apt name for him might have been Frankenstein.

As it was, he creaked persistently. No matter what Lionel did, he couldn't quite chase that squeak. But he was still Mordred, dented face and all.

The unit surveyed the contents of the cart with interest. When he spoke, his voice box wheezed alarmingly. "Master Lionel, she is beautiful."

Praise for Laura Strickland

Laura Strickland's novella *FORGED BY LOVE* won first place in the short historical category of the International Digital Awards.

~*~

"The world building is phenomenal."

~Daysie W. at My Book Addiction and More

~*~

"Laura Strickland creates a world that not only draws you in, but she incorporates it…seamlessly….the kind of book that keeps you awake well into the wee hours, and sighing with satisfaction when you've finished the very last page."

~Nicole McCaffrey, author

~*~

"As I read I became so involved with the story, I found it difficult to put down the book. …Definitely …an author to watch."

~Dandelion at Long & Short Reviews

***

Previous Buffalo Steampunk Adventures

Dead Handsome
Off Kilter
Sheer Madness
Steel Kisses
Last Orders
Tough Prospect
Cross Checking

Dedication

For my husband, Paul,
who is and has always been
a tinker of the very best kind

Chapter One

Buffalo, the Niagara Frontier, Spring 1885

"Excuse me, sir, but are you the man they call the Steam Tinker?"

The question came quietly from the doorway of Lionel's shop, and nearly failed to capture his attention. Engaged in a particularly delicate procedure on the steam unit that occupied the main workbench, he dared not let his focus waver. He detested interruptions at the best of times, and especially when a job required precision.

Indeed, nothing beyond the mere quirk of an eyebrow showed he'd heard the comment made, oddly enough, in a woman's voice. He didn't see many women here in his workshop, tucked away among a rabbit warren of streets and alleys off Niagara Street. The fact that this particular voice sounded rather attractive and carried a faint accent, pleasing to the ear, further threatened to distract him.

He maneuvered his pliers inside the head of the steam unit a mere eighteenth of an inch, and its eyes opened. The unit stared at him in inquiry, as if it too heard the voice.

Apparently deciding he hadn't heard her, the woman spoke again. "Excuse me! Am I at the correct shop? Are you Lionel Pike?"

Sammy, standing opposite Lionel and holding the steam unit's head between his hands at a precise angle, shot Lionel a look.

"Steady," Lionel told him in a low voice. "I nearly have it."

The steam unit trembled beneath his fingers. A small fire burned in its thorax, just enough to lend it possible life, but whether animation followed would rest on Lionel's skill.

He loved these moments almost as much as he hated interruptions.

The unit's eyelids—thin and rusty, barely able to cover the painted eyes beneath—sank shut before popping open once more with new determination. It gave a rumbling purr.

Sammy grinned. "You've done it, Mister Lionel."

"I am very sorry," persisted the voice from the doorway. "But—"

With a calm deliberation that belied his annoyance, Lionel laid aside the tool and turned to face the intruder. Immediately, he froze where he stood.

He did not see many female customers here, no, and certainly none like this. An occasional clerk or worker from one of the steam laundries perhaps, sent by her employer to ask if an ancient unit could be repaired. An elderly householder, maybe, who could not afford a new automaton and wanted to keep the old one going.

And there was Patsy—a female scrap dealer who operated from the back of a cart in company with her brother, George.

This woman, he now saw, was as different from Patsy as was a purebred hound from a stray mutt.

A lady, and no mistake. A further truth flooded in

upon Lionel's senses, one he rarely had cause to contemplate: a beautiful lady.

He possessed an appreciation for beauty, one rarely let off its leash. In his own way, he strove for it in the work he did, taking old units—the broken, the cast off, the ugliest of the ugly—and making them perfect, if only mechanically. The work he did, the beautification, did not show on the outside.

But he knew it was there.

Now he eyed the woman poised in his doorway, noting everything. Her fine clothes marked her as a stranger to this part of Buffalo. A black serge coat and a little, boat-shaped hat perched atop a wealth of tresses piled high, hair the color of the ginger his mother used to put in her spice drop cookies, long ago. Delicate bones acted as framework for a pale face marked by a haughty nose that had a slight bow to it. Large, brown eyes regarded him steadily from between fringed, dark lashes.

Lionel sucked in a breath. An entire world might rest in those eyes.

He strove mightily to master his senses even as Sammy stepped around the workbench to his side. Behind them, on the bench, the unit moved feebly.

Alive.

"I'm Lionel Pike," he confessed, mightily bemused. "Madam, you should not be here on your own."

Behind her, through the open doorway, he could see the cloudy spring day had dissolved into rain. No ordinary rain, this—it carried the scent of the river, a mere two blocks away, and came only in a Buffalo spring, when the skies tended to open without much warning.

Usually, Lionel welcomed the rain. It washed away the detritus from the streets, the only cleaning they received in this part of town. Now, however, the April sky had grown dark as night.

An ill omen? Did Lionel still believe in them?

The woman stepped farther into the shop and extended a gloved hand. "My name is Sofia Gregory. I am pleased to meet you."

Lionel stared at the glove—white, immaculate. His own fingers bore smears of grease and a generous coating of soot. He folded them behind his back and gave a slight bow.

Her hand froze for an instant before dropping back to her side. Uncertainty flooded the large, brown eyes. "You are the one they call the Steam Tinker?" she inquired again. "I've been told you can repair almost anything."

He could, though he didn't particularly appreciate the name that came along with the ability. *Tinker* implied a jack-of-all-trades mindset. What he did required a specific skill set. But he nodded. "Yes."

"Good. I hope you will be able to help me. I have someone outside. Might I bring her in?"

Someone outside—in this rain? Lionel exchanged incredulous looks with Sammy before he nodded again. From behind him he heard Mordred, his steam unit, start forward, his wheels giving off their familiar, faint-squeaky rumble.

"Sammy," Lionel murmured, "perhaps you can assist our guest."

Sammy hurried forward. At eleven, he had nearly attained a man's height, though he was all bones and

4

angles, no matter how much Lionel fed him. He outgrew his clothing at a prodigious rate.

Now Lionel and Mordred watched as the boy and the woman ducked outside, only to return towing a cart.

The cart bore an obviously aged steam unit in a state of woeful disrepair. It lay on the conveyance like so much scrap metal, only loosely connected at the joints, painted eyes staring upward.

Curiously, it wore clothing. The garments had been fashioned around its sculpted metal body and articulated limbs. At the moment they, along with the cart itself, were soaked through.

Lionel wondered if the woman—this dainty lady—had pushed the cart here by herself, all the way from wherever she'd come. The image near blasted his senses.

"Her fire has gone out," Sofia Gregory announced with a quiver in her voice that betrayed great distress.

Lionel, who observed much with little effort, could not miss that quiver. It made him far from happy. He didn't deal well with women. If this one started to weep, he had no idea what he would do.

In what he hoped was a soothing voice, he said, "If the fire in the thorax has extinguished, you have only to rekindle it." Surely she knew that. Why come here and bother him? But, eyeing the sprawled and sad-looking unit, he doubted lack of fire was the major problem.

Miss Gregory shook her head. Raindrops glittered on her hair and shivered—indeed, like tears—on her cheeks. "No, Mr. Pike, that is not all of it. She's—she's very old, near as old as me." A smile trembled across her lips. "I received her as a gift for my first birthday."

"I see." Again, Lionel ran an eye over the woman.

Not as young as he'd first surmised. She had to be nearly thirty. "Extraordinary. This must have been one of the first units made here in Buffalo."

"Yes."

"And it's been operative all these years?"

"She," Miss Gregory stressed the pronoun slightly, "has had many repairs. Her original components were rather—well, 'crude' is the only word I can employ. Since I reached my majority, I have purchased several upgrades. I had a man who worked on her—Darin Gordon. Did you know him?"

"I did," Lionel acknowledged. An elder craftsman, Gordon had a reputation for being fair as well as highly skilled and clever, an attribute, in Lionel's opinion, even more valuable. He'd died recently following a long illness. "I met him a few times."

"He was able to keep her running. But these last months, when he was too ill to take on jobs, I am afraid she deteriorated. Last week she just—just quit." Miss Gregory's lips worked for a moment before she spoke the next word. "Failed. I took her to another repair shop but they—well, they ruined her." She waved her hands over the object on the cart, distraught. "As you can see. Worse, I think they stole some parts."

"Where did you take her?" Lionel asked, surrendering the fight over the pronoun.

"Starr and Williams, on Pearl Street."

Lionel snorted. Sammy, who'd retired to his side, gave a soft echo.

Lionel said, "You would have done better taking her to the steamies." Over the course of the past year, the steam automatons of Buffalo—hybrid and standard alike—had formed a coalition and set about attaining their rights. Owners of the units were now supposed to pay them a wage. They pursued legitimacy that would prevent them from being turned off—which to them equated with death—without due cause. They married among themselves, and in rare cases with humans, and a human-steamie couple had just adopted a human child.

It was said, too, they hovered on the brink of creating children of their own—not pure steam units, but the highly sophisticated hybrid ones covered with skin, and with human hair and eyes. Steam units, so it turned out, were best at manufacturing more of their own kind.

"I did not think they would be interested in repairing so ancient a steam unit," Miss Gregory admitted. "I heard you do, on a regular basis." She looked around the shop, crowded with old components, before her gaze returned to him, compelling. "Besides, they say you are the best in the city."

"He is," Sammy spoke up staunchly, if without invitation. "He can tinker anything."

"If that is true, Mr. Pike, then save her for me. Please." Miss Gregory reached out and clutched Lionel's arm, her very touch an appeal. "I beg of you."

Women rarely came to Lionel's door, no. They certainly never begged. The fact that this woman had beautiful, expressive eyes that displayed her every emotion, that he could catch the scent of her sweet perfume as it competed with the smell of the rain, and that she had an endearing accent notwithstanding, Lionel could not allow himself to be seduced.

Slowly and carefully, he examined the unit on the cart once more before shaking his head.

"She may be past reanimation."

"She can't be." Miss Gregory's fingers tightened. "Anyway, I've heard you can perform miracles."

Lionel attempted to withdraw his arm from her grasp. She refused to release him; their joined limbs extended above the mess on the cart.

"He sure can," Sammy piped up. "Why, he resurrected Mordred here, and he was a right rusty mess when he got here."

"Mordred?" Miss Gregory looked startled, as well she might.

The battered unit rumbled forward. Lionel had done his best with him, polished his outer skin to a dull silver and replaced the worst of his battered parts. In truth, the unit had been put back together from a score of others that would never run again. A more apt name for him might have been Frankenstein.

As it was, he creaked persistently. No matter what Lionel did, he couldn't quite chase that squeak. But he was still Mordred, dented face and all.

The unit surveyed the contents of the cart with interest. When he spoke, his voice box wheezed alarmingly. "Master Lionel, she is beautiful."

That made Lionel stare at the unit in surprise. Mordred did not have many opinions. That was, he did, but he rarely bothered to express them.

And the broken unit on the cart possessed no beauty. Just worn metal and rust and wrecked gears. And that was only what Lionel could see in a cursory glance.

Slowly, and with regret, he shook his head. "I am sorry, miss. The damage here is—extensive. I am not sure these parts, as we have them here, can be repaired."

"Please." Miss Gregory leaned toward him in appeal. Her eyes gazed directly into his. "You are my last hope."

"I—" Lionel began unhappily.

"Her name is Verna, and she is my best friend."

Chapter Two

"Please," Sofia repeated softly, and hung on with all her might to the arm of the steam tinker. She could see refusal in his eyes, along with a measure of honest regret. And if he sent her away, she had nowhere else to turn.

She'd heard much about him during the past days, while Verna languished with those robbers, Starr and Williams. The best repairer of steam units in the city, so he was declared—aside from the hybrids themselves, of course. A genius and something of a recluse who took on only the specific jobs he chose. His shop, hidden away, was said to be shabby, and his nature difficult.

All that she'd heard had conjured an image so at variance with the man who now stood before her, linked to her by her desperate grip, it shocked her.

She'd imagined an aged, crotchety fellow, perhaps stooped and white-haired. No one had said anything to make her think differently.

But this man could not be above thirty and, though of average height and build, looked hale and hearty. He wore a neat pair of work trousers, a pinstriped shirt, and a shop apron liberally streaked with soot and grease, and had a crop of curly, dark hair that spilled with considerable abandon down his neck. He had a pair of intelligent, clear gray eyes that reflected his emotions far more than he probably realized.

Or maybe the link formed by Sofia's fingers on his arm let her sense what he felt. A bare, muscular arm it was, the sleeves of his shirt being rolled up to the elbows.

His gaze flew to hers, and he repeated carefully, "Your best friend? A steam unit."

Sofia drew a breath. "As I say, I have had her since I was one year old. My papa purchased her to act as my nanny and companion. She was a very good model back then, the best to be had. But that was well over twenty years ago."

"I see." Thoughts flickered through the steam tinker's eyes. Carefully, so as not to offend, he disengaged his arm from Sofia's grip. His fingers— long, quick, and clever—flew briefly over the components on the cart. "What happened to her?"

"An accident. She fell down the cellar stairs. They are in disrepair." The whole aging house on Woodlawn Avenue stood in a woeful state, more or less crumbling around Sofia's ears. "She tumbled over and over as she fell, and landed on the floor below, which is stone."

Sofia had begged Verna not to go into the cellar. Her wheels no longer operated properly and often failed to extend as they should to allow for a safe descent. But Verna took her duties seriously.

Had taken them seriously.

Sofia tried to see the items on the cart with objective eyes, the way the steam tinker must, and turned sick inside. It looked not so much like a steam unit on the cart as a random collection of components.

Lionel Pike asked, "Was she broken all apart like this from the fall?"

"No." Sofia's lips tightened bitterly. "She was

conscious."

"Conscious?" Startled, he returned his gaze to her face.

Sofia waved a hand. "Alive. Her fire did not go out at once. She was heavily damaged, but able to speak with me. I heard the crash, you see, and ran down—"

That awful moment remained burned into her.

"Damaged, how?" He sounded like the workman now, seeking facts.

"Her head was terribly dented, as you see it, and her thorax. Her left arm snapped off in the fall. She lost one set of wheels."

"How did you get her up the stairs?"

"We crawled." Sofia swallowed, remembering those terrible moments. "I carried her arm."

"Someone has disassembled her."

"That was Starr and Williams, at their shop. They said they needed to get a look at her inner workings, to see if they could match the parts."

"Butchers," muttered the young lad who stood watching with wide eyes, and who looked like a madman's conception of an elf.

"Did they take much of your money?" Lionel Pike gave Sofia a direct look. "They are thieves."

"I paid them, yes." More than she could afford. "Then they declared they could not get the necessary parts and refused to put her back together without them. Finally, I—I loaded her up and took her away from there."

"You will not find the necessary parts. Not for a unit of this vintage."

Sofia's heart fell violently. "Are you telling me she cannot be repaired?"

"I am not telling you that. Merely that the parts do not exist. They will need to be…fabricated." He waved a hand.

"Can you do that?"

The young man looked at Pike, awaiting his answer as did Sofia.

He hesitated. "Perhaps. It would be a great deal of work. And she would not be the same."

A cat appeared from nowhere, leaped with feline grace onto the edge of the cart, and examined its contents, much the way the steam tinker had. A ginger beast, it had rough fur and stripes on its sides.

"How—how would she be different? It is her personality I am most anxious to preserve."

Everyone stared at her, including the cat.

"Her personality," Pike repeated.

"Her—her essence. Her intelligence." Sofia explained more carefully, "What makes her Verna."

The steam tinker made a strange, humming sound in his throat. "These old units do not usually have much capacity for artificial intelligence. They do what they are told. That's about it."

"Verna is different."

The ancient steam unit at Pike's side, which had stood watching all the while, suddenly stirred. "Master Pike—"

"Yes, all right, Mordred. I know."

What sort of man named a steam unit after a mythical figure? Hope stirred in Sofia's heart.

"How long has her fire been out?"

Sofia's heart sank again. "Two weeks. It went out some time during the night after she fell down the stairs. I'm not sure how. I was asleep at the time. But I suspect she tried to get up, fell, and her water extinguished her fire. I—I was unable to restart it."

Though she'd tried, with trembling fingers and even desperate prayers. All in the echoing loneliness of the big house.

Again—sorrowfully this time—the steam tinker shook his head. "Miss Gregory, I don't think—"

"I will try to rebuild her," said Mordred, "if you will not."

The two of them—Pike and Mordred—engaged in a staring match.

With a rattle, the unit goaded its master, "I believed you could rebuild anything. Is that not your premise?"

Emotions flickered in Pike's eyes. "I did not say I could not rebuild her—"

"Well, then." A curious thing for a steam unit to say.

A grin broke over the elven lad's face.

"Please," Sofia said again. "It means everything to me. She means everything. If you are worried about the cost, I can pay you. I can sell some things. From the house."

Precious little remained. Some good clothing, mostly her own. A few of Mother's things. Her father's collection.

No, not that. Not yet. Though, if it meant getting Verna back—

"Look, Miss Gregory, this is a difficult and lengthy proposition. Moreover, it is one that may not result in the outcome you desire. I can get her, or some facsimile of her, running. She will not be the same. I will try my best to get close to the original components, but—to do so in whole would be impossible. And when it is all done, when she's restarted, she may be an empty shell." He added deliberately, his gaze intent on Sofia's, "No retention. Do you understand? She may not be the Verna you remember."

Sofia drew a quivering breath. "Then—then I will just have to teach her all over again." Teach her to be the supportive and loving companion Verna had become over the course of many years. Loving, yes, and she'd challenge anyone who denied it. "You say you can get her running. Does that mean you will?"

Pike glanced at Mordred. "I will undertake the commission—just so long as you are prepared for a less than favorable outcome, at the end."

"Yes. Yes, I will be prepared. I will try and be prepared. How long will it take?"

Pike shrugged. "Who can say? It all depends on whether I can find the components. I will, as I say, have to fabricate some of them."

"And—I suppose you have other jobs."

He gave her another of those long looks out of clear, gray eyes. "I am willing to put your job at the head of the queue. But that does not mean it will be quick. They've made a terrible mess of her."

"I know." Tears flooded Sofia's eyes, and she blinked them back desperately, determined not to cry in front of these strangers. She reached out and caressed some of the components that lay in the cart. Everyone—including the cat—stared at her.

Striving for a measure of composure, she said, "I will need time anyway to—to liquidate a few assets, in order to pay you. Have you any estimate for the cost?"

Pike shook his head. "She will need a new boiler— that will never hold water. Gears in all the joints.

Wheels, of course."

"And—and her mind?" Sofia lifted her gaze determinedly to Pike's. "What will it cost to rescue that?"

There came a weighty silence, broken by what might have been a murmur from the elven boy.

Mordred spoke with a wheeze. "I think, Master, our client speaks again of her companion's personality."

"Yes." Sofia turned to the unit in gratitude. He had painted, blue eyes, the left marred by a speck of rust.

"Miss Gregory, as I have said, I can't guarantee she will have a personality at worst, or at best one that, well, remembers you. I can't possibly estimate a price for that. Unfortunately, we will have to wait until we have her up and running."

"Yes, yes, of course. You did say." Hope, it seemed, was a treacherous thing.

"You might do better, after all, taking her to the hybrids."

"They have no reason to help me," Sofia said, ignoring the fact that neither did Pike. "That is, they repair other steam units who go directly to them, and they undertake to work on one another. But aren't they concentrating on creating others like themselves?"

"Yes. It's rumored they're close to perfecting the first hybrid steam child. No one's seen it yet, but I can imagine the workmanship will be highly sophisticated."

Sofia said nothing, trying to imagine a hybrid steam child—covered by skin, wearing hair and eyes, and presumably impossible to tell from a child who would laugh and run.

"However," Pike went on, "they have the

knowledge required to put a unit like yours back together properly."

"So do you."

"I'm called a tinker, Miss Gregory, because I'm mostly self-taught. If you're concerned about salvaging her intelligence, the hybrids may be a better bet. Have you heard of a fellow called Patrick Kelly?"

"He's a hybrid. And a policeman—a member of that Irish Squad of hybrids."

"And the leader of the steamies in this city, those who are pursuing their rights. Have you ever met him?"

"No." Sofia had seen him from a distance, once or twice. The steam unit looked like a big, strapping Irishman with reddish hair.

Again, Pike stared her directly in the eyes. "If you want the best outcome, you might do better to take this unit to him. It's said he's open to an honest appeal and, in fact, is a hybrid with a heart. He might accept your commission."

Certainty bloomed in Sofia's breast. Lionel Pike would send her to someone else, would he? Even as he stood there and spoke of a steamie with heart?

He was the man.

She shook her head determinedly. "You have already accepted the commission, have you not?"

He looked again at the jumble in the cart. "Yes."

"Then I assure you, Mr. Pike, I am satisfied."

Chapter Three

After Miss Gregory left, Mordred helped Lionel unload the steam unit from the cart onto the second workbench. They sorted as they worked, Lionel often pausing to scrutinize a component older than any he'd seen previously. Mordred had, indeed, been old when he got dropped off mysteriously at Lionel's door, some four years ago. That had been when Lionel had just opened the shop, with no real idea what he was doing—or just what he was getting himself into.

Even then, Mordred had been mostly intact. Heavily rusted, listing to one side, and barely operative, yes, but intact. Lionel had repaired rather than rebuilt him.

Since then, in a definite learning process, yes—he'd rebuilt many a steam unit, a few of which he would have considered near-hopeless.

None had ever looked so hopeless as this.

He glanced at the door, thinking about the woman who had disappeared into the rain, as completely as if he'd imagined her. Only she hadn't truly disappeared, had she? She'd left a measure of her presence along with her steam unit.

That could only be a flight of pure fancy, and Lionel Pike did not indulge in fancy. A practical man, he dealt in mechanical realities, such as whether parts fit together. He would not admit Sofia Gregory had rattled him.

He looked at Sammy, who stood by, watching the transfer to the work bench. Mainly because he refused to ask Mordred, he questioned, "What do you think?"

Sammy shrugged.

Mordred answered with his customary wheeze. "A challenge, and no mistake."

Lionel had tried to eliminate that wheeze, had done his best. He'd replaced Mordred's voice box several times, twice successfully. But in a mere matter of weeks, the wheeze had returned.

Lionel now considered it part of Mordred—a component of his essence, as Miss Gregory might say. Damn, there she was again.

"But, Master Lionel, I have faith in you. You can accomplish the task."

"You have faith in me, eh?" Lionel shot the unit a look from the corner of his eye.

"Explicitly."

"Huh," Sammy huffed.

"Sam, do you have something to say?"

"I agree, you can rebuild the unit. Whether it'll still be that lady's friend is something else."

Yes, that was what worried Lionel also. He could build a unit, utilizing some of these components. No question. But Miss Gregory wanted *Verna*.

Mordred put out an articulated hand and stroked the unit's dented cheek, on a head now dislocated from its body. When Mordred arrived, he'd had stubby hands equipped with clamps for fingers. In a feat of skilled engineering that had surprised even him, Lionel had given him better.

"Yes." Lionel could only agree. "But I fear her face

is too badly staved in for me to pound out."

The unit had originally possessed painted eyes and painted hair. Both had now been woefully worn away. But for the time of its manufacture, it must have been a first-rate unit indeed.

He wondered about Miss Gregory's family, whether she had money behind her. Her clothing had looked like quality, and she'd spoken in a cultured manner. That accent of hers still niggled at him, impossible to place.

Twenty-odd years ago, a unit like this would have cost a fortune. Now, most people would consider it scrap.

"I think," he said slowly, "I should begin from the inside out. The new boiler first. Then build onto it using whatever I can." Leave the "thinking" components for last.

In truth, they were operating components. Units like this, unlike the new hybrids, which were built to react and learn, had never been meant to think. Merely to operate and obey.

He sighed. What if he presented Miss Gregory with an operational unit, only to see her eyes fill with disappointment?

One step at a time, he warned himself. Don't worry about the outcome till you get there.

A knock at the door interrupted any further contemplation.

Sammy hurried to answer, and Ginny Landry came striding in. Miss Landry, daughter to the infamous Candace Landry who'd been a genius at the forefront of hybrid automaton creation, now provided refuge to unwanted and, usually, outdated steam units. She also provided Lionel with a large number of what she called "hopeless" cases, units beyond saving and destined for the scrap yard.

A forceful and intelligent woman who knew her own mind, she might not be the most likely candidate to entertain charitable impulses, especially considering her late mother's reputation for ruthlessness and exploitation. But a warm mercy lurked beneath her brisk exterior.

She'd once likened the units she rescued to stray animals. "Though, instead of taking them to Jamie Kilter at the Buffalo Animal Refuge," she'd told Lionel, "I bring them here to you. You're their last hope."

Lionel sighed, hoping she hadn't brought another sad load of broken units. But she shook the rain from her fringed jacket and gave him a bright smile.

"Good news, Master Tinker," she began, before catching sight of the unit on the workbench. "Holy crow, what's this?"

"A commission," Lionel said wryly. "Her owner wants her put back together again."

Ginny's clever hazel eyes flew to his face and back to the bench. "You must be joking."

"I wish I were."

"What a mess! What happened to it?"

"Reputedly, a fall down the stairs followed by an unsuccessful repair attempt. From what I can see, the wheels were largely inoperable even before the fall. You can see the extender springs were rusted nearly all the way through. She shouldn't have been anywhere near a flight of stairs."

Ginny made a tsking sound with her tongue. "If anyone can rebuild it, you can."

"I appreciate the vote of confidence," Lionel said sourly, and lifted his gaze to her.

An attractive woman and no mistake, with glossy brown hair and a lush form that promised to burst out of the western garb she favored. But Miss Landry belonged to one Brendan Fagan, a police captain of this city, and nobody in his right mind would cross him.

"You say you come with good news, Miss Landry? I could use some."

"I believe I do. I may have found a buyer—or at least a home—for some of the units."

Lionel stared. By "the units," she referred to those broken-down mechanicals she'd been bringing to him for repair. Even once operable, they were castoffs without a home. Some went on their way, determined to find jobs and attain independence. But most, being older units, wanted a place to belong. Currently, Lionel had more than two dozen of them in storage.

"That's wonderful. Where?"

Miss Landry leaned against the workbench opposite him. "You know about the efforts to reform the city's orphanages? A man named Mitch Carter's taken it in hand. You may have heard of him."

Lionel had. Big man in real estate, and with a dangerous reputation. "What would a man like that care about orphanages?"

"He was brought up in one, and his wife's a reformer. Anyway, she—the wife, I mean—is friends with Lily Michaels, who's a good friend of mine."

"Lily Michaels, the hybrid steam unit?"

"The one married to the human, yes, the same. She and her husband had been trying to adopt, and Tessa Carter made it happen.

"Anyway, the orphanages are woefully understaffed. It's been one of their main shortcomings. I suggested—quite cleverly, I thought—we put your restored units into service staffing them."

Lionel lifted his brows. "They're pretty crude, some of them."

"But operational, and in need of providing service. You know as well as I do, Mr. Pike, those units live to be of use."

They did not, technically, live. But Lionel wasn't willing to quibble over it. "How many?"

"I would say at least half a dozen to start, more as further orphanages get revamped. Mr. Carter is in the process of buying and refurbishing them, one at a time."

"He must be rich as Croesus."

Miss Landry shrugged. She possessed her mother's great fortune, though it didn't show in her manner, she being down to earth. And she'd proved generous with it, providing the money for Lionel to restore the units she pawned off on him.

"Ideally, of course, the orphanages should be staffed by humans. There's to be a nurse resident at each, and a number of teachers, as well as a housekeeper. But Tess feels there can't be too many steam units on hand. When the children need comforting or reassurance, someone must respond."

"Comforting." Lionel thought of the units back in storage. Most of them had, despite his repairs, seen far better days. How responsive might they be?

Still, storage made no life—so to speak—for them. By nature, steam units did need to be useful. And, ideally, appreciated.

"I find my own staff of steamies comforting," Miss Landry said. "They are there to greet me when I get home, often with a cup of tea. They are always concerned for me. They are, Mr. Pike, the heart of my home."

For some reason, Lionel glanced at Mordred, who worked at polishing components, on another bench. Was Mordred the heart of the shop? Nonsense.

"I will be more than happy to see those units assigned, in the orphanages or elsewhere."

"I can assure you they will receive good treatment. But I don't think I'll be able to get you much of a price per head, seeing as how so many are required."

"I don't mind." Lionel would be willing to donate them, if it got them out of storage.

"You should mind," Ginny chastised him. "You have hours of time and skill invested in those units. Would you like to deal with Mr. Carter yourself? Or would you like me to try and negotiate a wholesale price?"

Lionel shuddered. Happy hidden away here, working at his craft, he'd prefer not to venture out at all. Ruefully he said, "You will be better at such dealings than me."

"I think so. Good, then I'll go see the Carters today. And I'll do my best to obtain a deal that's fair to everyone."

"Thank you, Miss Landry. You've been very good to us here."

She flashed a smile. "I like nothing better than a deal that benefits both parties. You help my orphaned units, and we turn about and help the orphans. What could be nicer?"

Lionel just nodded.

Ginny Landry indicated the components on the workbench. "So, who's your new patron?"

"Patron?"

"The owner of this jumble. Who's hired you?"

"Her name is Sofia Gregory. Have you heard of her?"

Ginny Landry narrowed her eyes and shook her head. "But I haven't been in the city long. Brendan will know. He knows everybody. Would you like me to ask?"

"It doesn't matter."

"It does, if you're hoping to get paid."

"She has an accent. I can't place it."

Ginny Landry gave Lionel a long look. "I'll see what I can ferret out and let you know next time I see you. Meanwhile, good luck with that."

Lionel had no doubt he'd need it.

Chapter Four

The house felt too big and far too empty without Verna in it. The rain beat on the roof and windows, echoing through the half-denuded rooms. The fire in the parlor's grate smoldered and struggled, refusing to burn, and even after Sofia—drenched to the skin during the trip back from Lionel Pike's workshop—changed her clothes, she continued to shiver.

How would she ever manage, here alone?

She'd sold all the other steam units, with regret, beginning with the most valuable. She really should sell the house next. She didn't need so much space, and repairs had become prohibitive.

But the house represented her last tie with her parents. Her father had built it here on Woodlawn Avenue when he'd arrived, carrying a small fortune, from Riga. That had been before she, Sofia, was born. Those had been the grand days, when her parents entertained others who had come from Eastern Europe, when the house shone with light and vibrated with music and laughter.

Her father had been a clever man, who advised other men on handling their fortunes. For a time, life had been good. But he fell ill with a blood disorder. Consulting jobs no longer came in. The fortune, however carefully managed, did not last.

Father died following that lengthy illness, and

Mother, her heart broken, soon followed him to the grave.

Now Sofia found herself alone, doubly so with Verna gone. Away, she corrected herself swiftly. Verna was merely away, not gone. She would return. But Mr. Pike said it would take some time, and in loneliness, it felt like an eternity.

She had faith in Mr. Pike. She couldn't quite say why. Maybe it stemmed from the competent appearance of his grease-stained fingers. More likely, from the honest, level look in his gray eyes. She did not think Mr. Pike had lied to her.

She hadn't had the same feeling—not at all—about that pair of shysters Starr and Williams. They'd seemed shifty-eyed and had smiled entirely too much.

Never, so she'd learned, trust someone who smiled for no good reason.

Mr. Pike had not smiled. He'd looked serious, worried, and a bit annoyed, all emotions that made sense to Sofia.

If she ever did see him smile, she suspected it just might steal her breath away. A fine-looking man, Mr. Pike. But he thought her a little bit crazy. He would think her completely mad if she admitted she believed Verna had a soul.

She went to a window and peered out at the wet street. Dark swiftly fell, and the rain continued to pelt down, hard as nails. A horse-driven carriage went by, the horse's hooves clattering on the bricks. Sofia felt a rush of compassion for the animal, which was a real horse and not one of the new steam models now appearing around town.

People—most people—could accept that animals

possessed souls. Others treated their fellow creatures like things, and subjected them to all manner of abuse. But Sofia believed they had higher feelings. No one could deny they possessed personalities.

As did steam units, over time.

Granted, a new steam unit arrived from manufacture as pretty much a clean slate, ready to work for its new owner—employer. It might know only a few commands, as did a newborn human child, for that matter. Anyone who'd ever lived or worked for any time beside a steam unit could attest it did not remain that way for long.

Verna had a compassionate nature and a sense of humor. Sofia frowned and saw her face reflected back at her in the glass window. The frown made her look pinched and old.

Verna *had* possessed a sense of humor. Now gone? Forever?

No—no, she would not entertain that possibility. If Lionel Pike got her running, if there remained a glimmer of the Verna Sofia knew, Sofia would work with her—even as she'd told Pike—and get Verna back again.

Those hacks, Starr and Williams, had treated Verna like a thing. They'd torn her apart looking for flaws, for broken pieces, when all the while the thing that made Verna *Verna* couldn't be seen by the eye.

If Sofia wanted her back again, she had to keep faith. In what could not be seen.

****

"I don't want to go to school." Sammy stood in front of Lionel, tousled head at Lionel's chin, and delivered the words soundly, without a shred of doubt.

His dark eyes met Lionel's full on, and his lips set in a snarl of determination.

Lionel sighed. At times like this—and they seemed more frequent of late—he wondered at Sam's background, about which he knew almost nothing. The lad had appeared on a winter's morning three years ago, picking through the garbage bins in the back alley behind the shop. He'd had no coat, and only rags for shoes.

Against his better instincts, Lionel had brought him in.

The boy stayed and worked for his keep—off-hand jobs that allowed him to develop into a decent assistant. He was clever and did not steal from the shop, something Lionel refused to tolerate.

About his background, Sammy refused to speak. Small and quick, he had permanently tanned skin and liquid, dark eyes that argued a mixed ancestry.

Good-natured and willing, for the most part, he sometimes turned stubborn—like now.

Lionel gave him a level stare. He'd been in the shop late last night, sorting Verna's parts, and had been back at it early this morning. He did not need or welcome a battle of wills.

"Your attendance at school is part of our bargain," he stated flatly, and quirked an eyebrow at the boy. "Remember? We agreed you could live and work here, but you would get an education."

Sammy's face brightened. "I'm not getting an education at school."

"You certainly are."

"I'm not. It's all about sitting still the whole morning, repeating words and cyphers, and getting hit with the ruler." Sammy drew a breath and waved one hand. "I learn a lot more here."

"Nonsense. You're learning to read and write, yes? To do sums? If you want to run your own shop someday, you'll need all those skills."

"Then you teach me."

"I don't have the time. And that was not our agreement. Don't you know you are fortunate to have a place in a decent school—for free?"

Sammy muttered something under his breath.

"What's that?" Lionel demanded.

"It's a waste of time. That place is turning out students with less imagination than a raw steamie."

Lionel did not grow angry often, but now a bubble of annoyance rose and burst in his head. "You can exercise your imagination on your own time. If you're staying here, it's my responsibility to see that you can at least read."

"I can read."

"Not well. Not well enough." Coldly, Lionel said, "If you want to break our agreement, you can pack up your things and leave."

At that, Mordred rumbled up. Lionel could feel the unit's concern.

But now Sammy, too, was angry. "If that's what you want, I will."

"It's not what I want. But you're eleven years old. You need to attend school. And that was our agreement—you stay here, you go to school. So it's your choice."

"That's half-assed stupid!"

Lionel fixed the lad with a stern eye. "Then you never should have agreed to it."

"Master Lionel," Mordred interrupted, "where will the boy go?"

A worthy question. In truth, Lionel didn't know. He himself rarely ventured out into the city but knew it could be a cruel place with scant opportunities for disenfranchised steamies—or boys.

"Not my concern," he told Mordred. "Sammy knows the deal."

Mordred turned to the boy. "What is so terrible about attending school? It is in fact temporary. And we all have to do things that ill appeal to us. I, for instance, do not enjoy cleaning out the slop basins. But I do it."

Lionel raised his eyebrows. He used the slop basins to catch oil and other foul substances secreted by the various steam units under repair. He'd never realized Mordred disliked the task.

"Tell you what," Sammy proposed. "I'll do that, and you go to school for me."

"Smart ass!" Mordred wheezed.

Suddenly, Lionel wanted to laugh, his annoyance translated, just like that, to dark humor. But he couldn't let Sammy see he'd softened. Lose one battle with the lad and he'd lose them all.

"Go to school," Mordred said. "At least until you master words and numbers. You want to be a steam tinker someday, do you not?"

"Yeah."

"If you wish Master Lionel to keep instructing you, you must attend school."

Sammy weighed it, shot a look at Verna's components, now mostly sorted on the workbench, and abruptly conceded. "All right. But not today."

"What's different about today?" Lionel asked.

"It's the unveiling."

"Unveiling? Of what?"

"The hybrids are revealing their new child. At the Automaton Rights Center. Ten o'clock."

Mordred wheezed, and even Lionel caught his breath. So the day had come, when the hybrids at last revealed the project upon which they'd worked all winter. They said they would not present the child until it attained perfection.

"Where'd you hear this, Sam?"

"Word on the street. They've invited all the steamies in the city to see what they've done. A new generation of hybrid, they're calling it."

A hybrid's means of living on. They could not have children of their own, but they possessed the highly developed skills needed to manufacture them.

Lionel shot a look at Mordred, who had frozen in place. He told Sammy, "Well, look. Just this once, you can give school a swerve. We'll all attend the unveiling."

Chapter Five

Every steam unit in the city had gathered at the Automaton Rights Center on Niagara Street, or so it seemed. The place had grown up spontaneously from the ruins of a burned-out bordello called the Crystal Palace. Now it served as a meeting hall for automatons in the city, the property owned by a steamie consortium.

The current throng argued that most of Buffalo's mechanicals must indeed have come. The scene reminded Lionel forcibly of the standoff in Niagara Square last autumn, between the city's steamies and the human contingent, those who opposed machines attaining their rights, marrying, and even owning property.

No one could deny that since that encounter, the mechanicals, led by the hybrid Patrick Kelly, had attained a measure of power. They'd begun collecting a wage for their labors, and had pooled together to buy up a considerable amount of property around the city. It was whispered they backed politicians who looked favorably on their bid for equality.

Lionel cared little enough for all that. He detested politicians and tried to ignore the unrest in the city. But a chance to see the product of skill that, as he freely admitted, far outstripped his own, proved irresistible.

The difference between a hybrid and a regular

steam unit was like that between a bonfire and a struck match. So sophisticated had the manufacture of hybrids—mostly by the hybrids themselves—become, it was almost impossible to tell them from humans. With eyes, skin, hair—even fingernails—harvested from cadavers, and with an artificial intelligence capable of adaptation and boundless learning, the new steamies were forces unto themselves. Many secret construction methods were involved. The hybrids kept that knowledge to themselves.

No question that they—the hybrids—led the bid for automaton rights. But they welcomed all steam units into the fold, and Lionel saw various calibers of units around him here, from the most ancient, rusted units leaking steam to uniformed members of the Buffalo Police's Irish Squad.

Indeed, the crowd could not fit inside the Center, which had been rebuilt from the bones of the old Crystal Palace in brick and wood. In response, the ceremony had moved outside, onto the broad veranda.

At precisely eleven o'clock, a tall man stepped forward and lifted his hands. But no—he wasn't a man. Squinting his eyes, Lionel recognized Patrick Kelly out of uniform and wearing a pair of worker's pants and a white shirt, open at the neck. From inside emerged several other figures who took places at his side, one of them a dusky-haired beauty.

Lionel recognized her also. Chastity Greely, one of the hybrids manufactured by Ginny Landry's mother and now the foremost expert on hybrid construction.

His interest quickened. Mrs. Greely would have been instrumental in the manufacture of any steam-powered child.

He stretched his ears, eager to hear.

Kelly's raised hand quieted the crowd; however, a number of small children ran around the porch, in and out of the twin doors, laughing and squealing.

"Welcome!" Pat Kelly bellowed. "We did not expect such a large turnout here today, but are pleased to see each and every one of you. This is, indeed, a momentous day. Our team of creators has labored long to achieve a feat we hope will fulfill a wish held by many of you—that of being able to raise a child."

The crowd stirred with interest.

Kelly went on, "As you know, a number of us have formed unions of marriage. But until now, most have been denied the right to adopt, and that even though there are orphans in this city desperate for the good homes we might provide. Only a few of us—in mixed marriages—have been permitted to take human children from these institutions.

"But, my friends, there is another way. What is reproduction, after all, but the creation of others like ourselves? And what are we but steel and steam?"

He paused. Anticipation passed through the crowd in a ripple.

"It is true, my friends, that adoption for the likes of us will grow easier. The orphanages are in the process of being reformed by those not unsympathetic to our cause. And I urge you to adopt those children if you can. Here, before you, you will see a number of them recently liberated into good homes."

Again he paused. He lifted his head with what might be construed as pride. When he spoke again his voice, heavy with brogue, rang.

"But if you look more closely, you will see

something else. My friends, one of these children running and playing here is a hybrid steam unit."

Gasps came from the onlookers. Whatever happened here today, they hadn't expected drama. But Patrick Kelly, an intelligent hybrid indeed, employed it when he could.

"Children, please," he called. "Here, to me."

They came obediently and lined up in front of him, facing the crowd. A ragged row of heads—fair, brown, black, and one red—and scrubbed, shining faces full of light.

Kelly ran his hand lightly over those heads, with visible affection.

To the crowd he said, "Here you see six children—three boys and three girls. Five of them are human, born of the womb. Can you tell which is not?"

The crowd stilled. Lionel's breath caught in his lungs again, and he narrowed his gaze intently.

Three boys, rosy-cheeked and brimming with health. Three girls, each clad in a neat dress and with a bow in her hair.

With the eye of a professional, he scrutinized them best as he could from this distance. There should, he believed, be some telltale sign from a hybrid—jerky movements, or blankness of expression. But he saw none.

Sammy jostled his arm. "Mr. Pike?" The boy looked the way Lionel felt—awed and perhaps a little frightened. A thrall that masqueraded as a chill raced its way up Lionel's spine. He shook his head.

"I can't tell, Sammy."

Sammy spoke a word Lionel wouldn't permit in the shop. Lionel let it pass.

Kelly, still displaying showmanship, moved to stand first behind one child and then another, down the line. His audience waited for him to make an announcement.

Yet in the end, he didn't do anything so crude. To single out a child was not his way. Instead, when he reached the little redheaded girl, he stopped and very gently lifted her into his arms.

The two of them together looked out at the crowd. Cuddled against Kelly's broad shoulder, the child— hybrid—looked protected, even cherished. Her curls, brighter than Kelly's auburn, nevertheless complimented his.

I should have known, Lionel thought. She looks like him. I wonder if he intends to raise her?

Except—one could not raise an automaton, precisely. He might guide and teach her, but she would not grow like an ordinary child, and would remain the same size forever.

Kelly spoke, and Lionel would have sworn his voice carried tenderness. "We would like you all to meet Kiera. She is precisely thirty days old, today. She is the first hybrid automaton child."

The crowd broke into a babble, whine, and buzz— depending on various voice boxes—of conversation. The child, Kiera, gazed out from the shelter of Patrick Kelly's arms with what looked like wonder.

Soon, Kelly raised his voice again. "This achievement, this very difficult and important achievement, has been the effort of many. I would like to thank our team of hybrid experts, led by Mrs. Charity Greely, and her assistants, Averill Dwight and Thomas Morrow."

The others stepped forward. The human children scattered, some claimed by adoptive parents. The team—all but one themselves automatons—joined hands and bowed.

Then Patrick Kelly said something that made the hair stand up all over Lionel's body.

"Kiera Kelly is a miracle. Let us all give thanks, however we may worship."

****

"What did he mean, that old Patrick Kelly?" Sammy asked as the three of them made their way back to the shop. "Automatons don't worship anything, do they? I mean, I've never seen one go to church."

Lionel grunted. So, Sammy had picked up on that point too, perhaps the most important thing Kelly had said. An automaton—a machine, however sophisticated—speaking of miracles.

He said to Sammy, "How would you know? The closest you get to a church is when I send you on an errand past St. Mark's."

The city, inhabited as it seemed to be mostly by people from other places, was a veritable host of churches. The Irish in South Buffalo had their own, the Eastern Europeans on the east side had built a basilica. Other places of worship, big and small, dotted the main streets.

Lionel had never considered sending Sammy to one. Had he been derelict in his duty?

Sammy gave a snort. "If I was gonna seek the mysteries of God, I wouldn't do it in that po-dunk place. I'd go to the Cathedral downtown."

Lionel stared at him. "Do you want to attend services there and—and seek the mysteries of God?"

"No, I'm just saying that's the kind of building that might inspire a fellow."

Lionel contemplated it. He didn't spend a lot of time on the niceties of faith. He dealt with the realities of the fitting, the joint and the bolt, the practical basics of life. That didn't mean he believed in nothing. Because a man might build any number of machines. They ran only at the coming of the spark.

He looked at their other companion. "What do you think, Mordred?"

The unit rattled and, presumably, ruminated. "I am old and have operated a long while." Mordred never used the words "lived" or "alive" in reference to himself. He might be operational. He remained humble in it.

But, deliberately, Lionel used it now. "You mean you've lived a long while."

Mordred rumbled to a halt. Lionel and Sammy stopped with him. The old unit said nothing.

It was Sammy who asked Mordred, his voice brimming with curiosity, "Can a steamie believe in something, Mordred? If so, what would he worship?"

Mordred turned sculpted eyes on the boy in a long look and gave a mechanical kind of shudder. "I can answer for no one else. I, however, might believe in many things. The coal that powers me. The fire in my thorax." Slowly, he thumped the silver skin of his chest. "In a greater sense, in the air that feeds that fire. I have been relit many times. I was defunct when I got dropped off at Master Lionel's shop, destined for the scrap yard and oblivion. He rebuilt me from parts old and new, and I began a new *life*. I might, then, legitimately worship the Steam Tinker."

Sammy stared at Lionel, in bemusement, and Lionel at Mordred, in horror. "Please," Lionel begged, "don't do that!"

"I did not say I do worship you—merely that I could."

"Let's get home," Lionel urged. "There's work to do."

If he believed in anything, it was the work.

Chapter Six

Sofia's evil dreams came again during the night, and she had no defense against them. Usually, when she thrashed in her bed, mumbling and protesting, Verna would come to her, wake her gently, and make her a cup of tea. They might remain together for the balance of the night, and the dark would recede.

Now, with no one to wake her, she fell deeper and deeper into the troubling images. First she saw her father, looking as he had just before his death, body skeletal, eyes dark and brilliant in his skull of a face. He reached for her hand, his touch cold as the grave.

"Daughter, you have something important to accomplish." His voice reverberated through her hand, through her bones. "More important that any task you have ever undertaken."

Her? She was nobody—a woman of no significance, the last ember of what had once been a slightly glorious family, just hanging on.

The dream changed. Her father still clutched her fingers, but his hand was that of a mechanical. A battered steam unit lay in the bed where he had been, painted eyes like Verna's staring into her own. Rust covered its steel skin in wide patches. Even as Sofia stared, unable to look away, the patches of rust liquified and ran.

The unit bled. The blood trickled down and stained

the bedsheets where her father had lain.

Suddenly she stood in Niagara Square, the very heart of Buffalo. From here, streets fanned out like the spokes of a wheel, and the river lay at her back, mere blocks away. The square teemed with…

Automatons.

This had happened, it had actually happened. Last summer there had been a great confrontation between the automatons of the city, demanding their rights, and the human faction that opposed them.

But Sofia hadn't been there. Why would she dream she was, now? And—and the automatons that filled the square were not new or shiny. She saw no hybrids. These units limped and staggered or lay in a state of collapse, of decrepitude that rivaled Verna's. All old, all broken, all destined for—

What? Oblivion? What came after a steam unit's demise?

She woke from the dreadful scene and lay gasping, eyes fixed on the bare ceiling. What did the dream mean?

When small, she'd had dreams of her parents' home in Riga—a place she'd never been. For she'd been born here, in this city of steam and struggle, of river water and the wide, blue lake. Of disharmony and beauty. Of power.

Buffalo, equaled by no other city, with its streets like arms stretching wide, with its heart beating mightily, beneath the soil.

When young, she had described these dreams of Riga to her parents. She described the buildings, the bridges, a house that faced a broad square. The house where her father had been born.

They had marveled and whispered over it. They had tried to comfort her and had never suggested an explanation for her fits of mild clairvoyance. As if they feared she might be possessed, they had sent her to church.

The clearest thing she remembered about church was that Verna had not been permitted to accompany her. Sometimes her parents did. Far more often, they sent Sofia with a human nurse.

But Verna had been part of Sofia's life for as long as she could remember, her near-constant companion. Having her banned from the church colored the whole experience for Sofia. As soon as she could stop attending, she did.

Now she fought her way up from her troubled bed, feeling the weight of the empty house all around her. She had things to do today. She must decide which of her remaining valuables to sell in order to pay Mr. Pike for Verna's repairs. Getting Verna back with her was paramount.

She dressed with care instilled by her mother—*we must always look respectable*—and took no breakfast. Little food remained in the house, and anyway, she had no appetite. Most of her clothing had grown shabby around the edges. She had the costume she'd worn to take Verna to the steam tinker, but she kept that for true emergencies.

Roddy Stoeke's pawn shop could not be considered as such.

She'd sold all of her mother's good clothing and much of her own. Her father's exquisite suits had gone while her mother was still alive. She wished she'd retained a few of her mother's garments. A decent needlewoman, she might have fashioned them into new things for herself.

But that ship had sailed. No sense standing on the shore, mooning after it. She chose the most modest garments she possessed, a high-necked blouse and ruffled skirt. Roddy Stoeke was..."interested in her" was the best way to put it.

Sofia did not return his interest. She had no time for affairs of the heart, and only rarely felt genuine attraction. Her thoughts flashed to Lionel Pike, with his clear, gray eyes. She wondered from where his ancestors hailed—not a place like Riga, with its tall, narrow buildings and ancient, mysterious heart.

No, he made her think of the sea, though she didn't know why. She assured herself he was an entirely practical man and would have no time for the likes of her.

She went into the back room where she'd assembled the last of her valuables and made a grim inspection. She did, at least, trust Roddy Stoeke not to cheat her. Carefully, she wrapped two of her mother's glass perfume bottles and placed them in her bag. She hated to part with them, but better than tapping into her father's collection.

The pawn shop—called the Golden Dial—was a brisk five blocks' walk away on Dingens Street. Men, likely on their way to work, nodded at her in passing, interest flaring in their eyes.

You look like an old-world princess, Mother used to say. *Regal. Never lose that. It will bring the right man to you.*

So far, it had brought no one. Oh, men—like Mr. Stoeke—expressed their interest. But the inner sense that protected Sofia so well told her, always, too much about them. *He is greedy*, it might whisper. *Arrogant. Cruel. Corrupt to his soul.* Or, almost worse, *he is stupid.*

Ah, why did she have to possess such a voice, firmly lodged in her head? And when would it speak to her more favorably?

The front door of the Golden Dial creaked when she opened it and went in. The man behind the counter turned, and a big smile spread across his face.

Roddy Stoeke, big and bluff, was probably in his early thirties. He'd once confided to Sofia that he'd inherited the shop from his father. He seemed to enjoy his work, and lived upstairs in a flat of rooms. He had blue eyes, and yellow hair losing a battle and in retreat across the top of his head.

"Ah, Miss Gregory! My first customer of the day. And how glad am I that I opened early this morning?"

Actually, the name was Gregorovich. Sofia's father had Americanized it in order to do business here. Perhaps last night's dream put that thought in Sofia's head now.

She summoned a polite smile. "Mr. Stoeke, I hope you are well?"

"Much better for seeing one of my favorite customers. You do brighten this gray morning."

"How kind. Do you think it will rain again?" Small talk, she could manage. "So much rain we have had."

He shrugged. "It's spring. Nature wants to wash all the dirt out of the streets."

"Ah, a charming notion."

"My mother used to spring clean the very life out of our house. House proud, my father called her. But what can I do for you this morning?"

"I have some very special objects to show you, Mr. Stoeke."

Did the enthusiasm in his eyes cool? Sofia needed to keep him interested. She had to get a good price.

She hurried on, "These are some of my mother's favorite treasures." She unwrapped the perfume bottles and set them on the counter between her and Roddy Stoeke, where they gleamed ruby red and sapphire blue.

"Ah," said Mr. Stoeke softly, even as a faint whiff of Marya Gregorovich's scent trickled into the shop.

"Those were made in the old country, cut glass, as you see. These are but two of what I have. My mother had a collection of ten, in all colors. Amber, ruby, emerald, sapphire, as you see. They are very valuable."

That had been only one of the things that kept her from parting with them in the past. She only did so now for Verna's sake. She couldn't tolerate the emptiness of the big house.

"Perfume bottles," Stoeke said flatly.

"Yes, and in perfect condition. Each would make a lovely gift for any woman." Each had been a gift to her mother from her father, early in their marriage.

"No offense, Miss Gregory, but the sort of men who come here looking for gifts for their wives or lovers don't want something like those, and sure wouldn't pay big money for them. They want baubles, see. More like those earrings you're wearing."

He leaned over the counter toward her, and Sofia stiffened. Before she could protest, he lifted a beefy hand to cup the dangling jewel in her left ear, and scrutinized it. She felt his breath on her cheek.

"Now, if you want to sell these, I could do you a

good price."

"No. I could not." She had so little jewelry left. "My parents gave me these on my sixteenth birthday."

"They are exquisite." Stoeke stared into her eyes from a distance of mere inches. For one horrible instant she feared he meant to kiss her, and her entire body protested.

She withdrew so the dangling earring escaped his grasp. "Do—do you not want the bottles?" If he refused the perfume bottles, she didn't know what she'd do. They were treasures—or so she thought—she'd held in check.

Stoeke looked mildly disgusted, but he examined the bottles again. "They're pretty, I'll give you that. But my feeling is, I'll never move them."

"Oh." For an instant, she couldn't breathe.

"Tell you what. I'll take these two off your hands. But I can't use any more. All right? Next time, bring me the earrings."

"How—how much?"

"For the bottles?"

"Yes."

He named a price that made her heart drop to her feet. Oh, heavens, what was she to do?

"All right," she said, agonized. She needed the money. Even if she gave up eating, she had to pay the steam tinker. "And if these two bottles do sell, perhaps you will consider purchasing others from me?"

"If a miracle like that occurs, yes."

It seemed she must continue praying for miracles.

Chapter Seven

"Good morning, Duck! How's it hanging today?" Patsy Reardon greeted Lionel with the ribald question when he swung open the shop door in answer to her knock. A brawny woman with freckles and bright yellow hair, she dressed like a man and had the appetites of a she-cat in heat.

Her brother, George, equally blond and brawny, lingered behind her, the nose of their horse, Katie, at his shoulder.

Katie's presence meant they had a load of castoffs, and Patsy's smile meant they wanted to unload the rubble on him, Lionel.

He sighed. He'd been up late once again, working on Miss Gregory's unit. He had two other repair jobs on hold till he got hers done, and from the look of things, fixing Verna wouldn't be quick.

"Morning," he mumbled even as Sammy popped up at his elbow. For some unknown reason, Sammy liked Patsy and George.

Lionel turned and jerked a thumb at the boy. "You—school."

"Are we really going to go through all that again?"

Patsy reached in and ruffled Sammy's hair. "You do what your boss says, lad. Get yourself educated. Then you won't have to do what I do for a living."

Sammy's face lit. "I'd love to do what you do."

"Collect scrap?" Patsy looked astounded.

"Rescuing units. Keeping them from the yard. Saving their lives."

Patsy exchanged incredulous looks with her brother. "Lord love you, lad, they don't have lives. This is just a load o' junk. That is," she darted a glance at Lionel, "valuable components."

Another pile of stuff Lionel didn't need. Only, he did. "How old?" he asked.

"Eh?" Patsy returned.

"How old are the units you have there?"

"Don't know, governor. The usual, I guess."

George and Patsy drove around the neighborhoods and collected broken and irreparable units put out at the curb by householders, like so much trash. In the past, Lionel had been able to revive a few of them. Most would have been better towed away.

"Let me take a look."

They all went out into the watery sunlight. It had rained again during the night, and puddles spread across the bricks of the alley. Katie stood with her head down, and her load gleamed dull between patches of rust.

"I think there are five o' them," George spoke in a gruff rasp. "Not complete. The one's in two pieces. Still, a good load."

Lionel ran an expert eye over the contents of the wagon. His interest quickened. "What's that there, on the bottom?"

"A right old unit." George laughed. "Has a name."

"Eh?"

"Scratched on its thorax, like."

"Let me see."

Lionel heard Mordred rumble up behind him.

Sammy, who'd not yet left for school, stood with his chin propped on the edge of the wagon.

A horrendous clatter ensued as the scrappers shifted the load.

"There, see? That's a name, isn't it?"

It was, though Lionel doubted George could read. Five letters had been scratched across the unit's chest.

Wendy.

"Ah." The thing lay in two pieces and was pocked with rust. But it just might be the right vintage.

"I want that one."

"Eh?" George cocked his head.

"I'll take that one. Can't use the rest, I'm afraid."

George protested, "Ah now, Mr. Pike, you have to take the whole load. You know them's the rules."

Mordred bumped Lionel's elbow urgently.

"Yes, all right," Lionel agreed. "Unload it in the yard. Sammy, you get off to school."

The boy melted away with uncommon obedience. The weak sunlight disappeared, and by the time they unloaded the cart, isolated raindrops fell, pinging on the ancient metal.

Patsy held out her hand. With a scowl, Lionel dug into his pocket.

He'd sold six repaired units to Miss Landry for the orphanages and was flush. But that money should go to fund the shop, not Miss Gregory's steam unit.

Miss Gregory. He had the flash of an image— huge, dark eyes between spiked lashes, filled with unhappiness.

He needed to lift that sorrow from her. He wasn't sure why—he just did.

Patsy leaned close. "You know, I could let you

have this lot at a better price if you'd give in and take me out to dinner."

"Tempting an offer as that is, I don't have time to socialize."

"You wound me, Mr. Pike. Come on, Brother. It's fixing to rain hard."

So it did. No sooner did the wagon clatter off down the alley than the skies opened to admit a cold, pelting deluge.

Lionel told Mordred, "Here, help me get this inside."

They carted the unit in its two separate loads and set it on the floor.

"Do you think the components will fit Verna?" Mordred asked.

Lionel felt a stir of excitement. "I do." The word Wendy winked at him in the light of the steam lamps. The head and torso had been detached from the legs. The face, only a series of shallow depressions, had few distinguishing features. But at one time, the unit had meant something to someone.

"A rare find," Mordred observed.

"Indeed." Virtually a miracle, that it should fall into his hands now.

"Poor unit."

That made Lionel look at Mordred sharply. They dealt with ruined and even brutalized steam units every day. Since they'd begun seeking their rights, steam units frequently came under attack. Indeed, he'd met Miss Landry that way, when she called on him to refurbish a unit for her, one called Floyd.

Lionel rarely stopped to wonder what Mordred thought of working on, and sometimes condemning, outdated units. He couldn't doubt Mordred did think, in his fashion. He'd worked too long and too closely with the unit to mistake that.

But did Mordred now mourn?

Ah, no. Lionel merely needed to get more sleep.

"Here," he told Mordred. "Help me lift this torso onto the small bench. At least now she'll go for a good cause."

Mordred lifted, with careful reverence.

****

"Miss Gregory, I hate coming to you again, asking for money." Little Miss Warner, of the Automaton Aid Society, stared up at Sofia in blatant appeal. Behind her, trailing from the parlor into the hall, came a string of steam units, none particularly sophisticated. "But I know in the past you've been sympathetic to our cause."

Sofia replied, "I am quite supportive, yes."

"We believe automatons, like all other inhabitants of this city, deserve a place of worship. The mayor, as you know, stands steadfast against it. Such cruel bias should not be allowed to endure."

Automaton belief had become a hotly-debated topic in Buffalo. Most reasoning men agreed, steam units possessed no capacity for belief. Sofia, having lived many years with Verna, did not agree.

"But," she told Miss Warner starkly, swallowing her pride, "I have no money to donate."

"Posh!" Miss Warner regarded her with clear denial. "You live in this grand house."

"Look around you, Miss Warner. This grand house is nothing but a shell. I cannot help you."

Miss Warner withdrew in consternation.

"I suggest," Sofia said as gently as possible, "you go to the hybrids with this matter. I've heard it said they possess considerable wealth. I am sure if they want a church, they will build one."

"The hybrids," Miss Warner pronounced, "are focused on building more units like themselves. Children, now. What about units such as my followers? Are they to be shut out?"

"It's my understanding the Automaton Rights Movement has been very inclusive. All models are welcome."

"Welcome, yes. There's lip service paid. But why would they be making more like themselves if they think older models have value? Should our basic steam units not have a right to worship as they choose?"

"Of course. If they so choose."

"Our church will be built in Black Rock, which has become a gathering place for B.U.s, apart from the city. Buffalo, I fear, is falling under hybrid control."

"B.U.s?"

"Basic Units, as opposed to—"

"I see, yes." Sofia drew a breath. "Miss Warner, I advise you not to make these arbitrary distinctions. That will not serve you or your followers well. The way I see it, the Automaton Rights Movement gains its strength from its unity. You would do best to take advantage of that."

Miss Warner sniffed. "Once our church is built, the B.U.s will have a base and a refuge of their own."

"I am sorry." Sofia spread her hands. "I have nothing to contribute."

Miss Warner left promptly, and in a huff, taking her train with her. Sofia almost called them back. It felt so good having a steam unit, any steam unit, in the house again.

As opposed to the terrible, echoing silence.

Chapter Eight

"These will fit," Lionel said to Mordred as he ran his fingers over the components in a careful caress. "Of course, they're almost as worn as the ones we've taken out of Verna, but better, I think."

"I agree." Mordred bent so low over the disassembled torso of Wendy, he scribed a right angle. "Allow me to clean and polish these, to make them as good as they can be."

Lionel experienced a buzz of excitement. He loved it when a repair job began coming together, especially against terrible odds. Having Wendy delivered to their door had been an unprecedented stroke of luck. Miss Gregory would be so pleased.

"Yes," he urged his assistant, "go ahead with the polishing. If you can get the rust off, we'll be able to better assess the wear." He thought for a moment. "I'm worried about her springs."

"Which ones, Master Lionel?"

"The extenders on her wheels. These, out of the cadaver, are broken just like hers."

Mordred turned his face to Lionel. "'Cadaver', sir?"

"You know what I mean—Wendy."

A short silence fell.

"Master, Lionel," Mordred said then, "do you think Miss Gregory will be upset at the sacrifice of Wendy?"

"Sacrifice?"

The steam unit waved a hand. "Is that not what we undertake?"

"I suppose so. But this Wendy unit, like the others Patsy and George brought with it, were meant for the scrap yard. Oblivion."

"We are all meant for oblivion in the end," Mordred intoned. "Flesh and steel alike. But you, Master Lionel—you save many of my kind. It is by your hand that we stay, or go."

Lionel stared at his companion. "What nonsense is this?"

"I only say that you have a kind of power over us."

"Well, I don't want that power. I only want to repair whatever units I can. Right now, I want to repair Miss Gregory's unit because I suspect she's lonely without it." He saw again the expression in Miss Gregory's large, dark eyes. "This Wendy unit arrived already broken in two. I don't know if someone has tried to work on it or—or if they merely broke it up for ease of handling. These older units are very heavy."

"I am very heavy. I am an older unit. Tell me, Master Lionel, when first you saw me, was I in rough shape?"

"Very rough shape, yes."

"As rough as Wendy?"

"Perhaps not quite that bad, no, but broken down."

Broken down was a term Mordred frequently employed. It meant worn and aged certainly, but also implied what Lionel could only consider an emotional state—as when a man was down and out, with nothing left in either his pocket or his spirit.

"Then," asked Mordred, "what made you

undertake to repair me?"

Lionel considered the matter, perhaps for the first time. Mordred remembered his origins, the many years spent serving in one of the big homes just off Delaware Avenue. But what had happened after he'd been shut down and just how he'd ended up at Lionel's door remained a blank to him.

Lionel had, in fact, decided to try and tinker him back into operation on impulse. He'd wanted the challenge.

But he imagined no one—even a steam unit—wanted to know his existence pivoted on an impulse.

Besides, that hadn't been the whole story. There had been something about the unit's eyes, staring so blankly up at the sky, that had moved Lionel.

That had been several years ago. Now they were as good as inseparable. Lionel stood close enough to where Miss Gregory did to feel what she felt.

"I must have known," he told the unit, "what a good assistant you'd turn out to be."

"I do endeavor, Master Lionel."

"I know that."

Mordred's mechanical fingers touched Wendy's cheek, much as they had Verna's. "I just wondered, since Miss Gregory is so attached to Verna, if she might not rue Wendy's fate."

Lionel paused, thinking about that also. "The sacrifice must be made."

"Must it?"

"I took parts from other units to repair you."

"Did you?"

"Most certainly. And I've scabbed parts off other broken units since, to keep you going. The hybrids, when they build more hybrids, take the hair, eyes and skin from human cadavers and use them."

"Like that child we saw."

"Just like."

"Where did they get the sacrificed child?"

"I don't know. Maybe from a hospital. Or, I've heard children die at the city's orphanages, which aren't very good places to be. But folks are trying to reform those, now."

"Humans and steam units are alike, then, in that they are sometimes sacrificed after death."

"Some of them. And yes, we're more alike than we think." Lionel shot a look at Mordred's face which, despite being made of sculpted metal, managed to look troubled.

"Mordred, are you asking about Miss Gregory minding all this because it bothers you?"

"Perhaps. Wendy, just like Verna, was a *someone*."

"All those people lying under headstones in Forest Lawn were someones too. It's the way of the world. Look at it like this: if we're able to use some of her components, Wendy will live on in Verna. If she'd just gone to scrap—well, the scrap yard's like the graveyard, right?"

"Are you saying it's a worthy fate for deceased orphans to become hybrid children?"

"I don't know what I'm saying. Let's get back to work."

"That hybrid child looked very much like a human child, did she not, Master Lionel?"

"She certainly did."

"I could not tell the difference."

"Nor could I."

"What will happen to the child?"

"I suspect Officer Kelly and his wife will raise her, Mordred." With her red hair, the girl looked like she belonged to Kelly.

"Officer Kelly has a human wife."

"He does."

"How might that work?"

"I don't know, I'm sure." Lionel replied. He had enough trouble understanding relationships between human men and women. "All I know is, I'm going to have to find alternative adjuster springs for Verna's wheels, and I have no idea where they'll come from."

"You can do it, Master Lionel. You can do anything."

****

Sofia hesitated in the act of raising her hand to knock on Lionel Pike's shop door. She could hear sounds of activity from within, and a plume of smoke rose from the stack on the roof, probably from a steam plant. Similar plumes rose from homes and buildings all around and collected in the damp spring air. Buffalo smelled of burning coal, and steam.

And river water. This close to the waterfront, Sofia could smell that too. She drew a deep breath and knocked.

Would she see Verna, inside? Had she been put back all in one piece? Would she recognize Sofia?

The door opened. Lionel Pike stood there in his shirtsleeves, wearing the grime-stained leather apron. The dark hair—alive with curl—tumbled over his forehead, and he looked vital, and very competent.

"Good morning," Sofia said.

"Good morning."

"I hope I do not intrude."

He hesitated, which made her feel that yes, she did intrude. He gave off the air of a man who liked to be left strictly alone to do his work. Sofia wanted him to do that work. She also desperately longed to see Verna.

She lifted her handbag. "I have some money. For the job. Parts or—whatever else you will need."

"Ah, yes. Please come in."

The interior of the shop smelled like oil and steam. It stood empty but for a variety of parts, Pike's ancient steam unit, and Pike himself. Sofia's searching eyes could not see Verna anywhere.

Pike faced her with his back to a big workbench, as if barring her way.

Helplessly, she raised her eyes to his face. "Is there progress?"

"On your job? Yes. Oh, yes."

"Where is she?"

"Just here." He half turned and waved a hand at the bench. Walking forward, Sofia saw...

A vast clutter of metal components, only a few of which she recognized, spread wide. There—was Verna's face. There—a portion of her torso and—an arm?

Disappointment struck her, and she had to clutch the edge of the bench to stay upright.

"Oh—God!"

Pike looked puzzled by her distress. He shot a look at the automaton before he said, "No, truly, it is going well. We have everything sorted—the reusable components from those that must be replaced. I have my hands on a new boiler, and restoration can soon begin."

Sofia swayed on her feet. Of course, on some level, she'd always been aware Verna was a steam unit. A machine. On another level, though, she'd forgotten—or perhaps dismissed—that knowledge. Verna was her nurse, her surrogate mother, her friend, her confidante.

Seeing her this way, now, felt like seeing a dismembered metal corpse, and brought the truth of Verna's identity home.

"Perhaps, Master Lionel," suggested the automaton—Mordred, "Miss Gregory should sit down."

Pike drew up a wooden chair, scraping its legs across the floor and parking it next to the bench. Sofia sank onto it.

"Miss Gregory, are you all right?" Pike's face swam into view, keen gray eyes worried and brow furrowed with concern.

"Yes. It is just seeing her like this."

"You saw her like this before. You brought her to me like this."

"Yes, but she was—assembled. She looked like Verna, not—not—"

"I see. I'm sorry, but all the pieces have to be checked for wear, then greased and polished."

"I understand." Sofia concentrated hard. "Silly me, I thought she might somehow be put together already. So you do not know whether her mind—"

"We won't know that until she can be restarted, I'm afraid."

"I understand," Sofia repeated. Verna, in essence, lay in a deconstructed coma. This man with his intelligent eyes and competent hands must heal her, and wake her up.

Mordred's face swam into Sofia's view, his dished

eyes reflecting her face. "Miss Gregory, would you like a cup of tea? It is good for shock."

"That would be most kind."

The unit trundled off on noisy wheels. Pike drew up a second chair and sat facing Sofia.

"I assure you, Miss Gregory, it is going well. In fact, we've had a stroke of incredible luck. Scrappers often drop off units to me. I've just had one come in of a similar age to yours. Part of what's taken time is, we've been deconstructing that unit in order to salvage parts for Verna. Quite frankly, I have no idea where we could have found the right components, otherwise. I would have had to manufacture many of them, which would have taken far longer."

"How long?"

"Months."

Months. Alone in that house, without Verna. "As it is, how long will it take?"

"I can't say, really. We're off to a good start, so perhaps a few weeks."

Sofia took that on the chin.

"There are still some components I'll have to find or make—the leveler springs for her wheels, for instance. Those on the donor unit are as damaged as what you brought me."

"I know you're doing the best you can." Sofia fumbled with her bag. "I can give you partial payment, to help with purchasing supplies and such." She drew out what Roddy Stoeke had paid her for the perfume bottles. "It is not much, not as much as I'd hoped."

"We are all right for the time being. As I say, we've been fortunate."

"But I must pay you for your time."

He covered her hands, which clutched the thin roll of dollars, with one of his. His fingers felt warm, and strength seemed to flow from them in a current. "I've just sold a number of restored units, and we are well enough funded for the moment."

"But—"

He gave her a rather wry smile. "Miss Gregory, I do not do this work for the money. I am not helping you for profit."

Unexpected tears filled her eyes. "You are too kind."

"Not really." Hastily, he withdrew his hand. "I don't do it out of compassion either, but to prove I can. I don't expect you to understand."

"I think I do." Sofia mopped at the tears that wetted her cheeks. "I'm sorry. I didn't come here to make a spectacle of myself, but to pay what I owe."

"You don't owe me anything yet." He glanced at the money. "Put that away for now. You may need it for something else."

"But I might not be able to come up with more. You see, I have been selling things from my home. But the proprietor of the Golden Dial says he will not buy any more of the items I put aside for the purpose. You should take this now." She turned her gaze on the workbench. "I need her—back together."

"I will put her back together, Miss Gregory, I promise you that. I cannot promise she will retain all her memory. You said you would be all right with that outcome."

"Yes. I must confess, Mr. Pike, the house is so empty and—and bleak without her company. I do not know what I will do for several weeks."

Pike looked appalled. The steam unit clattered up bearing a steaming cup of tea in his hands. Sofia accepted it gratefully.

"Forgive me, miss," Mordred squeaked, "I could not help but overhear. Would it help you to participate in Verna's repairs?"

"What?" Sofia and Pike both stared at Mordred.

"I merely thought, Master Pike, it would get Miss Gregory out of her lonely house—"

"Get her out where?"

"Why, here of course."

"Mordred—" Pike began.

"And," the unit continued as if it did not hear him, "I am led to believe that keeping occupied helps humans deal with grief. Everyone," he added brightly, "likes to be useful."

Pike made a sound that most closely translated to, "Ack."

"And," Mordred went on, "we could use the help. With young Sam now attending school every day, we are without an assistant."

"But I…" Sofia said, "I know nothing about this work."

"You will learn. We need someone to soak parts in solvent, to polish them. You can do that, I am certain."

Pike ground his teeth. "Mordred—"

"Come spend your mornings," Mordred told Sofia, with an air of confidence. "We are busiest then."

Sofia looked from the automaton's silver face which, despite its blankness, somehow managed to radiate kindness, to Pike's, which—from his glare at Mordred—promised a dressing down, at the very least.

Carefully, she laid aside the teacup and got to her

feet. Looking at Pike, she said, "I cannot. I would not be welcome."

He rose also, his gaze fixed to hers, an expression there she couldn't hope to define.

He sounded strangled when he said, "Come, if you wish. You can...be near her."

"And," Mordred chimed in, "you can work to pay off your debt. How much is it you pay Sammy per hour, Mr. Pike?"

"Please, do not worry about that." Sofia shook her head. "All the owing, it is on my part."

"We will see you tomorrow morning," Mordred said, "and no thought of debt between us."

Sofia looked at Lionel Pike again, waiting for him to refuse.

He said nothing.

Chapter Nine

Lionel opened the shop door and peered out into the morning. The rain had stopped, and a watery sun shone through layer upon layer of gray clouds. The bricks of the alley gleamed slick and wet.

There was no sign of Sofia Gregory.

"I do not know why you told her to come," he grumped to Mordred, who rattled around behind him, tidying the shop. He added in a mutter, under his breath, "Or why I agreed to it. Sheer foolishness."

"Miss Gregory is clearly lonely in her home," Mordred replied. "And it is lonely here, with Sammy away at school."

"If he is actually attending school, and not just running wild in the streets. I should go down there and make sure."

"Yes. But not this morning."

"Perhaps she will decide not to come." Lionel hated people hanging around the shop. Yard apples, he called them—cluttering up the place and needing to be kicked out of the way. And a woman, of all things! He didn't need a woman here, especially one so beautiful and…well, possibly distracting.

"She will."

"She doesn't know the first thing about steam repair."

"She will learn. I will instruct her while you go

about your work."

Lionel glanced at Mordred. "You will?"

"Yes, Master Lionel."

"Why are you so set on this?"

"Miss Gregory is grieving. It is part of our mandate to alleviate that."

"It damn sure isn't." Lionel reflected on it. "Anyway, I'll best alleviate her grief by putting her unit together."

"Verna."

"Verna, yes."

"She has a name and, here, an identity. Just as I am Mordred."

"You are Mordred. And you take too much upon yourself. You'd best have a care, lest I decide to switch you off."

"You will never do that."

Lionel turned from the door. "So certain, are you? Why?"

"Because if you did, you would miss me."

The light tick of footsteps coming down the alley caught Lionel's attention. When he turned back, he saw Miss Gregory heading toward his door. She looked very small and rather exquisite in the watery light.

Hastily, he returned to the workbench, leaving the door standing open. It wouldn't do to let her think he'd been watching for her.

"Good morning." She paused in the doorway, looking uncertain. Lionel shot her a look. She'd come prepared to work, wearing a plain, dark skirt and blouse, and with her hair piled neatly atop her head.

He nodded, even as his pulse sped for some unidentified reason. Mordred rolled forward and ushered Miss Gregory in.

"Good morning, miss. Would you like tea before you begin work?"

"No, thank you. I have had my breakfast."

She approached the workbench where Verna lay and studied the contents gravely before lifting her gaze to Lionel's face.

"Mr. Pike, I must apologize for my discomposure yesterday. I will do better. No more tears, so I do assure you."

"Good." He could think of nothing else to say, so he repeated it. "Good." What incredible eyes she had. Dark and full of emotion, tipped up ever so slightly at the outer corners, and fringed with those sinfully long lashes.

She inhaled. "Do you still want me here?"

Lionel fought an inner battle, and lost. He did. "Yes."

"Then please, just show me what I can do to help. I am prepared to work hard."

"Mordred will be in charge of instructing you this morning, if that's all right."

She smiled at Mordred and the interior of the shop lit up. "That will be most enjoyable."

Mordred went into it, showing Miss Gregory where to hang her coat, and introducing her to the various stations in the room. Lionel, at work on Verna's new boiler, kept an eye on them, watching for Miss Gregory's reactions, but she said little. The automaton put her to work polishing Verna's outer skin, and the shop fell into surprisingly harmonious silence.

Despite her presence, Lionel soon lost himself in his work. He had no idea what time it was when Miss

Gregory paused beside him and said, "So that is her boiler? Ah, how strange—even though I've lived with her over twenty years, I confess I often forgot she had one. It was merely where her warmth came from, you know?"

Lionel glanced down at her. She wore her hat and coat. Was it already time for her to leave?

He said, "The boiler doesn't show, which is why I'm installing a brand-new one. The old tank was nearly rusted through, and if it leaked, you'd have trouble keeping her fired. Once her skin is on, you'll never know it's there. Best to do the job right, while we have the opportunity."

Miss Gregory reached out and caressed Verna's cheek, which Mordred had already polished diligently. "I'm sure you're right."

"Tomorrow I'll install her combustion chamber and the rest of the piping. Once we get her core built, we can begin attaching the other components, and she'll look more like the unit you know."

Her fingers, narrow and elegant, froze before she withdrew them. Lionel had a sudden—and shocking—vision of those same fingers touching him, moving over his body, followed by a wave of heat.

Damn, he didn't get that effect from other yard apples.

"Thank you, Mr. Pike. You've been very kind."

Lionel's throat went dry. He found it impossible to speak.

"I will be here at eight o'clock tomorrow morning," she told him.

"Ah—yes. All right."

Once more, she raised her dark eyes to his. "I hope

my presence here today did not disturb you too greatly."

Oh, she disturbed him—she definitely did, but not in the way she meant. "No, no."

She smiled. "Then I will see you tomorrow."

She left, and the quiet light also went out of the room.

****

"So," Sofia said to Mordred some three days later, as they worked side by side at the solution tank. "How did you come by the name Mordred? It's a very unusual one."

She wore heavy gloves and an ancient smock. The solution—a caustic and sharp-smelling stew—was used for cleaning components, a distasteful job from which Sofia did not shrink.

Mordred raised now-shiny hands from the tank. During their work time together, Sofia had grown ever more comfortable with him. Perhaps she just felt at ease with aged units, but he had a restful nature.

"Did Mr. Pike name you?" She still felt a measure of awe toward Lionel Pike, who worked so diligently and so devotedly. She rarely spoke to him.

"No, miss. I chose my own name."

"What do you know about Arthurian legend?"

"I beg your pardon?"

"In the old tales, Mordred was King Arthur's illegitimate son, who was responsible for his death."

Mordred turned his face to her. "I know nothing of that. I was a very decrepit unit when Master Lionel undertook to rebuild me."

"Like Verna."

"Not quite so bad, but I'd seen much hard service. I

never had a name."

"No? How did your owners address you, then?"

"You. Or Unit. That was all."

"Oh. How—awful."

"After Master Lionel rebuilt me, I wished for a name. I had learned the word 'mort' meant death."

"So I believe it does."

"And dread means—fear. I dread death, so I thought death-dread, or mort-dread should be my name."

"Oh, I see." Compassion stirred strongly in Sofia's heart.

"I still dread breaking down to a point where Master Lionel could no longer keep me running. Though, to be frank, I cannot easily conceive of such a point. The man is a genius. An unsung hero, so to speak. He can rebuild anything."

"Verna and I are fortunate we came to him, it seems."

"Oh, yes. I believe his hands hold a touch of magic, for us mechanicals."

"You believe?"

"Yes, Miss. I believe I am able to believe, despite the fact that I am a machine."

Who was Sofia to argue with that? But magic? She stole a look over her shoulder at Lionel and felt the small prick of awareness that always pierced her when she looked at him.

Over the course of the last three days, he'd fitted Verna's new boiler with other preserved components. When Sofia arrived today, Verna had been standing upright. At least, most of her was. Disquietingly, she had no head.

At the moment, he worked with intricate focus on the wheel assemblies which, she'd gathered from Mordred, represented a significant obstacle.

"Our wheels, feet and ankles—for want of a better term—take a great deal of abuse and wear," Mordred told her earnestly. "And they must function faultlessly. Master has been unable to locate any suitable springs, as yet."

"What will he do?"

"Engineer some. It will take time."

"I see." During the mornings she spent here, the time just seemed to melt away. She now understood why repairs tended to take so long.

But working here did, in essence, break her days in half and make the loneliness of the house much easier to bear. She spent her afternoons sorting through the last of her family's possessions, with an eye to selling the house.

She didn't need so much room, not even if she got Verna back. A set of rooms would do for the two of them.

A knock on the shop door interrupted her reverie. Lionel started and snapped out of his funk. "Mordred—door?"

Mordred trundled off obediently and admitted a man and a woman.

Were these the scrap dealers of whom Lionel had spoken? But no, both of them appeared far too well-dressed, if creatively clad in opposing manners.

The woman had glossy brown hair confined in a long braid. She wore a camel-colored coat made of what might be some kind of smooth hide, decorated with beading, and a pair of high-laced boots. She had a clever face made lovely by the wealth of life dancing in it.

Her companion, surely ten or more years older, appeared even more flamboyant. He wore a garish, multicolored jacket and a kilt of black-and-yellow plaid. A bobbled tam sat on his head.

Lionel Pike stared at this pair as if they'd just sprung up from the floor. The woman stepped forward eagerly and clasped his hand.

"Lionel, I've brought someone very important I'd like you to meet."

Lionel? Sofia's eyes widened. Who was this woman, and what did she mean to the steam tinker?

Lionel shook her hand briefly. "Miss Landry."

Miss Landry smiled. "Allow me to introduce Mr. Bruce Buchanan, newly arrived in our city from Ontario."

The man wearing the kilt produced a wide grin. He had fair hair and a rosy face lit by a pair of dancing blue eyes.

He seized Lionel's hand and pumped it vigorously. "I've heard a lot about ye. You're the steam tinker."

"That's what they call me." His hand swallowed by Buchanan's great paw, Lionel shot a questioning look at Miss Landry.

"Mr. Buchanan," Miss Landry said, "very much admires your work."

"You do?" Lionel asked the man in obvious astonishment.

"Och, dear me, aye. I live now in Ontario, but hail originally frae Scotland, where we tend to admire hard work and thrift."

"You heard of me in Scotland?"

"No—in Fort Erie. I admire your work and, even more, the spirit of your work."

"The—spirit." Lionel sounded stunned.

"Mr. Pike, I am a warrior for automaton rights. In Canada, I have fought for that, but north of Erie, steam units are scarce. Here in your city we find the center of the movement, and the heart of the fight, as I am certain you will agree."

Buchanan's brogue being thick, Sofia had some difficulty understanding him.

Lionel blinked incredulously. "I'm not involved in all that, Mr. Buchanan. I just repair steam units."

Mr. Buchanan laughed. "My good sir, do you not mend the disenfranchised, offer succor to the neglected, and provide equality to the forgotten?"

Lionel cast a desperate look at Sofia and Mordred, who once more stood together. "I suppose so, in a way."

"I declare, if automatons are to attain equality, it must be for all—from the sophisticated hybrids to the oldest and most decrepit." Buchanan grinned. "I must admit, I have a weak spot for these older units—like that one you're working on, there."

Miss Landry's face lit with enthusiasm. "Lionel, Mr. Buchanan is interested in acting as your patron."

"My, what?"

Buchanan took it up. "Mr. Pike, sir, I'm a wealthy man. I've been fortunate to ha' a number of things fall my way, and as I say, I canna' think of anything I'd rather spend my brass on than the cause of automaton rights."

Very carefully, Lionel Pike wiped his greasy hands on a shop rag. "I suggest you go speak with Patrick

Kelly then, of the Automaton Rights League."

"I do mean to take him to see Patrick," Miss Landry said eagerly. "But Mr. Buchanan is most interested in meeting with grassroots figures such as yourself."

"Can't get much more grassroots than Patrick Kelly," Lionel protested.

Buchanan's blue eyes twinkled. "This Kelly is a hybrid, right? Like that hockey star who helped beat our team last winter. Those are highly sophisticated pieces of machinery. I have confidence they will make their own way. I'm concerned, sir, about the ordinary, lowly units, the drudges, those destined for the scrap heap."

"Why?"

"Because I love an underdog. And I want to make sure those basic units, that have spent countless hours in our service, are not overlooked when the revolution comes."

Sofia stared. Revolution?

"Revolution?" Pike echoed the word. "What are you talking about?"

"It has to come, Mr. Pike. I would like to partner with you to make certain units such as your friend, there, are not overlooked."

He waved a beefy paw at Mordred, who returned his look with interest.

Lionel, seeming to recall the presence of Mordred and Sofia, started. "That is my assistant, Mordred, and a client, Miss Gregory. This is her unit I'm rebuilding."

"Miss Gregory," Miss Landry said with quickened attention.

"Ah, Miss Gregory." Buchanan turned toward her. "I am sure you can attest to the value of aging steam units."

Sofia glanced at Lionel before she replied, "I certainly can. But—I do my best to stay out of political matters."

"This is not strictly a political matter, Miss Gregory. 'Tis a moral and perhaps even a spiritual one."

"I—I have to go. Expected somewhere else." Hastily, Sofia shed the shop apron Mordred had lent her and gathered up her coat and bag. "It's nearly noon."

Before anyone could stop her, she fled.

Chapter Ten

"What happens at noon? Do you turn into a pumpkin?" The query, spoken in Miss Landry's teasing tone, stopped Sofia in her tracks, only a few steps down the alley. She turned around reluctantly.

Miss Landry grinned. "You know, like Cinderella, only in daylight."

"I am familiar with the tale. And no, I merely have obligations elsewhere."

Miss Landry leaned against the brick wall of the building. Her coat opened and revealed a neat, small steam cannon worn at her hip.

"What's Lionel Pike to you?" Miss Landry asked.

Sofia took a step back, her attention suddenly caught. "I am a client, just as he says. What is he to you?"

Humor flooded Miss Landry's hazel eyes. "Oh, don't worry. I belong heart and soul to a police captain called Brendan Fagan, and I assure you, he's all the man I can handle."

Sofia said nothing.

"Not that Lionel isn't an attractive man. Don't you think so?"

"I hardly suppose that is a proper topic of conversation."

"No? One thing I've learned, Miss Gregory, is that life is fleeting. You need to seize what you want while you can."

"I do not want Mr. Pike." A lie. Ever since she'd started coming to help out in the shop, Sofia had been aware of the attraction. She liked to watch those competent hands of his, and enjoyed eyeing the way his hair fell over his forehead. She lifted her chin. "I do need my steam unit repaired—quite desperately."

"I see." Miss Landry's amusement continued to shine, unabated. "Well, I just wanted to set you straight, in case you imagined you were possibly poaching on my territory."

"I do not poach," Sofia said indignantly, and then, when Miss Landry grinned again, felt embarrassed by her own vehemence.

Miss Landry gave her a salute. Sofia, devoid of cab fare, turned and walked the long distance home.

****

"So, Lionel, what do you think?" Ginny Landry posed the question while leaning on the workbench in a manner that put her impressive cleavage on display.

Lionel tried not to look. He liked Ginny a lot, admired her courage and her frank attitude. But she wasn't the kind of woman who attracted him, by and large.

Besides, the last thing he needed was that big Irishman, Brendan Fagan, taking exception to him. A copper, no less.

Lionel pulled his gaze determinedly from the front of Ginny's shirt to her face. The two of them were alone, Sammy still at school and Mordred gone off on an errand, probably washing the teacups with which he constantly plied Miss Gregory.

Mordred, so Lionel couldn't help but notice, liked

Sofia Gregory a lot. Lionel liked her too, in ways he didn't feel prepared to define.

He wondered if Ginny had picked up on that. Then he realized her question pertained to Bruce Buchanan, who'd also gone on his way.

"I know old Bruce is a bit full on and hard to take. But he's sincere in his desire to champion the cause of the lowly-and-dented."

"How in the world did you get mixed up with him?"

"Through Brendan, if you can believe it. A fight broke out at one of the hockey games. You know how the hybrids figured out a way to engineer reverse temperatures, so the ice stays frozen even when it's warm out?"

Lionel stared. "I didn't. Damn, those hybrids are just too clever, aren't they?"

"Too smart for their own good. Bruce was there, and in the thick of the brawl. Brendan and I were just passing by—he was off duty—and he went wading in." She gave her brightest smile. "I helped."

Lionel just bet she had, with her cannon in hand, no doubt.

"Anyway, you know how Brendan is. He demanded an explanation from the miscreants. Bruce was pretty drunk, but he was able to explain his position. Brendan told him I run what's more or less a rescue for broken-down steamies, and the big Scotsman attached himself to me."

Lionel thought about that. Any number of rescue organizations seemed to have sprung up in the city—for abused animals, for prostitutes, and now orphans. He didn't suppose that was a bad thing.

Ginny, still leaning on the workbench, went on, "I mean, you're already involved, aren't you?"

"Am I?"

"Look what you're doing. Half the stuff those scrappers bring you is beyond help. You're working on that mess, there." She nodded at the bench. "And you saved Floyd." Her face lit and her voice softened. "I, and my family of steamies, will be eternally grateful for that."

"I just rebuilt him."

"You're a genius."

Lionel shook his head. "Exactly what does Mr. Buchanan want?"

"To bring the plight of the lowly steam unit to the forefront, so they don't get forgotten in this movement. The hybrids are taking off, and I think he's right—a schism is developing between them and units like your Mordred. Patrick Kelly doesn't want that to happen. He's gone out of his way to make this a movement for all steamies. The banner they fly is equality for all. But I don't think anyone can deny there's a difference."

"What does Buchanan think he can do about it?"

"Raise awareness that ordinary units have value, and a reason to live."

"I ask again—what's made him take up the cause?"

"I think a unit once saved his life. Up in Canada. It's the one thing he doesn't talk about, but I can feel there's some kind of history. I know how it feels to owe a steamie. My Arthur saved my life." Her hazel eyes grew serious. "He didn't have to. He made a generous, moral decision. And I'm here because of it."

Lionel nodded. Nobody who worked around steamies could deny they had morals—sometimes rudimentary ones, but they existed. From whence the units procured those morals, he couldn't say. Perhaps some were programmed in. He'd be willing to bet others developed over years of service.

"I still don't see why you brought Buchanan here to me."

"You're both working for the same thing, in different ways. He truly is as rich as he says, Lionel, and he's come here looking to throw his money at a cause. Why shouldn't he throw some of it at you, in the process?"

"To what end?"

"I think he has some idea of building—or commissioning—a super steam unit, one to show off, that would rival the hybrids. I thought you'd be the man to accomplish that for him."

Lionel grimaced. "No basic steamie can ever rival a hybrid."

"You're sure about that, are you?"

"Besides"—Lionel gestured at the now-ordered clutter on the workbench—"I need to get this unit rebuilt. Miss Gregory is quite anxious for it."

"Well, you wouldn't want to disappoint Miss Gregory."

"You don't understand. I get the sense she's alone in the world, except for Verna here. She calls this unit her best friend."

"Everybody needs friends."

"Yes."

"So what you have here is more or less a sacred duty."

"It's a serious commission, for which I've pretty much put everything else aside for the time being."

"Mr. Buchanan will wait, as will the steamies." Ginny's eyes met Lionel's. "What other choice do they have?"

"Look, Ginny, you've been good to me, getting me commissions in the past, arranging to sell the units to the orphanages, even finding projects. But I'm not sure I want to get mixed up with a character like Bruce Buchanan. And I don't think I want to get involved with what's going on in the city right now. I just want to do my work."

"You poor fool, you're already involved. Every time you pick up one of those tools, you take part in what's going on. Every time you agree to salvage some battered steamie because it wants to live. Can't you see that? You've already weighed in on Buchanan's side. You might as well benefit from his largess."

Lionel thought about that. He'd been low-budget so long he didn't know what he would do with sufficient funding. What he could do. For an instant, a shining vision of the perfect rebuild rose before his eyes.

At the very least, funding would let him finish Verna the way she should be finished.

He'd have to weigh those options carefully, the good against the bad. As he'd learned, there were always two sides to every prospect.

Chapter Eleven

Sofia could hear the sounds of an argument when she tiptoed down the alley toward the shop, next morning. It had rained again during the night and mist—or steam—swirled between the dampened buildings in clouds. But already the sun had started to burn through.

Even in the short time she'd been working at the shop, this argument had become familiar. Lionel Pike attempted to send his lad, Sammy, to school. The boy protested.

As she approached the shop door, a lean orange cat emerged. The boy burst out after, the strap that secured his books slung over his shoulder and rebellion in his face.

"I can be more use here," he shouted before he caught sight of Sofia and silenced. He ducked past her and pelted off down the alley. Lionel stepped out in his wake and gave Sofia a nod.

He looked disheveled, and on this man, it looked good. His hair, in desperate need of a cut, spilled over his forehead and that, too, looked appealing on him. Sofia didn't imagine he wasted time thinking about his own appearance.

Sofia liked his hair, and wondered how it would feel to the touch. In fact, she ached to run her fingers through it, a thought that led to an awareness of other aches.

Ridiculous. She was immune to men. At least, she always had been.

Lionel brightened when he saw her. "Miss Gregory, good morning. Come in. I have something to show you."

She hurried inside, shed her coat and hat onto the now-familiar pegs, and looked at him expectantly. He gestured to the center of the room.

Verna stood on her feet. Wheels. Moreover, much of her steel skin had been reapplied. Disconcertingly, she was still missing her head, but from the neck down she looked like—well, Verna.

"Oh!" Sofia exclaimed. "You finished the springs?"

"I did. I just couldn't let go of it, so I stayed up late last night and—as you see—got her upright."

"The balancers are working?" This, as she'd learned, had been the thing worrying him.

"Faultlessly." He smiled, and the very room brightened. Lionel Pike, she'd also learned, smiled but seldom, but it invariably proved worth the wait.

"Oh, thank you!" Impulsively, she reached for his hand. His fingers closed on hers eagerly, and she stepped closer, to his side. "You've been ever so good about this."

"It's my pleasure. She's coming together at last."

"Her head…" Sofia faltered.

"Yes, the next hurdle. I did, in fact, want to speak with you about that." He drew her by the hand to the workbench. "Mordred worked hard and managed to get that terrible dent out of her face, but the finish is quite worn." He caressed Verna's cheek with those competent fingers. "Before her head goes on, I wanted to present you with an option. I know a woman—an artist called Beatrice Kormish. She takes on commissions and, among other things, paints faces for steamies. If you're interested in getting Verna repainted, now would be the best time."

"Repainted?"

"The eyes, cheeks, lips—I've seen her work. It's beautiful."

"But Verna is beautiful the way she is."

He smiled. "That's what Mordred said."

"It's true, her eyes used to be painted, long ago. Most of it's worn off, and I'm used to her this way. I just don't know."

Lionel hesitated. "Some customers, especially if they've paid a bit to get a unit rebuilt, like to include that finishing touch. People willing to spend a lot usually have an emotional attachment and—well, a picture in their minds of how their units should look. A mental picture."

"I see. I do have an image like that, yes. But it's difficult to imagine how it would transfer over to a painted face."

"Would you be interested in going to see some of Miss Kormish's work? I could accompany you to her studio, if you like. I need to go out anyway, to pick up some components for Verna's—er—head. Her studio is close by."

Sofia eyed him. "You and I, go together?"

He looked uncertain. "If you will not be ashamed to be seen with a mere workman."

"Why would you suppose that?"

"You're a grand lady, aren't you? From a wealthy

family."

"Wealthy no more. And my father always told me talent was the true wealth, that could not be purchased at any price." Sofia drew herself up. "I would be honored to be escorted by you, Mr. Pike."

Lionel nodded. "We'll go now, while Sammy is at school. Just let me grab my hat and coat. If I get those parts, I can work on Verna's noggin this afternoon."

Yes, Verna definitely needed her head. And Sofia had better remember to keep hers, too.

****

Out on Niagara Street, Lionel hailed a cab. A steam-powered model, it coughed and chugged and spewed dirty soot into the air. Sofia, who could only dream of having cab fare, still considered it a luxury.

"The engine needs an overhaul," Lionel muttered.

She gazed at him. "Could you do that?"

"Probably. I can tinker most anything steam-powered." No conceit colored the words, just practical acceptance.

Mr. Pike seemed different away from his shop, more talkative and less intense. During the ride, he chatted about the components he needed for Verna's so-called brain.

"It's not a brain as such, but an impulse center. There, she compares the instructions with which she was originally furnished with what she's learned since."

"You agree that automatons can learn?"

"No one can deny that. They learn with varying success—the hybrids at an astounding rate. A unit like Verna, that you've had in your company so long, has gained what I can only call experience. She's learned from and adapted to your reactions, almost as a canine might. What starts out as a simple edict to do as ordered, and so please the asker, develops into expectation, and in some cases even anticipation."

"You do acknowledge Verna has that capacity?"

"She didn't, at her time of manufacture, no. But she's been with you so long, it seems entirely possible."

"Mr. Pike," Sofia laced her fingers together, "I am going to say something that may shock you."

His clear gray eyes examined her face. "Not much shocks me. What is it?"

"I believe Verna has feelings."

"I don't find that surprising, Miss Gregory. Many owners do, especially those who grow close to their units."

"Do you believe Mordred has feelings?"

Lionel gave a tight smile. "Not 'feelings' in the biological sense, perhaps, but he has reactions, yes, and I accept that those reactions lend him the capacity for emotion. Mechanicals don't feel the way we feel, but they are capable of caring, and of loyalty and attachment."

Sofia nodded. "Verna is—or was—attached to me. I hope when you're able to reanimate her, she'll retain that attachment."

"Me too. It's one of the reasons I'm anxious to complete the work. Though—" He hesitated and stared out the window at the buildings streaming by.

Sofia's heart sank. "What?"

He looked at her again. "Whoever took her apart either stole or discarded some of the components from her head. I'm hoping that will not affect her memory."

"Oh."

"Miss Gregory, I did warn you at the outset—if I

get her restarted, her memory may be gone."

"Yes. And I told you then, if I can have Verna back, I'll take her in any condition. I'll just teach her to love me again." Sofia flushed. "You probably think me mad, going so far as to speak of love.'

He shrugged. "What do I know? The hybrids are marrying and seeking to adopt children. I assure you, Miss Gregory, I do not possess a definition of 'love.' "

The shop on Chippewa Street bore a large sign over the door that read, merely, Shop. When they entered, Sofia found out why.

It was run by automatons. Two of them stood behind the counter, and one trundled forward to greet them when they entered.

"Mr. Pike. What can we do for you today?"

"I need some very particular components. Is Geraldine in?"

The two shop clerks exchanged glances. Both were newer, high-quality units, and they operated with swift efficiency.

One said, "She is in back, working on a special project."

"Do you suppose she'll mind if I interrupt her for a moment?"

"Permit me to go ask."

The first unit hurried off. The other planted its hands on the counter and went still.

Very soon, a woman came through the door from the back. Tall and brunette, she wore a plain skirt and blouse similar to Sofia's, covered by a smock. Her blue eyes fastened on Lionel and did not waver.

"Mr. Pike, how are you today?"

"Very well, indeed. How have you been?"

"Busy and thriving, as always."

"I hear you have a special project going."

Geraldine smiled. "I am working on a delicate repair to a hybrid."

"I'm sorry to call you away from that. Let me tell you what I need."

The two fell into what Sofia could only describe as shop talk, most of which went over her head. She stood staring at the automatons, which had gone motionless until the woman sent one of them off, chasing down parts.

Lionel paid for a number of things with money from his own pocket and stowed the components he procured—all very small—neatly away there. Only then did he seem to recall Sofia's existence.

They left the shop together and stepped out into bright sunshine.

Concerned, she asked, "Did you get what Verna needs?"

"I did." He shot Sofia a look. "What did you think of Miss Geraldine?"

"She seems knowledgeable."

"That she is."

"It's an unusual line of work for a woman, steam unit repair."

"Yes. Except she isn't a woman."

Sofia stared. "She isn't?"

Lionel grinned. "Miss Geraldine is a hybrid automaton, one of the first built by other hybrids. Many of them have gone into automaton repair or manufacture."

"Really? I wouldn't have been able to tell."

"She's very sophisticated. Come, we can walk to

Miss Kormish's studio from here. Now, she's all human—and a bit eccentric."

A steam cab sped by them, brushing the curb, and Lionel took Sofia's arm, tucking her in beside him. It felt immensely protective, and comforting.

They turned up Franklin Street and approached a tall yellow house. It had a neat porch with bright blue flowers painted all around it. A posy of blue flowers decorated the door.

Lionel's knock was answered by a steam unit. When it swung wide the door, Sofia gasped.

The steam unit had been manufactured to appear male, but it had a painted face. Its silver skin, molded from steel, had been covered with a mask of matte in coffee brown. Delicate color tinted the cheeks and lips, and the eyes were painted deep brown, liquid, with artistically formed brows and lashes.

"Oh," Sofia exclaimed.

Lionel shot her a look. "An example of Miss Kormish's work."

Sofa leaned forward and touched the unit's arm, just as she might Verna's. "You are beautiful."

"Thank you, miss. Please wait in the parlor. I will tell Miss Kormish you are here."

In the parlor, Lionel asked Sofia, "Impressed?"

"Yes, indeed."

"I wanted you to see the work for yourself. There's no way I could convey how good it is."

A woman—a real one, this time—entered the room. She wore a ruby-red gown that spilled lace from the neck and wrists, and had auburn hair piled high on her head. Her carriage rivaled that of a queen.

"Mr. Pike," she greeted Lionel, "what brings you to

me today?"

"Miss Kormish, I have someone I'd like you to meet. This is Miss Sofia Gregory. She's commissioned me to rebuild her steam unit, and she's considering having a face repaint. I wanted her to see your work."

Beatrice Kormish's face lit. "Miss Gregory, I am happy to meet you."

"Honored." Sofia shook her hand. "Your butler—he's just wonderful. Until Mr. Pike told me, I had no idea such an artform existed."

"Come into my studio. See what you think."

"Thank you, I will." Sofia glanced at Lionel. "We will."

Chapter Twelve

The studio, a big room at the rear of the house, had a wall of windows that filled it with light. More than one form of art had been placed on display. Large canvases, most bright with flowers, stood propped against walls. Objects great and small, from tiny boxes to wooden cabinets, covered a number of plank tables. Colorful masks hung on the back wall. And several automatons stood about, all apparently on shut down.

The automatons had painted faces. Two of them—females—were also costumed. Lionel remained near the door and watched Sofia wander toward them slowly, as if mesmerized.

Miss Kormish shot him a look but said nothing as Sofia made her inspection, moving from one unit to another.

At last Sofia turned to her hostess and said, "They're exquisite. I would love this for Verna."

"That's your unit's name, is it?"

"Yes. When Mr. Pike told me about this, I wasn't sure. I mean, I want—wanted—her back the way she was. But now that I see your work, well, it would do justice to the beauty I see in her, if you understand what I mean."

"I certainly do."

"Why don't all automatons have faces like this?"

"Well," Miss Kormish said, "it does cost a bit, as it

takes considerable time. Most owners of utilitarian units such as these barely want to spend coin on maintenance, do they? They don't care enough to spend money on artwork for a unit's face, especially one that will be doing laundry or sweeping out a stable."

Sofia's shoulders sagged slightly. "Is it very expensive? I don't think I'll be able to—well, manage it, then."

Miss Kormish tipped her head. "It's a commission like any other piece of art. If your heart's set on it, we may be able to work out a payment scheme of some sort."

"They are so beautiful." Sofia raised a hand to touch a unit's cheek, but let it drop before her fingers met the metal.

"Go ahead. They're very durable."

"How—how does it work? They all look so different from one another, so individual. How—how would you determine how Verna should look?"

Miss Kormish smiled again. "Why, you would tell me. Only you know how your Verna should look. In fact, I encourage my clients to sketch pictures if they can."

"I am no artist. And—and as I say, I cannot afford to commission a job."

"Well, give it some thought. You are welcome to stop back here and take another look, any time. Perhaps next time, you will bring me a drawing."

****

Back out on the street, Sofia took Lionel's arm without thinking about it, and pressed close to his side.

"Thank you for bringing me here. It was wonderful to see. But I think, much as I'd like to honor Verna, it's quite beyond question."

"I told you, don't worry about that part of it. At least, not now." Lionel patted his pocket. "I got the parts I need. If I can get Verna's impulse center to function, everything else will fall into place."

Sofia looked up at him. "How soon will you know if you can get her impulse center operational?"

"Soon. Maybe later today." His eyes warmed. "Meanwhile, since we're out, will you allow me to take you to lunch? My rumbling stomach tells me it's time."

Sofia smiled. "I have noticed, while working with you, you rarely take time for meals."

"Which is why I need to take advantage now. There's a very nice café nearby. Shall we?"

Sofia wanted to. She discovered she very much desired a further helping of this man's company. But she said, "I'm afraid I shouldn't. I can't afford—"

"My treat, as I said. Will you deny me the pleasure?"

"Well, if you put it that way…"

The café on Franklin Street had checkered curtains in the windows and a number of tables with snowy coverings. It had been so long since Sofia had dined out—or been waited on by anyone other than Verna— she felt her spirits rise buoyantly.

A waiter brought them each a menu card, which she perused with pleasure. From the corner of her eye, she caught Lionel making an odd maneuver under the edge of the table.

"Mr. Pike? What is it?"

"I'm sorry. My hands aren't quite clean. I can't ever seem to get rid of all the grease, no matter how I try."

"I don't mind. You're an artist, like Miss Kormish. Think of it as the equivalent of paint."

"I'm no artist. They call me a tinker because I'm mostly self-taught."

"A craftsman, then. I've seen you work. You become so absorbed, you forget all else."

"Time does seem to melt away when I'm working."

"My father used to say that was when a man—or a woman, for that matter—knew his or her passion. When working at it made time just dissolve—poof."

Ignoring his stained fingers, Lionel leaned across the table. "What's your passion, Miss Gregory?"

"Call me Sofia, please. Passion? I'm not sure I have one."

"Everyone does, so I've been told."

Slowly, Sofia shook her head. "Then, I suppose I haven't yet discovered mine. I've always been happy with my parents—I was an only child, you see—and with Verna, after they died. I sometimes have strange dreams." She stopped there. Why would she initiate such a topic with him?

He frowned, and the waiter returned to take their orders. Not till the man left did Lionel speak again.

"What sort of dreams?"

"Please, forget I mentioned it."

His intelligent gray eyes assessed her. She flushed slightly.

"I've had recurring dreams of a place I've never been—Riga."

"Where's that?"

"In Latvia, from whence my parents came. I was born here and have never been to the old country."

"How do you know you were dreaming of this place—Riga?"

"I was able to describe the buildings, very distinctive buildings. My parents recognized them, and the streets around them. I would dream I walked along those streets and lanes, which had names they also knew."

"How remarkable."

"You will think me mad."

"No. A bit clairvoyant, maybe."

"Do you believe in clairvoyance?"

"I'm no longer sure what I believe. Miss Landry, whom you met, knows a woman called Topaz Gideon, who can see spirits."

"Those of the dead?"

"Yes. Apparently she's part gypsy—Romany, not a tinker like me. And she could look at you or me and see a kind of halo around us—that's our spirit."

"An aura," Sofia said.

"Even more incredible, she says automatons have them—these auras, I mean. Not so strong as ours, but they're there."

Quietly, Sofia said, "I believe that. I am convinced Verna has a spirit—an essence, as I said when we met. It's one of the reasons I want so badly to save her."

He covered her hand, which rested on the table, with his. "We will save her."

Sofia's eyes filled with tears.

"Here, now, I didn't mean to make you cry."

"You have been so good to me. You are one of the kindest men I've ever known."

Lionel looked nonplussed. His fingers tightened on hers in what could only be considered a caress.

"Sofia—"

The waiter returned, interrupting whatever he'd intended to say. Lionel withdrew his hand, but his gaze continued to rest on her, a sure connection.

"Mr. Pike," she began when the waiter had gone.

"Lionel, please."

"Lionel, I know we have agreed that automatons have feelings. But do you believe your Mordred also has a spirit? An inner life?"

"As I have said, I'm not sure what I believe. I've caught him contemplating matters a few times. And he's definitely developed what I can only call a moral sense. Of course, he's been operational a long while."

"There are people in this city ascribing religious belief to the automatons, and saying they deserve their own church."

That made him shoot a look at her. "Indeed?"

"Yes. I am in fact acquainted with some of these people."

"And what do you think?"

Sofia hesitated. Why had she introduced the subject? She did not want this man, to whom she felt such an intense attraction, to think her silly or fanciful. Neither—trembling on the verge of a relationship—did she want him to suppose her something she was not.

A man like Lionel Pike deserved honesty. Even if it cost his friendship, which she began to value so dearly.

Raising her eyes, she met his gaze. "I have to say, I agree with them."

****

Lionel finished his meal, all too aware of his disappointment. He liked Sofia Gregory. Moreover, he

97

felt for her a fierce and protective emotion. He never had much to do with women. He lacked the time, and on the few occasions—now well in the past—when he'd seen a woman socially, it had all blown up at him.

Women wanted attention. They specifically wanted his attention, and while this often started off well, with a woman—much to his surprise—finding him attractive, she soon grew resentful of the time and interest he spent on his work.

Yet there were always more units waiting for repair, their empty eyes staring at him and their need reaching out for him.

Trouble was, Sofia reached out to him, too. He felt different in her company. Even when she worked quietly in the shop, of the mornings, the mood of the place changed and brightened.

He felt an absurd desire to shelter her—in his arms, of all things—and make her world right. Not only could that wreak havoc on his existence, it was not what anyone, even women as fragile-seeming as Sofia Gregory, needed. Everyone should stand on his or her own feet. Even automatons, so he'd learned, needed a measure of—well, autonomy.

Yet he'd enjoyed her company, and learning she was a bit of a crackpot overset him. Yes, he believed steamies had personalities, developed over time. He might even buy into the premise that they *thought*.

But, worship? A far different prospect. He wasn't sure he, personally, believed in God. He was a practical man, a realist who dealt in the nuts and bolts of life.

A church for steamies?

Best he found out she was a little cracked now, before his feelings for the woman got out of hand.

He told himself so over and over again, while they left the café, when he offered to see her home and hailed another cab. When they arrived on the doorstep of a big, imposing house on Woodlawn Avenue, where she told him she lived.

His mind agreed with the good advice he gave it. Trouble was, his body didn't want to listen. It craved contact with her. His hand tingled with the desire to catch hold of hers, to raise it to his lips. He ached to take her in his arms.

How lovely she was as she turned and raised those dark eyes to his face. Incredible eyes, wide and brimming with emotion. Too bad they belonged to a loony.

"Lionel, will you come in?"

He shouldn't. Temptation lay beyond that door, and anyway, he had work to do. Back at the shop. But his body hammered at him.

"All right."

The interior of the house looked and felt bleak. From the foyer, into which they stepped, a flight of stairs swept upward. Stained glass in the windows turned the daylight dirty and grim.

No wonder she didn't want to remain here alone. No wonder, for that matter, she'd developed odd ideas.

"Can I offer you a cup of tea?"

"I have work back at the shop. I shouldn't stay." He said it aloud this time, and she smiled tremulously.

"Of course, you do. I've already taken up far too much of your day."

"I didn't mean that." He couldn't take his eyes from her face, from the full lower lip that quivered slightly beneath his gaze. He wondered how it would feel trapped between his lips.

Soft, so soft. Hot.

She put out her hand, placing it in both of his. "I won't keep you, then."

Keep me, keep me.

"Thank you for such a lovely time and—well, for everything."

He drew her toward him, using her hand. She came quite willingly, her body meeting his flush, and just like that she rested where he'd wanted her all the while, in his arms. Before he could let himself think about it, he bent his head and captured her mouth with his.

Gently, tentatively, he bestowed the caress, his mouth fitting to hers, seeking and wooing. He expected her to stiffen in horror and pull away—perhaps to strike him for taking such an unwarranted liberty. Instead, she melted into him, gasped, and parted her lips.

He lost all capacity for rational thought then. His practical, reasonable mind flew away, seared by pure lust. She tasted of the raspberry tarts they'd shared, and of another incredible sweetness that eluded identification. Heat flowed from her into him—or perhaps from him into her—forming an indelible bond.

He'd kissed women before, sure, and been kissed by them—on one memorable occasion by Patsy, which had seared his consciousness, although not in a good way.

Not like this. Never like this. Now his heart pounded, and Sofia Gregory seemed to reach inside him and capture it even as it raced. She captivated him.

He tried desperately to rein in his passion. He didn't want to frighten her—a gentle, untried lady. Yet the embrace went on and on.

When at last the kiss ended—merely because, so he suspected, the two of them needed air—the dirty light still filled the foyer, but everything else had changed. Sofia clung to him, both arms curled around his neck, and her fingers tangled in his hair.

"Oh, God," he whispered, addressing the deity in which he wasn't sure he believed.

She made a sound in her throat that might be a sob, and pressed her cheek to his shoulder. He began to shake and had to fight hard not to wrap his arms around her.

I want you.

He ached to speak those words. He wanted this woman as he'd never wanted anything, and not just physically, though that need screamed through his veins and pooled in interesting places.

But he couldn't tell her that. They barely knew one another. He'd terrify her with such ferocity.

Instead, he caressed her cheek, the one that was uppermost, with his lips. A staggering wave of tenderness swamped him.

He whispered, "I hate to leave you here alone."

"It's all right. I'm used to it."

He forced his arms to release her, drawing hard on any remaining shreds of composure. Gazing into her eyes he said, "Tell me I'll see you tomorrow."

"I—yes, of course."

He wanted to ask her for promises. He wanted to kiss her again, so much it shook him, to chase that sweetness which lay inside her and claim it for his own. Instead, he stepped away, hauled his cloth cap from his pocket, and put it on his head.

"Be sure and lock the door behind me," he told her.

"I will."

Out in the street, he stood and listened till she did.

Chapter Thirteen

The last person Lionel wanted to see at his door the next morning was Bruce Buchanan. He'd been waiting anxiously for Sofia to arrive, wondering how things would be, between them, after that searing embrace. Eight o'clock—her usual arrival time—had come and gone. So had nine. He began to wonder if she'd thought better of their association.

He'd been too forward, damn it. What sort of man pushed his way into a woman's foyer and forced a kiss on her? Well, in truth he'd neither pushed nor forced. She'd enjoyed that kiss, so far as he could tell.

But what if she now decided to keep away? The thought had him feeling desperate. Fool—he couldn't be falling for the woman, could he? He had no time or patience for it.

Now he threw open the door and found himself staring into Buchanan's broad and rosy face.

"Good morning, laddie!" the Scotsman greeted him. "Are ye no' going to ask me in?"

"This isn't a good time." Lionel searched the alley behind his visitor. No Sofia.

"Miss Landry's no' with me," Buchanan said, misunderstanding. "But I do ha' a proposition I believe may interest you."

Lionel growled, unwelcomingly, "Come on in, then."

At the smaller workbench, Mordred worked sorting through the last of Wendy's parts. Next to the main bench, Verna stood, her head still unattached.

After returning from Sofia's house yesterday, Lionel had worked on the unit all afternoon and late into the night. He'd installed the new components he'd bought from the hybrids, but he sensed something was still missing from the assembly. It had not left him in a positive mood.

"Ah." Buchanan looked at Verna. "Making progress, are you?"

"Not as much as I'd like."

"You'll get there." Buchanan looked Lionel in the eye. "You won't quit till ye do. I ha' known other men like you, in the past. It's what makes you so successful."

Lionel lifted his palms and indicated the shop. "Does this look like success to you?"

"Aye, it does. Och, the place may no' be grand or cutting-edge. I've been in the modern shops—those who run them would not deign to visit here."

"Well, thank you very much," Lionel said, his mood deteriorating further. Even Mordred turned around to regard Buchanan.

Buchanan laughed. "Do no' take me the wrong way, laddie. 'Tis no' all about shiny equipment, or money. Pfft! I ha' money, and what does it get me?"

A comfortable life, presumably, and the temerity to horn in on other people's business. But Lionel didn't say that.

"You, my lad," Buchanan went on, "ha' something better than riches."

"Oh, have I?"

"Aye. You ha' inspiration, and magic in those fingers."

"How do you determine that? You, begging your pardon, don't even know me."

"No, but Miss Landry does. What a woman, eh? If I were twenty years younger—" Buchanan shot Lionel a sharp look. "Anyway, I can sense what's inside you, lad. It's one of my talents. I can read people. That's what's helped build my fortune."

Lionel didn't know what to say to that. He kept silent.

Buchanan grinned. "I have for you a proposition, one that may solve most your monetary problems."

"I don't have any, really." Not at the moment. He had the funds from the sales to the orphanage, and Ginny always slipped him a bit.

Of course—a little extra with which to wine and dine Sofia might be nice. And what if he were able to gift her a commission with Miss Kormish, to get Verna's face repainted?

He fixed his gaze on Buchanan. "I'm listening."

"Look, lad." Buchanan leaned on one side of the workbench. "I don't like bullies. Never have and never will. Did you get bullied in school?"

"No," Lionel said shortly. He'd spent as little time in school as possible, a truth he didn't intend to share with Sammy. He'd slipped away often as he could to old Phil, who'd taught him everything he knew about steam units.

Old Phil had been a true tinker who could take apart anything, and put it back together again, and had. He'd mostly worked on junk, and taught Lionel its value.

"I was," Buchanan admitted. "My parents brought us over frae Scotland, where I was born. There were eight o' us, brothers and sisters. We settled in a place called Caledonia, but it wasna anything like home. Believe it or not, I was puny in my youth—that was before I got my growth, see—and I got picked on mercilessly." Buchanan's bright blue eyes grew reflective. "That made me—sensitive to it, like."

"I see," Lionel lied, completely at sea. What had this to do with him?

"I began working at six years old and made good in the glass trade. You wouldn't think a fortune could be made in something so fragile, would you?"

Lionel shrugged.

"I moved to Fort Erie and started a factory. I could see all the trade lay on this side o' the Niagara. But I got a look, while doing business, at the use o' the steam units here, first in manufacture and then in people's homes. They're being bullied, lad, pure and simple. They're being used and neglected and cast aside in a shameful fashion."

Mordred had straightened from his bench and listened as if rapt.

"I might well agree with you," Lionel told Buchanan, with a stir of pity. "The state of steamies in this city is in flux. As more new hybrid units are built, the older models are being cast off. People don't want to spend money on maintenance. I've seen shocking things, for the want of a bit of grease. Under the new ordinances, steamies are supposed to collect a wage. Ordinary folks, who may have had a steam unit chugging along for years, put it out for scrap rather than give it a pay packet."

"And…" Buchanan's bright gaze prodded Lionel's. "Do you think those units mind?"

"I know they do." It was why Lionel took many of the units off Patsy and George, even though he doubted he'd ever use them, why he did the work he did.

Buchanan nodded in satisfaction. "Yet their wishes—their fears—are disregarded. I believe it's because people just don't value them."

"So what can be done?" Every aging steam unit couldn't be saved. Again, Lionel's eyes moved to Wendy's bench. She couldn't be.

Buchanan followed his gaze and smiled at Mordred. "That unit will, in essence, live on because you're utilizing it in this rebuild. Do you have any children, Mr. Pike?"

Lionel shook his head.

"We have children, lad, so that bits of us live on after we die. Everyone dies, humans and steam units alike. Steamies can't reproduce. Och, I ken the hybrids are, after a fashion. I saw that new, wee lassie they made. Miss Landry took me to meet her. But an ordinary unit cannot pass on its talents, its beliefs."

Beliefs. Lionel thought of Sofia. Where was she? Surely, with his clumsy embrace, he'd destroyed whatever lay between them.

"So," he asked Buchanan, "what's to be done?"

"How does one put an end to bullying? I believe 'tis by proving value. And how to do that? By shining a light on the worth o' what's being belittled."

Buchanan, so Lionel decided, was a madman. "Those are all high and fine ideals." He shook his head. "But what can I do? I just work on steam units."

"Wrong. You work on the downtrodden. You

tinker them, lad, and bring them back to life."

The shop door opened. Sofia came in, dressed in her dark coat, with her head bent.

Lionel's relief felt so staggering, he stumbled where he stood. She'd come. Late, but here after all.

Buchanan, intent on convincing Lionel of whatever crazy thought he pursued, ignored her arrival.

"I want you, lad, to build me a steam unit."

"Eh?"

"One beyond compare, of superlative quality. A steam unit above all others, strong and clever and magnificent, able to accomplish astounding things. But"—Buchanan held up a finger—"I want you to tinker it for me."

"What does that mean?" Lionel stared, his attention well caught.

Buchanan smiled. "I want you to build it all out of scrap, from the wheels up. Not a new part on it. I want it to have the attributes of all its donors, and I want it to be able to best any steamie in this city."

Lionel croaked a single work. "Hybrids?"

"No, not them. No mechanical can best a hybrid, can it? That's part of the problem. But I want it to take on even those new units that are being turned out by shops like Starr and Williams, and hold its own."

Mordred had straightened, and Sofia stood listening also, arrested.

Lionel asked, "What good will that do?"

"It will make people take a look at their own aged units, will it no'? Make them think twice about failing to invest in them, and casting them off."

Would it? Lionel experienced a rush of interest that started deep in his gut, and spread outward. Maybe, just maybe.

"I'll fund ye, lad. And I'll stand by ye, because I believe you're the man to accomplish this, the only man in the city who can."

Chapter Fourteen

After Mr. Buchanan left, giving both Sofia and Mordred a smile in passing, the interior of the shop grew very quiet. Though Sofia received a few glances from Lionel, he didn't ask why she was late. She offered him no explanation.

Quite clearly, he had Mr. Buchanan's offer on his mind. Sofia had heard only the end of what Buchanan said to him, but even that much had been astounding. A challenge to best all others, it must seem, to a man like Lionel Pike. And one with far-reaching implications.

Sofia thought about the implications while she worked alongside Mordred, sorting Wendy's components into those usable and those destined for the scrap heap.

She agreed with some of what Buchanan had said. Anyone who'd ever formed an attachment to a mechanical unit experienced frustration over the difficulties of repair as it aged. And more and more units were abandoned out on street corners like stray cats, or left to wander until their supplies of coal ran out.

The Automaton Rights Movement insisted that, as an inclusive entity, they worked toward equality for all units. But any fool could see the old units were getting left behind.

In Mr. Buchanan, it seemed they had a champion,

and Sofia felt glad about that. What would have happened to Verna, had she not, in turn, had Sofia to stand up for her?

Or had Sofia not, in fact, found the steam tinker.

Sofia's heart sped up at that thought, not because he was clever and carried a little magic in his hands, but because of what had happened between them yesterday afternoon. She'd thought about it—and relived it—all night. She'd experienced over and over again the heat of it, and the absolutely thrilling excitement. No lady would have acted as she had, gone so willingly into a man's arms and melted against him, offering her mouth to his.

By morning, she'd come to the conclusion she should not see Lionel Pike again. He was too tempting, and far too dangerous to her state of mind. He didn't need her help to repair Verna. Sofia had merely wished to be near the unit—near him.

All that must end now. She'd told herself so over and over again while she performed her ablutions, washed in cold water, and put up her hair. While she dressed in what she now thought of as her shop clothes and, two hours late, set out on the long walk to Niagara Street.

Now Lionel labored over Verna, who stood on her new wheels and still had no head. And Sofia felt very certain he thought only about Mr. Buchanan's offer.

Not about her.

Which meant she'd been right to come. That fiery kiss they'd shared had meant little to him. Not like her—for it had altered her world. Altered her inside, if she were honest.

He quite likely kissed women all the time. The

thought made Sofia feel a bit wild in the head, started a protest in her breast that clamored for release. She did not want this man to want any other woman.

Not when she, Sofia, wanted so badly to kiss him again.

She sorted and sanded and polished, while she thought about ways and means. She'd need to get Lionel alone. That meant persuading Mordred to leave the shop. She'd need an excuse then to get near Lionel. To touch him. To lift her face to his.

Risky. Especially since he appeared completely absorbed in his work, focused on Verna. Had he forgotten she existed?

She felt singularly ill equipped to garner his attention. She'd been raised by old-world parents with strict ideas about how a lady should behave. A lady had dignity within herself, she knew her value. She exercised restraint and always displayed decorum.

She did not throw herself at a man with grease stains on his hands, who very likely didn't return her interest.

The time dragged by while thoughts bounced around inside Sofia's head. At last, Mordred turned to her and asked, "Miss, would you like a cup of tea?"

"That would be most welcome."

"One moment.

The unit squeaked away. Sofia wiped her hands on a shop cloth and went to Lionel's side. "How are Verna's repairs progressing?"

He glanced at her. "Not as well as I'd hoped. I've installed the components we purchased yesterday, but I don't think she's ready for start-up yet."

Yesterday.

"Why not?"

"Something's missing. For the life of me, I can't tell what. This afternoon, I may take another look at Wendy's control center. Maybe I'll be able to figure it out from that."

Sofia edged closer, hungry to touch him, even if she merely pressed her elbow against his. "Once Verna is started, then we'll be able to tell what she can and can't remember?"

"Should." Again he looked at her. "I hope you won't get your expectations up too high. It may take several attempts."

"I understand." Sofia waved her hands. "You're more than patient, taking all this time from your regular work, as I understand, and devoting yourself to her."

"To tell you the truth, I'm enjoying the challenge of it. But I'd hate to let you down."

She met his gaze. "You will not. I believe in you."

Something sparked in his eyes. His arm gently encircled her, and just like that—so easily—she was where she wanted to be.

She turned to face him. "Thank you," she whispered, and went on her tiptoes to kiss his cheek.

He shifted, though, so his mouth rather than his cheek met her lips. A thrill shot through Sofia, swiftly followed by a rush of raw delight. He was not immune to the desire that rode her so persistently. He too reveled in this sensation so strange to her that she couldn't tell what to do with it.

But, as the steam tinker knew so much, he also seemed to know about this. He drew Sofia closer, wrapping her tight in his arms and slowly—delectably—began to consume her.

Mother would be shocked, Sofia thought, and then *Mother is not here. I am, and this is the most alive I've felt in—well, possibly ever.*

Swiftly, swiftly, all rational thought flew away. Just like yesterday, Sofia became lost in sensation. The steam tinker's lips wooed her. His tongue swept the interior of her mouth, and a moan escaped his throat, one that served to intensify Sofia's desire.

Desire. To mold her body to his—which she did. To stretch up on her tiptoes and wind her arms around his neck. To give a groan of her own, that answered his—a sound of approval, a demand for more.

Whatever it was, he understood that also. His palms flattened on her back and slid downward until they cupped her buttocks. He drew her up and into him, and for the first time in her life she began to understand how a man and woman were made to fit together.

Her knees went weak. Suddenly she felt desperate for more. She wanted to shed her clothing, the better to feel him. She wanted—

A sound interrupted the outrageous impulses streaming through her. It was a strange rasping scrape, and it made Lionel stop kissing her, and direct a glance over his shoulder.

"Yes, Mordred? What is it?"

"Miss Sofia's tea is ready."

Lionel gasped. "All right. Set it down there."

"Would you like me to serve?"

"I'd like you to return to the back room for a few minutes."

"Yes, Master Lionel. How long?"

Lionel's eyes met Sofia's in consternation. "Ten minutes?"

Mordred squeaked away. Lionel, still breathing hard, captured Sofia's face between his palms and asked, "What am I to do about this?"

"This?" she faltered.

"How I feel about you. I suppose I should apologize—again."

Earnestly, she told him, "I suspect, this time, it was my doing. I wanted, needed to know—"

His gaze quickened. "Yes?"

"If what happened between us yesterday was an aberration."

"Ah, yes. Good. Experimentation is always a worthwhile endeavor."

"Perhaps," she suggested tremulously, "we should experiment farther."

"I'm not sure I dare. You're like fire to dry tinder."

"Yes," she could only agree.

"I've never—" He halted abruptly.

"Neither have I." Sofia did her best to think despite the fog of desire filling her head. "Perhaps, since this is unfamiliar to both of us—new ground, so to speak—we should see how far it may go."

His eyes widened. "Eh?"

"I suggest a learning experience. A—a kiss here, an embrace there." Her cheeks flushed. "A touch. A—a caress."

Sweat appeared on Lionel's brow. "I would not wish to do anything to offend you."

"How can I be offended by a learning experience? If ever one of us wishes a lesson to stop, he or she need only say so."

"Lesson, is it?"

"Is it not?"

"Sofia, it doesn't seem quite proper."

"Perhaps not. But, Lionel, I discover I'm a bit weary of being proper. It's a lonely position in which to find oneself. And very, very boring."

"Master," Mordred called from the back room, "may I return now?"

"That wasn't ten minutes," Lionel shouted. "It couldn't possibly be."

Sofia giggled. "I trust you, Lionel."

"You shouldn't. You really shouldn't."

"I know you will keep to the rules."

He groaned and kissed her hard.

"Master Lionel," Mordred called again, "the tea is growing cold."

Sofia smiled at her erstwhile instructor. In return, he delivered a slow wink.

"Then, Mordred my fellow, I suppose you'd better come out and serve it."

Chapter Fifteen

Surely, Lionel thought with weary acceptance, he was losing his mind. Events had conspired to make it happen.

He'd once had a fairly well-ordered life, doing more or less as he wished—scraping along financially, yes, but that had never mattered much to him. Now his mind struggled under Buchanan's fascinating offer, and his body responded helplessly to Sofia's suggestion. What was she thinking? An innocent, he'd considered her. And there remained a certain innocence in her offer, still.

Yet little innocence lingered in her kiss, and her body called irresistibly to his. This game, or lesson, or whatever she called it, offered possible liberties of which he might only dream. A touch. A caress.

She had used that word.

Did she know what she wanted? For certain, he would lose his mind, unless choice parts of his anatomy exploded first.

He wanted to play her game. Oh, yes, he did. And that surprised him.

It shook his dull, predictable world.

He tinkered in steam units, little more. Now, he had the challenge of repairing Verna, who proved unexpectedly stubborn.

And he had the prospect of building a steamie to

best all others.

From scrap.

Plenty to occupy him. Still, even after Sofia left for the day and Sammy came home from school, thoughts of her dominated Lionel's mind. He relived again and again how they'd parted.

Sofia had towed him to the door, leaned up in that confiding way she had, and laid a kiss on him that parted his lips.

"Till tomorrow," she whispered as she slipped out.

God, he could hardly wait.

"You want me to answer that?" Sammy's rather shrill voice cut through Lionel's heated thoughts.

"Eh? What?"

"Someone's at the door." Not waiting, Sammy went. The door swung wide to reveal a tall figure in a blue uniform. Dull sunshine lit the alley behind him, making him look something like an avenging angel.

"Yeah?" queried Sammy, not impressed by the uniform.

"I'm looking for a Mr. Lionel Pike."

Well, that couldn't be good. Lionel laid aside the part he'd been fitting and wiped his hands on a rag.

"What for?" Sammy demanded. "What's he done?"

"He's done nothin'," The officer had a mellow, rolling Irish brogue. "Is this his shop?"

"Sammy." Lionel went to the door and nudged the lad aside. "Officer? I know you, don't I?"

The officer topped six feet, with a set of shoulders like a bull and bright blue eyes. He examined Lionel keenly. "Mr. Pike?"

"You're Captain Fagan, aren't you? Miss Landry's—er—friend?"

"Ah, yes. Miss Landry is, in fact, the one who's directed me to you today. She says you're a genius with steamies."

"I'm not sure I'd use that term. What can I do for you?"

Captain Fagan stepped in and shut the door behind him. "We police have an ugly situation on our hands, *sor*. We need an expert to take a look and help make sense of it."

"Take a look at what?"

Fagan gave him a hard stare. "You've heard of the fighting pits?"

"You mean, dogs?" Lionel's stomach rebelled.

"Aye, *sor*, but most of those have been shut down. Oh, they're constantly reopening in back alleys and such. But Jamie Kilter's been getting after those. You know Jamie Kilter?"

Lionel shook his head.

"He's a real warrior, *sor*, from the Anti-Cruelty League."

"I see," said Lionel, who didn't.

"With the dogs out of the picture, miscreants are pitting other things against each other."

"Things?"

"Men against men. Men against machines. Now we think it's machines against machines."

"Steamies, you mean?"

"I do. We've heard of it before. We haven't had the laws to put a stop to it." Fagan glanced at Mordred. "Steamies are just things, so these pit masters say. Right?"

Wrong.

"New laws are going on the books. We have a

chance to legislate against it. What we need is documentation. From an expert. I'd like you to come down with me to view this current scene and document what we've found."

"Document? I'm not much for formal writing."

"You just state your findings, *sor*, and I'll have a man write it down. You can sign it, after."

"Well—uh, I'm a bit busy here."

"I can see that, Mr. Pike, and I wouldn't ask if this weren't so important."

Lionel glanced at Mordred who, or so he fancied, stared at him pleadingly.

"All right, I'll come."

****

The pit—a fully enclosed yard in the back of a warehouse on Seneca Street—stank of coal smoke and scorched metal. It looked like a butcher's floor, if the things being butchered were steam units. The sand in the pit had been flooded not with blood but water and grease which, to Lionel's dismay, he saw came from severed joints.

Severed everything.

"God," he whispered when Fagan led him in.

The police captain gave him a cool look. "Just so, *sor*. This is a disgrace, and needs to end."

Other police officers made a presence. One, short and stalwart, stood stationed at the door. Two more, both big men, examined the terrible tangle of rent boilers and limbs that littered the place.

"I've brought the expert, Pat," Fagan called. "Will you take it from here? Mr. Pike, Officer Banks, here, will record your findings." He nodded at the officer by the door. "Officers Kelly and Riley will show you around. I'm needed back at the station. You have my thanks, for doing this."

Officer Kelly. Lionel turned back to see that yes, one of the officers was the now-famous hybrid automaton, the same he'd watched introduce the hybrid child, Kiera, last week. In fact, narrowing his eyes, he realized both officers facing him were hybrids, no doubt members of the Irish Squad.

"Mr. Pike, is it?" Kelly asked. He stepped forward and put out his hand. "This is my colleague, Officer Riley. We appreciate your assistance."

A remarkable work of engineering was Officer Kelly. The only thing that gave him away as other than human was a slight click from his voice box when he spoke.

"Glad to help," Lionel said, and nodded at the second hybrid.

"This scene was reported around noontime, when a deliveryman stumbled across it. By then, of course, all the patrons were long gone, as well as the operators. This yard is listed as rented to a Mr. Cornelius Quinn, who denied all knowledge of these goings on."

"How can I help?"

"If you can, Mr. Pike, please sort out how many units were sacrificed here, and how they met their demise."

Lionel gazed around helplessly. "It's a litter of parts. It will be difficult, at this point, to tell."

Kelly said gently, "That is why we require an expert, *sor*."

Ironic that, Lionel thought—a mechanical unit calling upon a human for expertise. Yet Kelly and his companion were hybrids, and might not have as intimate a knowledge with older mechanicals as he did. "Look," he said, "the hybrids have the market cornered on expertise. Can't you call your people?"

Kelly smiled. "Thank you for acknowledging us as people, *sor*. But if hybrid experts are called in, those in this city who oppose laws to protect automatons—on the premise they are in fact mere machines—will lay an accusation of prejudice. We need a human expert. And you are reputed to be the best. If you prefer, we could call in Starr and Williams."

"No, don't do that. They're not honest."

Riley spoke suddenly. His voice box also clicked. "We have one over here in this corner, who's still alive."

"Alive?" Lionel repeated, startled.

"He means operational," said Banks, who now had his notebook in hand.

"Oh. Can't you ask him what occurred?"

"We would, but his voice box is smashed." Kelly eyed Lionel. "We hoped you might be able to take him back to your shop and get that mended so we can obtain a report from him."

"Yeah, all right. Let me see him first."

The unit in question half leaned and half slumped against one wall amid a pool of spilled liquid. An older unit that had obviously seen better days, he had glass eyes—one cracked—that fastened on Lionel when he hunkered down. The top of his head, his chin, and his throat had all been smashed and his torso staved in, though his boiler still retained enough water to keep him operational.

Steam leaked from several joints, and he flailed weakly against the rough boards.

Compassion flooded through Lionel. Poor old unit. He reached out to touch the torso, and the unit's pincer hand closed on his wrist.

He felt a jolt of connection.

"Bastards," he muttered.

"Precisely," Kelly agreed. "We need to close these kinds of operations down permanently."

"Amen," said Riley, and Lionel stared at him.

Who said hybrids didn't care about the old, primitive units? These two clearly did.

"I'll take him back to the shop and see if I can rig up another voice box. Of course, if his memory's damaged—"

"We understand, *sor*."

Lionel patted the leaning steamie and got to his feet. "Let's look at the others."

Together, they moved from pile to pile, sifting through the detritus of tortured metal and spilled coal. Banks jotted notes on his pad while Lionel did his best to make sense of the components. These units were aged—no new models used here—and many looked as if they had been scabbed together. At one point, he found part of a unit, headless, with what after some struggle he identified as a weapon still clutched in its hand.

"Here," he called to the hybrids, "look at this. What kind of weapon is that?"

Patrick Kelly, answering his call, turned his head and examined the object, a spiked metal ball on a chain. "Mace," he replied.

"Eh?"

"Medieval weapon. I've read about them."

The slow anger simmering in Lionel's heart burst

to life. "Somebody's patching these old units together, only to make them destroy each other. Why?"

Kelly gave him a look from keen, green eyes. "For entertainment."

"But I mean, why would the units take part in such an awful display?"

"Mr. Pike, *sor*, these units have been created to obey orders. Over many years, it's been their sole purpose in life. It's what they will do."

"Well, it makes me sick." Lionel glanced around. "I estimate there are at least a dozen steam units here."

"Good, Mr. Pike. That's exactly what we need to know."

"But where are the rest of the weapons? And where's the—the winner?"

"I expect the weapons were all collected at the end of the show, save that one, which was overlooked. So was the victor, being, in a minor way, valuable. He," announced Kelly, "will have to fight again."

Not if I can help it, Lionel resolved.

"Thank you for your assistance, Mr. Pike. If you'll permit, we can run you and the damaged unit back to your shop in the paddy wagon."

"Right," Lionel agreed. "Though I don't know what the neighbors will think."

Chapter Sixteen

Once again, Sofia thought about Lionel all night. She relived the moments they'd shared in the shop yesterday and saw once more the look in his eyes— intent and heated—when he'd agreed to her experiment.

She thought about all the things she'd like to build into the lesson plan.

She got little actual sleep, but her thoughts made the hours pass and staved off a little of the loneliness created by Verna's absence.

As she dressed in the chilly dawn, she asked herself how daring she should be. How far should she go with the attractive Mr. Pike? She required more of those heated, knee-melting kisses. She wanted far more than kisses, truth be told.

But what did that make of her? What might her mother have said? Well, she could guess the answer to that. For the first time in her life, however, she found she didn't care.

It felt as if Lionel's kisses had freed her, burned through the moral restrictions that held her in a place she didn't want to be—bereft and isolated. Starved for a helping of all life had to offer.

She wanted Lionel Pike. And, as she walked to his shop that morning, she determined that, shocking as it seemed, she would have him.

But when she arrived at the shop, she found chaos.

Ordered chaos it might be, but upheaval all the same. A strange unit stood, front and center, in the middle of the floor with a clutter of tools and body parts all around it. A large unit, it dwarfed Verna, who still stood beside the work bench and who now, as Sofia saw, had acquired her head.

Lionel, Mordred, and Sammy—apparently playing hooky from school—all stood around staring at the new unit.

"Good morning," Sofia said as she slipped in. Lionel turned and gave her a vague smile, so she went to his side and joined in the staring.

The new unit appeared heavily damaged, even to her eye. Every part of its metal skin bore dents, some quite severe, along with scrapes and stains. The torso and lower half of the face seemed to have sustained the worst of the damage but, astonishingly, the unit still operated, leaking wreaths of steam and giving off fearful heat.

"What is this?" she asked.

"A fallen warrior," Mordred intoned.

"I beg your pardon?"

Lionel explained, "After you left yesterday, I was called to a fighting pit."

"Called? By whom?"

"The police, who required my assistance."

"Oh!"

Lionel glanced at her and shook his head. "Not a dog pit—this one put steamies up against one another. Only wreckage left when we got there—and him. Police thought if I can get him talking, he'll be able to testify."

"Oh." Sofia said again, and wrinkled her nose. "He

126

stinks."

"That's scorching. Plus, with his boiler staved in like that, he isn't getting an efficient burn. And, his hopper's stuck shut. I have to figure out how to give him more coal, because we need him running."

The unit had blue glass eyes. Sofia experienced a kind of chill when they adjusted to look at her. She felt the touch of horror.

"How terrible. Can you help him?"

Lionel didn't answer.

"I say, pry him open," Sammy declared with what sounded like ghoulish relish.

Lionel didn't so much as look at the boy. "Go to school."

"I told you, I'm already late."

"I don't care, Sam."

"I'll get detention."

"Then you accept the penalty and resolve not to be late again."

"That's bull—" Sammy looked at Sofia and hastily amended, "crap."

"Go," Lionel ordered.

"I don't want to miss this."

"It's going to take hours. I'll still be working on this one when you get home."

The boy went off, grumbling. Sofia struggled to see how the presence of the damaged steam unit changed everything. What of their game? And what of Verna's repairs? Did this put those on the back burner?

"Mordred," Lionel requested, "go find me the good lubricant from Verna's bench."

Mordred trundled away, and Lionel said to Sofia, just as if he read her mind, "I'm sorry, but this will delay Verna's repairs a bit. I have to try and get this unit communicating. I did manage to fit the missing part to Verna last night, and I reattached her head."

"I see that. She looks much better."

Lionel gave her a look from the corner of his eye. "I must confess, it's one of the first things I did when I got back from that fighting pit. Seeing all those units without their heads attached turned my stomach. I must apologize—I never realized how distressing it must be for you to keep seeing her that way."

"Yes, well—"

"I don't have her running yet. To tell you the truth, I'm a little leery of trying, because if her intelligence is lost, well, that presents a whole new hurdle. But she's about ready to refire."

"Thank you. I do appreciate it."

To Sofia's surprise, he took her hand in his and clenched it tight. Still looking at the damaged unit, which looked back at them, he said, "I simply must get it to speak. It might be able to say who runs that fighting pit."

"He's so large."

"He's an old unit, rebuilt to fight. They've added to the girth and height, as you can see, and double-walled the torso, which probably kept him alive. But it's making things harder now. You can see all this metal's crumpled. I need to get that hopper open, before he runs out of fuel."

"The way he's leaking steam," Sofia observed, "he's going to need water, too."

Mordred returned with the lubricant. Lionel released Sofia's hand in order to apply it to the unit, which watched him with those careful, blue eyes.

"Do you think he has a name?" Sofia asked.

"Probably not. Most units intended for labor don't. but they're built strong, which would be an advantage to the kind of people who run a pit."

"What sort of labor would he have done?"

"I don't know." Lionel caressed the folded skin with one hand, and the unit fixed its gaze on him. "Shoveling coal, perhaps? Loading and unloading ice? Some backbreaking job men don't want to do. Yet," Lionel added in a mutter, "those same men sneer at these units and call them worthless."

"Can you fix him so he'll be able to speak?"

"I hope so. His voice box has been smashed, along with the bottom half of his face."

Sofia wondered aloud, "What kind of weapon would do damage like that?"

"You don't want to know."

"I'll help," Sofia decided. "Give me a task to do."

"You don't have to. He's filthy, and leaking something fierce."

"That's all right. I want to hear what he has to say."

****

In the hours that followed, Sofia was treated to a rare spectacle—the steam tinker at his best. She'd seen him intent before, since coming to the shop, watched him engrossed in Verna's repairs. This felt different. A man on a mission, he poured himself into mending the battered unit, and Sofia virtually held her breath.

There truly was magic in his hands she decided as she watched him gently uncrumple the battered torso, fold upon fold, and eventually pry the hopper open. The boiler tank proved so damaged, it could only be half refilled with water.

"Worry about replacing that later," he muttered, and began disassembling the bottom of the unit's jaw—or what was left of it.

A disconcerting sight. Sofia glanced repeatedly at Mordred, wondering what the unit thought of the process, but he displayed only calm. Mordred had probably seen it all while working with Lionel.

In the end, Lionel used Wendy's voice box and part of her chin.

"He won't sound right," he admitted, "but we don't care about that right now, do we?"

"No," agreed both Sofia and Mordred, in time, and Lionel gave a tight smile.

It took five attempts to get Wendy's voice box working. Noon came and went. Sofia did not leave. When a knock came on the door, she went to answer it and admitted a tall, handsome police officer who identified himself as Brendan Fagan.

"Does Mr. Pike have that fighting unit going yet?" he asked Sofia.

"Just about to start it. Please come in."

Lionel greeted Fagan with a nod. They all stood rapt and silent as, with a bit of jiggling, Lionel adjusted things.

"Can you speak?" he asked the unit.

"Yes."

Lionel had been right. Wendy's voice sounded too high and squeaky for the big unit. Ludicrous. No one cared.

"Does it have a name?" Sofia asked.

Lionel glanced at her before repeating it to the unit. "Do you have a name?"

"Dammit Twelve," it uttered.

"I beg your pardon?"

"It is what my owner always called me. *Dammit Twelve, move faster. Dammit Twelve, pick up that ingot. Dammit Twelve, how can you be so stupid?*"

"Oh, goodness," Sofia breathed.

Fagan gave a hard laugh. "Employed in the steel trade, were you?"

The blue glass eyes fastened on him. "Yes, sir."

"What happened?"

"I broke down."

"Pushed to the curb, were you?"

"Yes, sir, along with others. I'm the last one left…alive."

A small silence fell. Lionel cleared his throat. "How did you get to that fighting pit?"

"I do not remember, sir. I ran out of coal shortly after being put out, and so I shut down."

Sofia asked, "Why didn't you—run away after being put out?"

"And go where, madam?"

Imagination, so Sofia gathered, must be limited in these models. She knew Verna's reached only so far and, while she'd been able to recite stories for Sofia as a child, she really couldn't vary or expand upon them.

Now Sofia suggested, "You might have looked for a way to get some more coal and keep yourself going."

The unit looked at Captain Fagan. "That would be stealing. And stealing is forbidden."

Captain Fagan puffed out a breath. "Most commendable of you."

Lionel asked, "So you woke up at the pit?"

"No, sir, at a workshop not unlike this one, only bigger and cleaner."

Lionel gave a frown.

"Someone refitted him," Fagan said, "to fight."

"Yes, sir," the unit agreed in his—or rather Wendy's—high whine. "I reignited to find my body had been reinforced and some of my faulty parts had been replaced. Not all of them, unfortunately."

Fagan took over the questioning. "Do you know who ran the fighting pit?"

"No, sir."

"But you'll have seen them."

"Sir, I saw many persons. The area around where we fought was full of screaming humans. I was given weapons and ordered to fight others like me. I did so. I survived many battles though badly damaged, as you see. The last I faced was someone I knew."

"Eh?" said Lionel, startled.

"Someone else from the steel works, who was put out with me. He was also refitted. I—" the unit paused, or rather froze, and Lionel cursed softly.

"He must have broken down again—"

But the unit jerked suddenly back to life. "I killed him."

"Aw, shite," Fagan breathed.

"But I was badly hurt in the combat. I fell against the wall. My captors thought me dead."

Captors, Sofia thought. An apt description.

"You must have seen these men," Fagan pressed. "The ones who ran the pit. The ones," he added with precision, "who did this to you."

"The ones," Sofia put in, "who gave you the order to fight."

The blue glass eyes—one so disconcertingly cracked—moved to her.

"Yes, madam."

"Can you describe them to the police captain, here?"

"I do not understand—describe."

Of course, he wouldn't. Impulsively, Sofia reached out and touched his scuffed arm. "Tell him what these men looked like. So he may apprehend them. That may stop this happening again to other units like you."

"Yes, madam. They were—persons."

"How tall? Like—like the captain, here, or like Mr. Pike?"

"Shorter than me."

Anyone would be shorter than him. "Captain, please," Sofia whispered to Fagan, "stand straight. As tall as the captain's head? High as his eyebrows?"

"One to his eyebrows and very wide. The other— the other smaller with hair the color of Mr. Pike's."

"Good. Very good, indeed. How old were they?" Sofia took the unit through a number of other questions, and Fagan wrote the answers down carefully.

"You're good at this," the captain whispered to her, when they had what he considered decent descriptions.

"I've lived with a steam unit most my life." She nodded at Verna. "You learn that they think quite literally."

"Well, er—Dammit," Fagan addressed the unit, "I thank you for your assistance. I think I will leave you here for the time being, if that's all right with Mr. Pike."

"Yes, fine," Lionel agreed.

Fagan extended his hand to Lionel. "Pat Kelly and Sean Riley said you were respectful to the steam units yesterday. I can see that's true. Would you be willing to testify in court for this case, if it comes to it?"

"Well…" Lionel looked at the battered unit. "Yes, all right."

"Good. Thank you, *sor*. And you, Dammit? You're happy to stay here for the time being?"

The unit focused on Verna, who stood directly across from him.

"I would like that, sir. I would like that very much."

Chapter Seventeen

"Do we have to call him Dammit?" Sofia asked in an undertone, once the police captain left.

Lionel looked from her to the unit in question, which seemed to have gone into voluntary standby mode. It still leaked steam horrendously and appeared too damaged to operate.

"He thinks that's his name."

"I know, but—" Her luscious lower lip—the one he'd kissed—came out in a half pout. "But it's so degrading. Can't he learn another name?"

"Possibly."

"How about Damian? It sounds similar."

"We'll try that." Lionel edged closer to her. "It was kind of you to stay on this afternoon and help out."

"I'm hoping to see Verna restarted. Plus," she turned to him and lifted glowing dark eyes to his, "we have our own experiment to run."

Lionel's pulse leaped. "So we do."

"Delayed by all that's happened here this morning but—I hope—not canceled?"

She hoped. "Certainly not."

"I wonder, for instance, what would happen if I placed my hand here."

With deliberation, she flattened the palm of her delicate hand against the skin of his chest, where his shirt collar lay open. Her eyes immediately widened.

"Oh, my. I can feel your heart."

"Can you?"

"Oh, yes."

"And," he asked, greatly daring, "what if I returned the gesture?" Very gently, he placed his palm over her left breast. Oh, and he could see everything reflected in those dark eyes of hers—surprise, wonder, and delight.

"You must feel my heart also. It's racing."

"I can feel that, yes."

She leaned closer and brushed her lips across his. "What would happen if—"

He claimed her mouth, unable to hold back from it. Minutes ticked by while their heartbeats synchronized and they breathed as one.

At last he ended the kiss and said, "Sam will be home soon. We—"

"He's not here yet." Sofia could not imagine what had got into her. She was not a bold woman. Never before had she thrown herself at any man.

Only, this didn't feel like she threw herself at Lionel. It felt like she melted, or melded into him. Wanting. She wanted, from this man, things she could barely imagine.

She unfastened one of her blouse buttons in order to afford him access. "Much better," she said, "skin to skin."

Interest flared in Lionel's eyes, the sort of intent fascination she'd so far seen him spend only on steam units.

"Sofia," he whispered.

A second button, and he began to sweat. "God, Sofia."

She wore a chemise beneath the blouse, a thin,

filmy thing most utilitarian in appearance. It had narrow straps, and after the fourth button came open, she slid it down her shoulder to expose the top of one breast.

"Let's see," she breathed, and pressed his palm against the exposed skin.

He closed his eyes, as might a man tasting heaven. The heat of his palm penetrated Sofia's flesh, and it warmed and stirred her even as his kiss had done. Her body responded, and her nipple peaked. Lionel slid his hand inside the fabric of the chemise and captured it.

Sofia's entire body came alight, and her spirit followed. So it was this of which women whispered. This—these teeming sensations—allowed a woman to shed her clothing for a man and welcome him where no other man had ever been.

"Oh," she whispered. "Oh, mercy—"

He swallowed the words as he captured her mouth, his lips hot on hers. His hand cupped her breast and moved softly, causing the heat to build deep inside.

How long they stood there, she could not say. She didn't wonder where Mordred might be, or if the clock raced toward Sam's arrival. Mouths molded, bodies crushed together, they existed only for each other.

Lionel withdrew his hand from her bodice and caught her face between his palms. "Sofia," he breathed.

She loved the way he touched her—gently, carefully, and yet with the ability to enflame. She loved the way he said her name.

She gave him a tremulous smile. "A favorable experiment, I should say."

"Maybe so, but, Sofia, this isn't wise—"

The outer door opened with a rattle. Lionel and

Sofia sprang apart as Sammy came in. Sofia, facing the workbench, hastily rebuttoned her blouse, even as Lionel retreated behind the bench.

"Why's she still here?" Sammy demanded at once. "It's long past noon."

"Don't be rude," Lionel chastised him. "Miss Gregory is very welcome to stay."

"Is she?" Sammy shot a look between Lionel and Sofia. Could he perceive what had just happened?

And what had just happened, precisely? Sofia wondered. What had gotten into her head? She'd never before behaved in such a manner. Gently raised, taught never to put herself forward, she'd never imagined it. But Lionel made her feel weak at the knees. Strong at the heart. Bright and victorious.

Lionel nodded at the unit from the pit. "The police have asked us to keep our friend there for the time being. His name is Damian."

"That's a dumb sort of name."

"Better than the original," Lionel muttered.

"Eh?" Sammy returned. "Where's Mordred?"

A good question. Perhaps hearing his name, the unit trundled out from the back room.

"Welcome home, young Sam. Are you hungry? There is bread and jam in back."

Sammy disappeared with alacrity.

Much as Sammy had, Mordred looked from Lionel to Sofia and back again. "Master Lionel, are you going to start Verna?"

"I am."

"May I stay and watch?"

"I'm sure I'll need your assistance. Miss Sofia, please don't be upset if the first few attempts are abortive. We'll keep at it till we get her going, all right?"

"Yes." Sofia went breathless again, though for a different reason.

But Verna, her new boiler full of water and her hopper stocked with coal, fired immediately. Lionel let the fire build, adjusted the burn, and fiddled with the air flow below her throat.

"She may not—" he began.

The unit jerked to life. Her head swiveled back and forth, her arms twitched, and she shifted on her wheels.

"Damn," said Sammy, who'd returned from the back room.

Lionel didn't seem to notice. He raised his head. "Wait." Then he called commandingly, "Verna? Verna, can you hear me?"

The unit jerked more violently, its only response.

"Let me try." Sofia stepped forward and laid her fingers on Verna's arm. "Verna, my dear, it's me."

The unit withdrew. It rolled back several feet till it fetched up against the workbench and flailed its arms, almost delivering a blow to Sofia's head.

"It doesn't remember her." Sammy stated the obvious.

Sofia's heart sank with sickening disappointment. She'd tried, yes, to prepare herself for this. But now tears threatened.

"I'm going to shut her down for the moment." Lionel moved forward, but Sofia caught him back.

"No, please. How will she get used to us if she's shut down?" She wrapped her arms tight around herself. "Maybe it will just require some time."

"Maybe so." But Lionel appeared neither happy

nor certain.

****

"I did warn you," Lionel told Sofia some time later, while she donned her coat and hat, preparatory to leaving the shop.

Several hours had passed. Verna continued to operate faultlessly, except for the fact that her memory had apparently gone.

Sofia turned toward Lionel and tried to smile. "Yes, you did."

"There were no guarantees. I did try—"

"It's not your fault. You're a very good mechanic."

"It seems I'm just a tinker after all, nothing more."

"Far more. And believe me, I'm grateful. Somehow, I just thought—well, I didn't think she'd forget me. I didn't think she could."

"Don't worry. If you leave her here with me, I'll continue to work on her. Maybe some fine tuning—"

"Yes. I—I won't take her home just yet." Sofia gulped. "I'll come back and visit her tomorrow, if that's all right."

"Of course, it is." Lionel longed to take the misery from Sofia's eyes. He'd failed her, and when it mattered most. "Why don't you let me see you home just this once? It's late."

"No. need. I'm used to the walk."

"You're not walking at this late hour. It's pouring rain out there." He shed his shop apron. "Sam, I'm going to see Miss Gregory home. Tell Mordred, will you?"

Sammy's only response was a grunt.

"Really," Sofia began again, "you don't need—"

"Hush."

They went out into the wet darkness. The narrow alley caught very little radiance from the street beyond, and Lionel used that as an excuse to tuck Sofia's arm close against his side. Out on Niagara Street, he hailed a cab and gave her address.

"You never should have walked so far every day," he fretted.

"No, it's all right."

Inside the cab, he put his arm around her and tucked her head into the crook of his shoulder. How well she fit there, as if made for him. He wanted to kiss her, wanted it so much he ached, but this did not seem the right moment to continue their experiment.

"I'm so sorry about Verna," he said.

"Not your fault."

"Who else's?"

"Those cretins who took her apart. Lionel, I was thinking—I saw Stein and Williams' shop. It's much bigger than yours. Newer. You don't think—"

"That's where Damian was altered? The same thought crossed my mind. I really don't know. We'd need some proof before making any accusations."

"What if we took Damian there? Might he recognize the place?"

"Dangerous. Now that the police are onto this, whoever's responsible will be on the alert."

"I suppose so."

She turned her cheek against his shoulder, and their lips met. Fire exploded into the darkness inside the cab. The kiss lasted till the driver drew up in front of Sofia's home and he cleared his throat.

"Wait, please," Lionel told the man as he got out. "Just let me see the lady to the door." The house looked big, and very dark.

"No, don't wait," Sofia told the cabbie.

Lionel stared.

She told him, "Won't you please come in?"

He asked her in an undertone, "Sofia, are you mad?"

"Please, Lionel, stay with me."

"I'd stay, buddy," the cabbie advised. "She has the look of a woman who knows what she wants."

Silently, Lionel paid the man. Hand in hand, Lionel and Sofia entered the house, and Lionel heard the cab pull away from the curb behind him.

Chapter Eighteen

Sofia is merely lonely, Lionel told himself as they entered the dark foyer of the house. And who wouldn't be, in a place like this? The interior of the structure felt cold and damp from the rain, and even after Sofia switched on the nearest steam lamp, pools of gloom lay everywhere.

She's distraught because Verna failed to remember her. She just wants company, not—not anything more.

He was a decent man. He wouldn't take advantage of Sofia's vulnerability. Would he? No, certainly not.

She turned toward him. "I'm sorry. I don't leave any lights on when I'm away. I'm almost out of coal for the steam plant in the cellar, and quite frankly don't know how I'm going to pay for more."

Lionel glanced around. "You live here all alone?"

"Me and Verna, yes."

"Seems like an awfully big place for one person and one steam unit. Did you ever consider letting some of the rooms?"

"Yes. But it seems so risky. You don't know who these people are, really. And you're locking yourself in with them."

"True."

"Would you like something to drink? I can stretch to a cup of tea."

"Sofia, I shouldn't stay. I—"

She stepped up, toe to toe, and kissed him. No soft kiss this, nor that of a refined lady. It had all her will behind it, and a great deal of passion. It sent fire through Lionel's veins, just like fever. Did she mean what he thought she meant by that kiss?

He groaned. "I can't. It's not right. Not proper."

"Who's to say what's right? I've lived by other people's rules all my life. But those people are all gone, and I'm still here. I think it's time for me to make my own choices."

Lionel said hoarsely, "I don't want you to do anything you'll regret."

"I won't."

"How can you be sure?"

She answered the question with another. "What about our experiment?"

"It involved touching. Kisses—"

"So touch me. Kiss me."

"If I stay, Sofia, things will go way beyond that."

"Good."

She towed him up the stairs by the hand. In a bedroom halfway down the hall, she lit another lamp.

This must be her room—slightly shabby yet very feminine. Ruffled curtains framed the windows, which reflected their images back at him as she moved into his arms.

"Are you cold? Would you like me to build a fire?"

"No, that's all right." Lionel felt anything but cold. Heat still roared through him, and the very prospect of being alone here with her had him upstanding.

"Perhaps," he said, his throat working to release the words, "I'll just stay with you. For company. Nothing else needs to take place between us."

She raised those incredible, bottomless dark eyes to his. "Is that what you want?"

"No. I just—"

"Ask me what I want."

"What do you want, Sofia?" But he knew, he knew.

"I want to feel again what I felt in your shop, when you touched me. Only—only all over."

"Oh, God."

"Leave if you wish," she told him. "But I don't think you want that."

"You're right. I don't."

He kissed her, and his feelings broke loose like a dam bursting. Suddenly nothing mattered, nothing existed outside this room, beyond this woman. No shop. No steam units. The world might end, and he'd disregard it.

"Shut the drapes," he whispered, and she moved to obey.

****

The bed felt cold when they tumbled onto it, and as damp as the rest of the house. She shouldn't be living in a place like this, Lionel thought before she fastened her mouth to his once more, and his mind flew away.

Beyond the bed curtains, she'd left the lamp burning. She'd also unfastened the buttons on her blouse, just like at the shop, and when the kiss ended Lionel didn't hesitate to invade—not with his hand this time, but his lips.

Her skin was soft, smooth, and heated. She smelled like heaven and tasted even better. As he worked his way downward, she shrugged the blouse open wider and shed the straps on the garment beneath. When his mouth found her breast, he thought he'd surely die.

"Oh," she breathed. "Oh—oh."

She'll stop me now, he thought. She'll recall herself, realize she doesn't want me here. Sure enough, Sofia drew away from him. But it was only so she could shed her blouse entirely, wiggle out of the chemise, and present herself to him again.

A haze came over Lionel's brain as he took what she offered, and feasted. He lay like a man drunk with pleasure, his tongue caressing first one breast and then the other. At last she claimed his mouth again, stretched her body against his so her naked, damp breasts pressed into his shirt.

Suddenly she ended the kiss and stared into his eyes, hers sparkling with daring light. "What comes next?"

He would, if this kept up. But he said hoarsely, "Take down your hair for me."

She complied willingly, sitting up and raising her arms so her breasts swayed out at him.

Perfect breasts, they were. Full and delicate as the rest of her, just the right size to fit into his mouth. Her hair looked perfect too, when it came down in a glorious shower over her shoulders.

"You're so beautiful." He raised both hands to her breasts, and she closed her eyes in unabashed pleasure.

"I'm glad you think so, Lionel. Perhaps we need to remove some of your clothing?"

"If—if we do, you know what's likely to happen. Either I leave now, or—"

"Or we take off your clothes." And she reached for his trouser buttons.

****

Surely she'd done this before, Sofia thought. Only, she hadn't. She'd rarely ever been alone with a man. And the carefully selected beaus her parents approved would never have dared attempt anything approaching this. She was whole, and untried.

Yet the sensations Lionel aroused in her felt familiar. The heat and the urgency. The thrill of it when, having successfully divested him of his shirt, her naked breasts met the hair on his chest.

Surely she'd experienced this before, in some life, with some man. Perhaps in some house on a street in Riga, where she'd never been.

This man, though—this man lying here in her bed—he fitted her like her own skin, only a hundred times better. Everything about him appealed to her, from the taste of him to the hardness between his legs.

For she'd managed to divest him of his trousers after all. Now he wore only a pair of short pants that concealed little.

"Sofia," he groaned.

She loved the way he said her name. She crawled up his body and asked, "What comes next?" Though she knew, oh, she knew.

"You'll be the death of me."

"Wait. I need to remove this skirt."

Was that a sob she heard from him as she slipped from the bed in order to shuck the rest of her clothing? When she came back to the bed, she draped herself over him, and he began kissing her like a man starved for the taste of her.

Rain dashed against the windows. The lamp had dimmed—probably, Sofia thought madly, because the steam plant in the cellar had run out of coal. Did she care? No. Only the two of them existed.

Soon, soon the two of them would become one, complete.

"Are you sure?" Lionel gasped just before he rolled her onto her back and cradled her in his arms.

"Yes, oh, yes."

He pressed his mouth to hers and at the same instant slid into her, below. Time promptly suspended; sensation did not. Sofia could feel so very much—his heart beating against hers, breast to breast, and the heat of the fire coursing through her. His hardness, and her slickness that welcomed him. The tenderness that blossomed between them. A blessed madness. So this was what it meant to be a woman—this feeling of utter desire and power, of no longer waiting for life to tell her how to live, what to do. This was her choice, and she claimed him for her own.

The urgency they shared built to a crescendo, like a burst of beautiful music, and left her gasping. She clung to him, clung to him as the echoes died away, feeling safe in his arms.

"Sofia." His breath fanned her cheek, and his hair lay caught against her temple. She ran the palms of her hands across his back, and awe flooded through her. This man was like no other.

"Sofia?" He whispered her name again.

The very movement of his lips made her want to kiss him again. She loved the way it felt when she touched them with her lips. She loved how it felt when he parted her thighs and—

"Don't speak," she begged. "Oh, don't ruin the spell."

"Spell?"

"Can't you feel it? The magic of us being together."

He made a sound like a strangled groan. "I did not hurt you?"

He was not a man who hurt others. Some men did, as casually as they breathed. Sofia knew, to her soul, Lionel would never be one of them. He was gentle when he touched the battered steam units. He harbored a basic goodness.

"No." Oh, no.

"Still." He raised his head from the pillow. "We shouldn't have done that. I shouldn't have."

Now she wished for some light, so she could see what lay in those perceptive gray eyes of his. All at once, she knew he would leave her. He would rise from the bed, reassume his clothing, and abandon her to the cold, dark house.

She asked, "Did you not enjoy what we shared?"

"Yes. God, yes. But a man, a decent man, doesn't treat a woman this way—a decent woman. One he's just met. Especially a woman who's never—"

"Never. Until now." He'd changed that—she had, with her choice, and her world would never be the same.

"Oh, God," he groaned again. "Sofia, allow me to apologize."

Apologize, for bringing her to life? The way he did the broken steam units, the way he had Verna?

"You are on your own in the world, and vulnerable. I took advantage." He drew a breath that, for their proximity, she felt all the way through her body. And then he spoke the words she'd feared, for the last several minutes, must come. "It was wrong. We probably shouldn't see each other again."

"But—"

"Sofia, Sofia—" He smoothed the hair from her face, his fingers clever in the dark. "You're the kind of woman who means forever, and I don't have room for a woman, any woman, in my life. I'm obsessed with my work, poor company, a terrible prospect."

"But I've been coming to the shop."

"Yes, and I've been grateful for your help there. I think, though, it will be too much of a distraction for us to continue working together. You—you're a temptation I just can't resist."

"What about Verna?"

"I'll continue working on her, do my best to mend her intelligence. Then I'll send her back here, to you. Give me three days."

Three days. Without him. Without the company of Mordred, in the shop. The comfort of Verna's silent presence. How would she endure?

He slipped from the bed and began searching for his clothing. "Is there a light?"

"It went out. There's no coal." Was that her voice? Fragile and heartbroken.

"I can't see a thing."

She lay there on her back, as he'd left her, while he fumbled around and the cold came rushing in, making her ache.

At last he said, "Wrap up and come down to lock the door after me. I want to know you're safe."

In the hallway, she found a candle to light their way down the stairs. Her hair, still loosened, streamed out behind her when they descended and when, at the front door, he turned to face her, she could at last see what was in his eyes.

Regret. Burning, as the passion had.

"Please," she said.

"Sofia, this is for the best. A woman like you—well, you deserve better than me. Far better. I'm nothing but a tinker. No wealth, no education—"

"If you suppose I care about those things—"

Very gently, he told her, "I think you should." And he went out into the pelting rain.

Chapter Nineteen

Four pairs of eyes greeted Lionel the next morning, when he entered the shop from his upstairs rooms. Mordred, always astir early, turned a bland face toward him, one which also managed to appear curious. Sammy, also there ahead of him, produced what looked like an accusing stare.

In addition, Verna—still operational—regarded him intently with her chipped, painted eyes. And the battered unit, Damian, having come off standby, presumably on his own, regarded Lionel steadily with those startling blue marbles.

Lionel found it disconcerting. He turned on the one person available for chastisement.

"Sammy, why haven't you left for school yet?"

"I was waiting to see if you were alive or dead. What happened to you last night? You didn't stay with that woman, did you?"

The others all seemed to hold their breaths for his answer. Well, Damian didn't; steam still leaked from him woefully.

Lionel wanted to tell Sammy it was none of his business where he'd been last night. However, it was actually Verna's business—except at the moment Verna couldn't recall her connection with Sofia.

Sofia. At the thought of her, sensation poured through Lionel again. The satin feel of her naked skin beneath his fingers, the softness of her breasts. The scent and taste of her. The warmth when he'd—done what he never should have.

Resolve made his voice sound hard when he said, "I saw Miss Gregory home."

"For four hours?"

"Don't be cheeky, boy. I wanted to make sure she was secure in that house of hers."

Sammy snickered. "And did you make her all safe?"

Curse it, when had Sammy discovered what went on behind closed doors, between men and women? As his ersatz guardian, Lionel had never informed him, though he supposed he should, if only to keep him out of trouble.

The kind of trouble in which Lionel now found himself. But no, he'd put that behind him, put Sofia Gregory behind him.

Saved himself.

Hadn't he?

"Watch your lip," he growled at the boy.

"I suppose she'll be here any minute now." Sammy promptly disregarded Lionel's prohibition.

"And what's that to you?"

"Women like that don't belong here. No reason for her to keep hanging around, anyway. Her unit's buggered, and don't remember her."

"Miss Gregory won't be helping out here anymore. When I finish repairing her unit, which I will, I'll send it to her."

"Fine, that."

"Now get your books and go to school."

Sammy moved off. Mordred immediately edged up

153

to Lionel.

"Is it true, Master Lionel? Miss Sofia will not return?"

"It's true. We—discussed the matter last evening."

"Might I ask why, Master Lionel?"

"Much as I hate to admit it, Sammy is right. This is no place for a lady."

"I am sorry to hear that. I liked her."

After so many years together, Lionel did not attempt to tell the aged unit he could neither like nor dislike anything. He knew Mordred had…well, preferences.

"We got on well. She was respectful of me."

"Yes. But Mordred, you must see how improper it is. A woman of quality should not occupy her time with the likes of us."

"What is there about us, Master Lionel, that is improper?"

"For one thing, Sammy's a little rascal," Lionel said, making sure the boy—on his way out the door—heard.

"But, Master Lionel, Verna is here. And I thought Miss Sofia wanted to be near Verna. The lady seems so lonely, does she not?"

She did, which unquestionably made the reason she'd fallen into Lionel's arms. That big, empty house and her need for company had seduced her into it.

"I do not understand why everyone supposes he can question me," he grumped. "Now let's get to work. There's much to be done."

He set about dismantling Verna's control center—once again—more than half his attention fixed on the door of the shop, just in case Sofia disobeyed his request and decided to come after all.

She never did.

****

Sofia awoke from a deep and terrible dream, on a pillow still damp from the tears she'd shed after Lionel left her last night. He had, in fact, fled with an alacrity that she could only find insulting, given the circumstances.

And she had sobbed herself to sleep, where she'd fallen victim to the dreams.

Having been touched by Lionel, she would never be the same.

Physically, that was all too true. Mentally and, she feared, spiritually it was also true, even more so. She'd given Lionel Pike everything she was, everything she had, and he'd walked out on her.

Could anything be more humiliating?

He didn't want her to return to the shop, did not wish to see her again.

She stirred in the cool, damp sheets even as the emotions stirred inside her. Not all humiliation. She felt regret also. Not for what they'd shared—that had been far too beautiful to regret—but for the way it ended. And anger. She felt anger, which in a curious way lent her power she'd never had before.

She dragged herself from the bed and dressed before opening the drapes and regarding the day. Last night's rain had come to an end, and bright sunlight flooded the streets below. Spring at last? Perhaps.

What should she do today? Volunteering at Lionel's shop had eaten up some of the hours emptied by Verna's absence. She'd grown accustomed to the quiet industry there, and Mordred's gentle company.

She longed to be there now, to be with Verna and see how Damian fared. Did she want to see Lionel also? Yes, oh, yes. She wanted to tell him off, give him an earful, denounce him for treating her so shabbily.

At the same time, the ghost of her mother whispered in her ear. *What did you expect, after throwing yourself at the man that way? Of course he would take advantage. To him, it meant nothing.*

But, Sofia argued helplessly, would a man to whom the act they'd shared meant nothing employ such tenderness? Lionel Pike had worshipped her last night.

And then left her cold.

With a sound of disgust, she went downstairs and emptied out the Wedgewood vase that stood on the mantel in the parlor. There she kept her coins, and they numbered pitifully few. She needed to get down to the local shop where she ordered coal. And food—she had almost nothing in the house. Following last night's exertions, her body demanded sustenance despite her crushed spirit.

After she visited the shops, she just might drop by and see Verna.

Because she'd be cursed if she allowed Lionel Pike to dictate her actions.

****

As she walked from shop to shop, searching out not the best goods but the most affordable prices, she thought about last night's dream. Once more, she'd visited Riga, and found herself hurrying along its narrow, twisted streets with pain in her heart.

In the dream, she felt desperate to reach someone—a man. One for whom she cared a very great deal. He meant all the world to her, but he lay in danger.

Faces leaped out at her as she went, terrible countenances that appeared from the darkened buildings. They leered, they grinned and spat at her spitefully. Some of them appeared to be mere masks, some constructed of metal. Automatons? But no, steam units were not inherently evil. These beings, on the other hand, most certainly were.

In the dream, the malevolence nearly overwhelmed her. Worse, twisting and turning in an effort to avoid them kept her from reaching the man who lay injured.

The one she loved.

She spent more than she should in the shops and, walking home, determined she'd need to visit Roddy Stoeke again, distasteful as that prospect might be. She intended to drop off her purchases at the house and commence the walk to Lionel's shop.

But she found someone at her door when she arrived, in fact two someones pealing the bell.

She supposed she might consider Miss Pyatt and Miss Rumple friends. Both spinsters and both in their early thirties, they occupied themselves with good works, mostly on behalf of automatons. Sofia had, in fact, first met them at fundraising functions. The two ladies had more or less taken her under their joint wing.

Now, however, her heart sank at the sight of them. She respected and, yes, harbored liking for them but was not in the mood to socialize.

"Miss Gregory!" Jane exclaimed as Sofia walked up. "We were just about to give up on you."

"I'm sorry. I'm just back from shopping."

Jane Pyatt had mouse-brown hair drawn back into a severe bun and truly lovely brown eyes. Tillie

Rumple, shorter and stouter, had a round face with rosy cheeks and—though Sofia shouldn't say so—always reminded her of an adorable piglet.

"But," said Miss Rumple now, "surely you are not out on your own. Where is your dear Verna?"

"She is in for repairs."

"Still?" Jane tilted her nose up. "I thought you brought her away from that dreadful Mr. Starr and Mr. Williams."

"I did. She's at another repair shop now."

"Never mind. We've come to collect you for a function. There's a lovely brunch and fundraiser at the First Lutheran Church. You simply must come."

Fundraiser? Sofia's heart sank.

Her cheeks flushed. "I'm afraid I have little to contribute at this time."

Both women's expressions turned kind. Jane glanced at the house, and Tillie said, "Of course you do. Your good energy and your opinions are needed. Working for a cause is not always about monetary donations."

Sofia experienced a wave of consternation. She could scarcely think of anything she'd like to do less than accompanying these ladies to a meeting. Still, brunch. Her stomach rumbled, reminding her she'd been able to afford only a half-pound of chicken livers and a small loaf of bread.

The hunger made the decision for her. "Let me put my purchases inside, and yes, I'll come along."

The two women chatted nonstop as they walked to the church, which wasn't far. The subject of discussion today, so it seemed, was Faith for All. A joint coalition of automatons and concerned citizens, like them, gathered to debate ways and means of allowing mechanicals their own place of worship.

"There's a contingent dead set against it," said Jane as they drew near, and Sofia saw a sizable crowd outside the church. "They, as you know, insist machines can't believe in anything. But, Miss Gregory, you and I know that even the most humble steam unit is far more than a machine."

"Yes," Sofia agreed.

"Why, my Ogilvie—he is wiser than I am, and believes in a wealth of things."

Sofia had long suspected that Jane might be more than half in love with Ogilvie, her steam manservant. She'd had him upgraded many times and spoke of him the way another woman might her husband.

Tillie, on the other hand, had a little family of steamies that gathered in her parlor every week to share Sunday services.

Both women were admirably devoted to the cause of automaton rights. But yes, the city might explode if steamies tried to build a church here, as well as the one proposed for Black Rock.

She mused, "Ogilvie is quite extraordinary."

Jane broke into a bright smile. "Isn't he? I swear, I can confide anything in him, hopes and fears. Dreams like this one, which he and I share."

"Isn't he here today?"

"Already inside." Jane looked proud. "Part of the presentation."

As the three of them crossed the street to the church, Sofia became aware of a contingent stationed up against the buildings opposite it, mostly men, but with a few ladies included. These began hurling insults and derogatory remarks at their approach, everything from "steamie lover" to "blasphemous sinners," which Sofia did her best to ignore.

The crowd at the church proved far more welcoming. Sofia recognized most of them from past gatherings. They gave her nods and even a few smiles, though most looked focused on the matter at hand.

A clergyman moved among the crowd. Reverend Tile, so Tillie murmured, who served at the First Lutheran Church. He stood firm in the assertion that everyone, everywhere, should be free to worship.

Accompanied by the jeers of the dissenters, they all filed inside, as many of them as could fit. A number of steam units remained outside on the steps.

Once seated, Sofia marked the presence of Patrick Kelly along with a woman she knew to be his wife, Rose, and a small girl with red tresses.

"That's Kiera," Jane whispered in Sofia's ear, "Officer Kelly's new daughter."

"New?"

Tillie, seated on Sofia's other side, lowered her voice also. "The hybrids manufactured her in their own image, so to speak. Just the first of many, they claim."

Chapter Twenty

Lionel worked on Verna's impulse center all afternoon, without any real progress. He took it apart and put it back together once and was about to do so again when Sammy got home from school.

"She's not here?" the boy asked, tossing his books in the corner. "Good."

Lionel replied in a grunt. With half an ear, he'd been listening for Sofia all morning and afternoon. He too felt relieved she hadn't turned up, as well as bitterly disappointed.

His body craved her—both the taste and feel of her beneath him—even though he knew he shouldn't see her again.

Oh, he might have to see her when he returned Verna, a thing he wanted to do almost as much as he wanted to see Sofia. But he needed to return the unit in perfect working order. That had, after all, been the reason Sofia came to him in the first place.

Not for comfort. Not for kisses or that deep and mindless passion they'd shared.

It had been perfect. He froze with a tiny crescent wrench held aloft in his hand, arrested by that thought. The way she'd yielded to him without hesitation, offered her body without restriction. The way they fit together, and the emotions that accompanied their joining—possessiveness. The need to hold, to protect.

He'd never experienced anything like that, or hoped to. He'd never even imagined a woman like Sofia Gregory existed.

Ah, well, the way he could best protect her lay in not seeing her again.

"You all right?" Sammy stood behind him, eyeing him suspiciously.

"Sure, why?"

"I asked you a question three times, and you just stood there. Didn't you hear me?"

"Of course I heard." Lionel gestured with the wrench. "I'm just concentrating. What is it?"

"Some of the lads are playing ball down at Prospect Park. I wondered if I can go."

"Do you have much homework?"

Sammy shrugged. "I'll be home by dark. I can do it then."

"All right." That would leave Lionel alone with Mordred and Damian once again. Mordred, no fool, had been keeping out of his way. All Damian did was stand where they'd put him and stare at Verna.

"Thanks."

Sammy left. Lionel turned to Mordred, who busied himself cleaning tools. "I think I've found what's wrong here. There's still a part missing."

Mordred trundled over. "Yes, Master Lionel?"

"Look, the connections look complete, and that's what threw me off. But someone's rigged it, or should I say diverted it. In models this old, there needs to be a distributor box, here."

"I see. Where is it?"

"Gone. Either it was worn out—burned out—and whoever tried to mend her thought they could bypass it,

162

or they wanted the box for something else and stole it."

"Which, sir?"

"I don't know, and it doesn't really matter. The result's the same."

"If you replace the distributor box, will she recall who she is?"

"I think so."

Mordred brightened. "A fine result, Master Lionel."

"It's not quite that simple, though. Those boxes are rare, which is what makes me think hers might have been stolen." Lionel stepped back from Verna and said, "Miss Gregory says she took Verna to Starr and Williams for repair, and they are suspect in providing units for the fighting pit."

"You think there is a connection?"

"Possibly. They had no reason to disassemble Verna as extensively as they did—not unless they scab the units they repair, for parts. Units as old as our friend Damian, there, require components that are difficult to find. Just as Wendy proved a godsend to us, Verna may have proved to them."

"That is despicable, Master Lionel."

"They may well be despicable men, if they're fitting steam units to fight each other to the death."

"Where will you find an appropriate replacement box for Verna?"

"That's the question."

Damian stirred, giving off several gouts of steam. "Sir, if I may speak?"

Lionel glanced at him. "I beg your pardon?"

The unit fixed him with its blue glass stare. "I am of a comparable vintage with Miss Verna, yes?"

"More or less."

"Then open me up, and if I have the required component, use it for her."

That caused Lionel to blink at him. "But then you'll no longer operate correctly, or remember who you are."

"I barely do remember."

"This seems a bit extreme," Mordred posed.

"I agree. It's a handsome offer, Damian."

"I do not mind. She is so beautiful. She should continue to function."

"She is beautiful," Mordred agreed. "Perhaps I have the required part."

"I can't have you down," Lionel told him. "Actually, I can't have either of your down. Damian, we need you to remember everything you can from your time in the pit. You may be required to give evidence in court. We need your memory intact."

"Yes, sir. But perhaps after that matter is settled, you can disassemble me."

"I don't know whether you possess the right component. Wendy—there on the other bench—does not, and she's the right vintage."

Damian rolled toward him a few feet. "Disassemble me, borrow the unit, and see."

Lionel exchanged looks with Mordred. "I would just have to put you back together again."

"I do not mind."

"Oh, hell," Lionel said, and got to work.

****

Hope springs eternal, Lionel thought as he waited to see if Sofia would arrive the next morning. Sammy had already left for school, and the shop door stood open to what looked like a beautiful spring day. He'd worked late taking Damian apart and putting him back together again. During that process, a few things had come straight in his mind.

He wanted to keep the old unit running and—for want of a better word—cognizant. He also very much wanted to keep Sofia Gregory happy, even if he never saw her again.

Which looked quite possible, from where he now stood. *Of course she won't come,* he chastised himself. *You made yourself quite clear when you left her. A lady like that isn't about to chase after you.*

Maybe he should go and see her, though. Apologize again for what happened. Tell her about the progress he'd made with Verna.

Make sure she was all right.

But if he saw her, he'd want to touch her. If he touched her, he'd want to kiss her. If he kissed her, he was lost.

"What will you do, Master Lionel?" Mordred asked.

Lionel wiped his hands on a rag. "I think I need to report my suspicions to the police. Can you hold the fort here while I'm gone?"

"Certainly, Master Lionel. If Miss Sofia arrives, what should I tell her?"

That I want her here. Beg her to wait for me. Make her promise she will.

He hauled himself up firmly. "That I'm out on an errand. Nothing more."

****

"Here, just march up and down the sidewalk with this placard," Miss Pyatt instructed Sofia. "Aren't we fortunate we have such a lovely day for this?"

"Yes," Sofia concurred without much conviction. The sun shone down through the branches of trees just budding with new leaves. Those branches arched above Linwood Avenue, where she'd been assigned to demonstrate.

The plot of land that had been purchased for raising an automaton church, as Sofia understood it, lay close by, and the residents of the quiet, pleasant street were up in arms.

This peaceful demonstration was the automatons' answer to that.

"We have a right to raise a community building," Patrick Kelly had said at the end of yesterday's gathering at the Lutheran church, "even as we have a right to express ourselves. We must stay strong for the sake of future generations." He'd said it while holding his daughter, Kiera, in his arms, which made quite an impact.

Still, for all that Sofia agreed with him, she wondered how she'd got herself into this situation. Committed to walking the same stretch of sidewalk all morning, carrying a sign that read *Freedom of Faith for All!* While wearing her one remaining good hat and a pair of shoes that pinched.

With, of all people, Jane Pyatt on the adjoining patch of sidewalk.

Sofia liked Jane, she truly did. She admired the woman for her devotion to the cause. And Sofia believed in that cause. Having lived in close proximity with Verna so long, she knew steamies had thoughts and beliefs. Verna hoped for things—or she had before those crooks tampered with her. Sofia could not count the times Verna had, during dark moments, told her to keep believing.

Now, Verna's memory had been destroyed on the basis that she was just a machine, a thing, to be used and manipulated. So Sofia had lost her.

Unless the steam tinker could bring her back again.

That got Sofia thinking about Lionel, which hurt. But at least it distracted her from her pinched toes. The way he'd looked there in her room before the lamp gutted out. The intent expression in his eyes, one of passion barely restrained—passion for her, of all people. All for her. His lean, hard body when she at last got him out of his clothes and—

"Get out of here, you despicable woman! Get off my property."

The enraged directive rescued Sofia from her dangerous thoughts. She swung around and saw a man on the front stoop of the house in front of which she paced. He glowed with anger and indignation, all his ire directed at her.

"I beg your pardon?" she returned.

"I said get off my property, you demented automaton sympathizer!"

Jane hurried up from her section of the sidewalk and shouted back at the fellow. "She is not on your property, sir."

"She most certainly is." He waved an arm wildly.

Jane pointed one tightly-laced boot at the man's lawn. "That may be your property, but this sidewalk is city property, and thus available to all. If you do not believe me, call the police to settle the dispute."

"God, no," Sofia whispered.

"Just be gone," the man bellowed. "Go pester

somebody else."

"Maybe we should go, Jane."

"Nonsense, we just got here. You stand your ground." To the enraged man, Jane added, "We know our rights."

"Rights, is it?" He marched down the steps of his house and charged along the walkway. Sofia tried to withdraw, but Jane grasped her wrist firmly.

Close up, the homeowner proved florid and well-fleshed. He wore a fine suit, and his forehead glistened with sweat. His eyes burned like two coals, red deep among the brown. "You biddies should be ashamed of yourselves."

Jane recoiled. " 'Biddies'?"

"Making a scene like this," he ranted. "Where's your dignity?"

"Sir, we are not the ones making a scene."

By now, a scene had definitely been made. People—demonstrators and passersby alike—stared. Sofia flushed with mortification.

"You most certainly are. Old maids with nothing better to do."

"I beg your pardon! What makes you think we lack husbands?"

The man sneered. "Madam, if you had a husband, he would keep you in line far better than allowing you to cheapen yourself marching up and down like a strumpet in this fine neighborhood."

"How dare you?" Jane cried. Sofia could no longer tell which of them was angrier.

Hastily, she attempted to defuse the situation. "Sir, I do believe we have a perfect right to espouse a cause in which we believe. There is no reason for you to become abusive."

"A cause in which you believe?" he howled. "A church for machines? Perhaps we should build an altar in the terminal for the trains as well, or allow the steam cabs to hold sacrifices."

People drifted closer to listen.

Sofia raised her chin. "Sir, it's not the same. You must acknowledge there is much more to the typical steam unit than mere machinery."

"I acknowledge nothing of the kind."

"And," Sofia persisted, "even if you don't consider steam units capable of believing in a higher power, where's the harm in letting them build a church? People build meeting halls, don't they? Community centers?"

"Those are people."

"Does it matter?"

"It most certainly does." He drew himself up. "Do you think I want to be the man who owns a house a stone's throw from an aberration? A mockery of other genuine churches? A joke?"

"Whether the steam units congregate there to discuss their place in the city or to pray should have no bearing on you." Sofia's nostrils flared. "Have you, sir, so little self-esteem your status relies on where your house is situated?"

"And have you, madam, nothing better to do than harass your fellow citizens? Get off my property at once."

He reached for Sofia's elbow, presumably to hasten her along.

"Don't touch her!" Jane screeched, and brought her placard down dangerously near his bald head.

"She attacked me! Tried to brain me!" the man

howled and pointed a trembling finger at Jane. "You all saw her."

"What's all this, then?" A tall figure in blue came hurrying up. Seeing him, Sofia wanted to sink through the sidewalk from humiliation. Someone had called the police and, in fact, she recognized this officer.

"This woman attacked me." The homeowner gestured dramatically at Jane.

"I never touched him," she declared stoutly.

And both these women are trespassing. I want them removed."

"Removed, *sor*?" the officer repeated.

"Arrest them. For assault."

The officer peered at the top of the man's head. "I do not in fact see any wound, sir."

"Not for want of trying. Officer, these women and their companions are crackpots."

"Yes, *sor*?"

"Just look at their signs."

The officer dutifully read Sofia's placard. "Freedom of Faith for All."

"The 'all,' " the man rejoined, incensed, "being bloody automatons."

Sofa caught her breath, and her gaze flew to the officer's face. She knew who he was because she'd seen him at one of the meetings. He was, in fact, a hybrid automaton and a member of the Irish Squad.

"Have you ever heard the like?" the homeowner demanded.

"No, *sor*, I have not. It is a true wonder, so it is. Might make a man believe in miracles."

The homeowner stared, perhaps feeling a bit of doubt for the first time. "Arrest them," he urged again.

"They're dangerous. And ridiculous."

"Well, now, we can't be after having ridiculous people on the streets."

"Just so."

The officer bent a look on Jane. "Did you in fact, madam, threaten this illustrious citizen with your placard?"

"Officer Greely, isn't it?" Jane smiled at him. "How is your lovely wife?"

"Thriving, madam."

"Glad to hear it. I did threaten this person with my sign, but only because he first threatened to lay hands upon Miss Gregory."

"I'm afraid I'll need to take you down to the station."

"Ah!" the homeowner grunted in satisfaction.

"Am I being arrested, Officer Greely?"

"We merely wish to de-escalate things, madam." He looked at Sofia. "I think it best you come also."

"Oh, oh, dear." Sofia's heart sank.

Officer Greely turned and gave a whistle; a paddy wagon rolled up from around the corner.

"Must we ride in that?"

"Yes, but you may ride in front with me."

The homeowner stomped off with a smirk on his face. The crowd which, Sofia saw in shock, had now increased considerably in size, stood and stared.

This, she thought, was not at all how she'd hoped her day would go.

Chapter Twenty-One

"You are not, in fact, under arrest," Officer Greely told Sofia and Jane as they rumbled along over the brick streets. He'd asked his fellow officer, who brought the vehicle, to keep an eye on the demonstration before they headed downtown. "I removed both you ladies from that situation for your own welfare."

"Oh?" Jane said.

"I do not know if you noticed, but an Undesirable Element had begun moving in. That tends to happen whenever there is the slightest confrontation between humans and automatons. In this case, the Element had rocks in their hands."

"Oh," Jane repeated in a far different tone. "You were protecting us."

"It is what I am sworn to do."

"But," Sofia spoke up, "do we actually have to go to the police station? I've never been there before."

"Nor have I." Jane wiggled. "It's so exciting."

The officer said, "I would like you to file reports against that man for harassment. You were in fact demonstrating within your rights. And if he makes an official complaint later, yours should be on file."

"How thrilling," Jane enthused.

Sofia could think of far more thrilling events. If she went to the police station, she had no idea how she would get home again. She had no money in her pocket and therefore no hope of cab fare. Could her life get any worse?

"I would just like to say," Officer Greely confided, "I appreciate you ladies' efforts on behalf of automaton rights."

Jane beamed. "That man back there didn't even realize you are, in fact, hybrid, did he?"

"No, madam. He thought me human, and every bit as prejudiced as he."

****

"I'm sorry, sir, Captain Fagan's not here," the desk sergeant told Lionel. "He's off on other business at the moment. He is in fact what you might call a hands-on sort o' captain."

Lionel gazed across the teeming station room and saw Patrick Kelly sitting at a desk. "Might I make my report to Officer Kelly, then? He was involved with the case in question."

"Certainly, sir. Go right on over."

Patrick Kelly got to his feet when Lionel approached, and extended his hand. "Mr. Pike, sir, I'm happy to see you again. What might I do for you?"

"It's more what I hope I might do for you," Lionel replied.

Half an hour later, Kelly had a page of meticulous notes and what looked like an interested gleam in his eyes. "Sir, I will make certain Captain Fagan gets this information."

"Thank you. Has any more been uncovered about the fighting pit, or aren't you at liberty to say?"

"I am not at liberty to say. That being stated, we have run to ground the individual who sublet the space for leases of which the landlord was unaware. That space was supposed to be used to store equipment. Which, the subletter argues, it was. He denies all knowledge of any fighting pit, even though the evidence was there before our eyes."

"Yes."

"You say you are willing to testify in court, Mr. Pike?"

"Yes," Lionel said again. He hated to get in the middle of a messy tangle, but abuse such as he'd witnessed couldn't be ignored.

"Thank you," Kelly said. "Also, the subleasee matches the description Dammit Twelve gave of one of the promoters present at the fight."

"Uh—we've renamed him Damian."

Kelly cocked his head. "Why?"

"Well, Dammit didn't seem entirely respectable."

"Mr. Pike, sir, you are a considerate man. Would you be able to bring Damian here to make a statement, if we find it necessary?"

"I would, of course."

"Thank you again, sir, for all your cooperation."

Lionel rose from the chair beside the desk. "Officer Kelly, how's your little girl doing? I saw her with you when she was introduced."

Kelly's face lit. "Kiera is very well indeed, thank you for asking."

"Something of a miracle, isn't she?"

"And a long time coming. We worked most carefully and diligently on her design."

"If you would not mind me asking, from a purely professional perspective—"

"Go ahead, Mr. Pike."

"Well, I've never worked on anything nearly as sophisticated as your Kiera—or yourself, for that matter. But it makes a man curious, all the same. She's metal, underneath?"

"She is. High-tensile steel with the most intelligence we could build. Already, she's learning quickly and voraciously."

Lionel already knew the answer to his next question, and anyway it seemed rude to ask. The skin, hair, eyes, and such for hybrids had always been harvested from corpses. In this case, Kiera's had presumably come from a deceased child. He remembered hearing the hybrids had lately come into possession of a hospital, and they had access to orphanages where, unfortunately, all too many children perished—though that was changing.

"So," he mused, "she will always remain small, a child?"

Kelly's face blazed with enthusiasm. Anyone, Lionel thought, who insisted hybrids did not experience emotion need only take a look at him.

He lowered his voice so his words became barely audible in the busy room. "No, sir. Kiera will remain a child for the time being, so we might all enjoy her company. Eventually, an adolescent model will be built—as materials become available, you understand, and her intelligence will be transferred into it."

Lionel's stomach turned queasy at that, but curiosity prompted him to ask, "You can do that?"

"Not me, sir. I am but a humble policeman. We have a team, however, headed by Mrs. Chastity Greely, the wife of Officer Greely, whom you may have met."

"So your daughter will outgrow her current—er—

housing?"

"As children tend to do. At the last stage, she'll be transferred to an adult version. But that will be far in the future."

"I see." Transferred. And Lionel struggled to repair and regain the memory of one aged client. He truly was a mere tinker in comparison with these craftsmen.

Maybe he should turn Verna over to the hybrids, if only for Sofia's sake.

"Well," he said, "thank you for being so forthcoming with me."

"Of course, sir. And thank you again for your kind assistance."

They shook hands once more, and Lionel turned for the door. Occupied with the one question he absolutely could not ask—what would happen to Kiera's former bodies when she outgrew them—he stumbled out into the spring sunshine.

Only to collide with someone else—a woman—who'd also just exited the station.

Two women, in truth. They'd paused abruptly outside the door as if they didn't know where to go next, and Lionel smacked into the nearest, so hard it hurt.

She spun, and he found himself gazing into Sofia Gregory's wide, dark eyes.

****

"Lionel? What are you doing here?"

The man who'd blundered into her reached out and grasped her elbows, presumably so she wouldn't tumble down. He had his cloth cap tucked into his pocket, and his dark head gleamed in the bright sunlight. The warmth of his fingers—quick, clever fingers—

penetrated her sleeves and spread heat through her flesh, just like the sunshine.

"I might ask the same," he said. His gaze moved from Sofia to Jane, who looked extremely interested, and back again.

Sofia said, "We were here making a report. There was a bit of trouble."

"Trouble?" Concern flooded his eyes. "Are you all right?"

"Yes. A bit shaken, but…"

"What happened?" He stepped closer, and she could feel the heat of his body. Just like the night they'd shared themselves with one another, powerful and inexpressibly arousing, the night that quite clearly, in his opinion, should never have taken place.

"Oh, my," Jane said. She extended a somewhat dusty white glove to Lionel. "Allow me to introduce myself. Jane Pyatt of the Freedom of Faith for All campaign."

Jane's pale blue eyes inspected Lionel from head to boots. "And who might you be, my good sir?"

"Jane, this is Lionel Pike. He's the repairman who's working on Verna for me."

"Ah, yes. Pleased to make your acquaintance, Mr. Pike."

Sofia, dismayed by how much she disliked this, spoke quickly. "Are you here in connection with Damian's case?"

"I am."

Lionel appeared to fight an inner battle and lose. He wetted his lips before he said, "Might I see you home?"

An entire scenario blossomed in Sofia's mind. He

would see her home. They'd go inside the big, silent house and once more up to her bedroom. This time it would be flooded with sunlight. She'd leave the drapes open in an act of daring, and she'd be able to see all of him when he took off his clothing. No, no—when she took it off. That rough tweed jacket and the shirt beneath. His vest and—and his trousers.

She grew weak at the thought and had to seize his arm for support.

It wouldn't happen. He'd finished with her. Hadn't he?

"Well, well," Jane murmured and shot Sofia a perceptive glance. "Sofia, I know we said we'd ride home together, but I just remembered I need to go and meet Ogilvie. Will you forgive me?"

"Of course," Sofia could only reply.

"Perhaps Mr. Pike could see you home."

"I will." Lionel bowed his curly head in a strangely courtly gesture. Sofia experienced the mad desire to run her fingers through his hair in a lingering caress.

Gazing into his eyes, she said, "If it's too much trouble—"

"It isn't."

"I can certainly see myself home. I'm quite used to doing so."

"I know. Here, we'd better step aside. We're blocking the doorway."

People were trying to come and go from the station, giving them exasperated looks.

Lionel towed Sofia down to the sidewalk, his fingers linked with hers. Even that innocent contact stirred her and heated her blood, bringing one fact very much into evidence.

She desired this man. She wanted him again.

A cab miraculously appeared, and Lionel hailed it. When they climbed in, the interior smelled like old coal smoke, perspiration, and somebody else's lunch. They sat in silence, their linked hands resting on Lionel's knee.

At length he said, "Your friend mentioned there was a bit of trouble. Might I ask what sort?"

Sofia smiled faintly. "We were protesting, and I fell into a confrontation with a homeowner."

He looked astonished. "A confrontation? You?"

"Does it surprise you so much that I might believe in something enough to take a stand?"

"No, not at all. I just don't like the prospect of seeing you hurt."

You hurt me, her heart cried. But she bit her lips to keep the words in.

"The cause," he said, "is automaton rights?"

"Specifically, the right to worship. The automatons of the city, at least some of them, wish to build a church on North Street. They've already purchased the property. But citizens are blocking the undertaking."

"I see." He thought about it. "I assume you're acting on Verna's behalf?"

"In part. I'm acting mostly because I believe it's right. Why shouldn't all citizens have a place to meet and perhaps educate their children, get married if they choose? There's no harm in it."

"I agree. But it's a lot for ordinary members of this community to swallow. A true sea change. May I ask you a question?"

"Please do."

"Do you truly think automatons—like Verna, like

Damian—have a capacity for spiritual experience?"

"Why not? They have a capacity to learn everything else."

"But no imaginations. One might argue an individual needs an imagination, to conceive of an afterlife."

"It's not just about the afterlife. Even humans don't agree on that." Sofia thought of the streets of Riga, which she'd trodden most likely in another life, and of being here now with him. "There are as many concepts of that as there are churches and temples, probably more."

"That's true."

"If you're asking me if I think automatons have spiritual awareness, and perhaps a concept of a power beyond themselves, I should have to say yes. I know Verna does."

"Indeed?"

"Indeed. I have lived with her a long time. Lionel, would you accept the fact that steam units are capable of sacrifice?"

"Yes."

"Of love?"

"Some of them."

"There is where we disagree. I think even the least of them is capable of love."

"What is love, though? Can you define it? I will agree wholeheartedly they are capable of attachment, deep and unswerving loyalty. I'm not sure that's the same thing as love."

"For them, it is. And it gives them strength."

"Still different from faith."

"I'm not so sure."

"Perhaps I've taken too many steam units apart to accept that, entirely. I've seen what's inside them—components and steam."

Sofia turned her head and looked into his eyes. "And, were you a surgeon, you might take humans down to their bones and muscles. Could you see faith then?"

The cab drew up in front of Sofia's house, and she stirred, not waiting for his answer. "Thank you, Lionel, for the ride."

"Wait a minute." He climbed out of the cab after her and laid his hand on her arm. "I wanted to say—"

"Yes?"

He shook his head and turned away, back to the cab.

"Wait," she said in turn.

He looked at her, a wealth of emotion in his eyes.

"Do you want to come inside? We can talk."

For the space of a dozen heartbeats, he hesitated. Two dozen.

"Hey, buddy," the cabbie called, "do you want me to wait, or what?"

"No," Lionel said, not even glancing at him. "You can go."

Chapter Twenty-Two

"I'll make tea," Sofia said once they got inside. She wondered if she had enough to make a full pot. Scrapings in the bottom of the caddy, most likely.

She led Lionel to the kitchen and bustled around, bringing down what was left of the best teacups and putting the kettle on to boil. There had, at one time, been a whole tea set of china so delicate you could almost see through it. She'd sold the tray first, and then the pot, creamer, and sugar tub. The three remaining cups had chips, though not where you could see.

"Don't fuss for me," Lionel said.

"I beg your pardon?"

"Don't fuss on my account. This"—he waved a hand—"all this just goes to show why it would never work between us."

Sofia's heart dropped. She stared at him, standing there with desire bright in his eyes and a denial on his lips.

"And this," she said, "demonstrates why it just might." With that, she laid aside the cups in her hands, stepped up, and kissed him. Pressed close in his arms, she molded her mouth to his, giving in to irresistible impulse.

What has gotten into me? she wondered even as the heat gathered low in her belly and spiraled up to her head. What became of the woman I was? Replaced, it seemed, by another self, ravenous for the taste of this man and unashamed to show it. A powerful feeling, and a demoralizing one.

For an instant, Lionel stiffened beneath her touch, and she feared he would push her away. Reject her once again. If she had any pride, she'd step away from him first, salvage what dignity she could.

But in that breathless instant, even before her tongue touched his lips, his resistance melted. She felt it go, like a wall of ice before a flame.

"Sofia," he gasped.

The next few moments proved chaotic, blinding, and wonderful. Her mouth fastened to Lionel's, Sofia pressed close and tangled her fingers in his hair. When the kettle began to wail, she thought it a side effect of the heat between them.

"Kettle," Lionel said, speaking into her mouth.

"Eh?"

"It's going to explode."

She unfisted his hair and ran her hands down his body until they met the weight between his legs. "No doubt. Maybe we should go upstairs."

He laughed helplessly before he swung her up into his arms. Pausing only to drag the kettle off the heat, he carried her up the stairs and into her room, where he placed her on the bed.

****

It must be a dream, Lionel thought as Sofia unbuttoned his shirt, and then her blouse, before pulling the latter off. The middle of the day, in broad sunlight. A proper lady did not shed her clothing with such alacrity, nor with a slightly wicked gleam in her dark eyes.

Yet for all that, Sofia Gregory still managed to look very much the lady, even with the pink tips of her exquisite breasts bobbing up at him as she shifted on the bed.

It was without qualification the most titillating thing he'd ever experienced.

In fact, he was able to see a number of things he'd missed last time, in the dark. The warm ginger gleam of her hair against the backdrop of the pale bedcurtains. The fact that her stockings went all the way up to the thigh, beneath her petticoat. The milky perfection of her skin, all of which he ached to kiss.

He wanted to start at her toes and work his way upward. Or perhaps begin at the corner of her mouth and go down, lingering a while over those luscious pink buds. Either way, she had him hard as a stallion at stud.

"You're so beautiful," he told her hoarsely.

"Do you think so?"

"I know it."

She began pulling the pins from her hair, at the same time kicking off her shoes over the side of the bed, one at a time. The last, tattered shreds of Lionel's control abruptly snapped.

He'd never before taken off his clothes for a woman, at least not lacking the cover of the dark. Usually, he felt neither ashamed nor particularly proud of his body—it served its purpose. But now, with the sunlight pouring through the windows, he felt he was on display. And, God help him, he wanted her to be impressed.

He shed the shirt she'd already unbuttoned and unfastened his trousers. He shucked them also, and watched as her dark eyes left his for the first time, to trail down what he revealed. They widened, and a flush rose to her cheek.

A good sign? God, he hoped so.

He put a knee on the bed and bent to slide his palm slowly up her leg, all the way to the top of her stocking. "Allow me to remove these for you."

"Please. Do."

She had sweet little, highly arched feet, and the skin of her thigh felt like velvet. When he eased her bloomers down off her hips, she made no protest. When he placed a kiss on the reddish cluster of curls between her thighs, she shivered like a woman with fever.

"Please," she whispered, and closed her eyes.

So perhaps he did believe in prayer, or magic, or whatever she wanted to call it, he thought several minutes later. There could be no holier experience than worshipping this woman with his lips and tongue, feeling her open herself to him, and the bonds tighten between them. Quite possibly, the last thing he should be doing on this bright, sunny afternoon. But if he died thus, he would regret nothing.

After she broke apart in his arms, she gasped—or maybe sobbed—and drew him up to her breasts, where he feasted further. And then she rocked him—wound her legs around his body and rocked him till he slid more and more deeply into her.

Sanity returned some time later when he realized what he'd done. Again. They lay with their bodies still joined and her arms tight around him. He could feel the beat of her heart.

What to say to the woman? He'd escorted her in the cab, carried her up the stairs, and ravished her more soundly than he'd ever imagined a man could.

Obviously, she took him beyond himself. And when they got near each other, all self-control flew out the window. Quite clearly, they shouldn't be allowed in one another's vicinity.

Or perhaps he should ask her to marry him.

That thought shocked him so violently, he jerked like a gaffed trout.

"What is it?" she asked. "What is the matter?"

He raised his head and gazed into her eyes—dark eyes, deep and fathomless, fringed with black lashes. At that instant, he forgot where and even who he was.

"Nothing. Nothing at all."

****

"I'd like to come back to work at the shop." Sofia spoke the words idly while playing with the hair on Lionel's chest. She loved the way it felt between her fingers and how her touch made the lean muscles of his stomach quiver.

What a magnificent body he had—so perfectly sculpted, hard and powerfully muscled. Who would have thought something so different in form would fit with her body so well?

Yet they might have been made for each other. When they were connected, while he was inside her, she felt so much more than her ordinary self, and her spirit soared.

Now they lay side by side beneath the covers, still in her bed. She'd lost track of the time, but the light had begun to fade, so she knew they'd been here a while.

"Um?" he replied.

Had he fallen asleep? But no, his eyelashes twitched and his hand, on her naked belly, stirred.

Oh, how she wished he'd slide that hand just a few

186

inches lower.

"I want to be near Verna," she told him. "And—" greatly daring, she added, "and you."

He opened his eyes and his fingers tensed.

"Not a good idea."

"There are many ideas in this world that may be considered less than good. The manufacture of steam units, for example. But once they are, they are."

"What have steam units to do with it?"

She raised up on her elbow and leaned over him. "I am saying that they, like our relationship, are a *fait accompli*, and impervious to change."

He frowned. "You'll need to speak English if you want me to understand."

"What has happened cannot be undone."

"I see."

"And"—she waved a finger in his face—"do not tell me we should not see each other again. That will not work."

"No?"

"Today, fate led us to one another. At a police station, of all places. And only look what came of it."

He raised a hand and touched her naked breast. Her body reacted without her volition, tightening marvelously.

"What a miracle you are," he breathed.

"Yes, it is a miracle. And an abomination to doubt such things when they are presented to one in life."

"Even so, Sofia, I have nothing to offer you."

"Oh, have you not?"

He shook his head.

"And I suppose I am used to living in the lap of luxury, am I, with my great, barren house and my baubles even the pawn dealer refuses to buy? It is, indeed, a grand existence."

"Still, I barely earn enough to keep myself, Sam, and Mordred going."

"I am not asking to come and live with you. Merely to resume helping out mornings."

"Mornings, is it?"

"Yes. Afternoons, I will be otherwise occupied. I mean to continue my efforts toward raising a place for automatons to worship."

"And"—he waved a hand—"what about this?"

"This?"

"The fact that you and I can barely be in the same room without…getting all het up."

"That is a very strange term."

"You know what I mean."

She did, and found that, quite shockingly, she enjoyed it. She wanted more of him—already.

She leaned down so her lips hovered above his. "Why do we not just play it by ear and see what happens?"

"We already tried that experiment. I know very well what will happen. So do you."

"And you suppose keeping away from each other will put an end to the desire? To the ache?"

"No, I suppose not."

"Well," she whispered against his lips, "I am glad you see sense. Or, to prove my point, do I need to seduce you again?"

A smile creased his lips. "Come to think of it, perhaps that's exactly what you need to do."

Chapter Twenty-Three

Lionel smiled in satisfaction as he straightened Verna's limbs and flipped the switch at the small of her back. Four days had passed since the afternoon—the long afternoon—he'd spent in bed with Sofia. Indeed, it had been growing dark when he'd stumbled home, feeling as if he'd been drained dry and put through a laundry press.

In a good way.

The next morning, she'd arrived at the shop looking so unassuming and demure, he could scarcely believe she'd given herself to him so completely. Of course, one look from her dark eyes and he was in a sweat, each and every memory flooding back upon him.

Torture, being in her company. And torture also, when she left around noon.

Sammy had kicked up a fuss and demonstrated his disgust. Mordred seemed happy to see her, and Damian, who remained at the shop, mostly indifferent.

That term could not in any way describe Lionel's feelings. He remained aware of the woman, wherever she moved in the shop, even though she mostly kept quiet and never interrupted his work.

He forbade himself to touch her. Once, when he'd asked Mordred for a tool, Sofia brought it instead and their hands met in passing. That innocent contact had left him shaking with desire.

Quite honestly, he'd not believed he was capable of desiring a woman this way, with raw and painful abandon. He was a simple man, and had simple needs. A place to work, occasional food, his tools, and time to tinker.

Now a new desire had come to life inside him. He didn't know what to do with it.

The fact that Sofia seemed to share that desire further inflamed him. He'd rather innocently supposed that women—well-bred ones—didn't harbor such feelings. But Sofia wanted him. He could feel that every time she looked at him. It existed in the memory of every kiss and touch they'd shared.

And he wondered now, gazing into Verna's worn, painted face, what of Sofia's insistence that fate had brought them together at the police station? Did he believe that?

He couldn't deny fate—or some such unnamed power—seemed to be at work in his life. Even as he'd considered Damian's offer to be disassembled for Verna's sake, George and Patsy had arrived with another load of what, at first, appeared to be genuine scrap.

Lost in his thoughts, Lionel had almost refused to look through the pitiful, broken units in their cart. Something prompted him to do so, and there at the bottom he'd discovered a portion, just a portion, of a unit the same vintage as Verna.

It contained the missing component.

He'd tried and failed to calculate the odds of such a thing happening. A component so rare that whoever had worked on Verna felt compelled to steal it, but turning up in such a way… George told him someone went about the city ahead of him and Patsy, picking up the older units.

Yet exactly what Lionel needed fell into his hands.

He couldn't help but ask himself whether the same thing had happened for him, when it came to Sofia. But he'd said nothing to her about finding the missing part. He didn't want her to be disappointed if, due to its age, it failed to operate correctly.

Hence, he'd waited till after Sofia went home today to fit the part, and had worked on into the evening. Now, when Verna stood ready for a trial, he, Mordred, and Damian were alone, Sammy having gone off to bed.

Both the other units watched him avidly as he worked, Damian from his corner and Mordred close at hand.

Verna had built up a fine head of steam. None of her joints leaked, and the movement of her limbs had become smooth and easy. But could she now access her memories?

Lionel asked her softly, "Can you tell me your name?"

She turned her head so her scratched, painted eyes faced him. Before that, she'd gazed—if such a term might be employed—at Mordred.

An innocent question, to mean so much. And one full of doubt. The found component hadn't quite fit. He'd had to alter it, and—

"Verna. I am Verna."

Mordred emitted a strange sound, something between a whoop and a hiss. Lionel experienced its human equivalent as a big grin spread across his face.

"Excellent. Verna, to whom do you belong?"

"Miss Sofia Gregory."

Oh, thank God. Lionel pictured Sofia's face lit with gladness when she beheld her unit, her dark eyes—that revealed so much emotion—aglow.

"And," he posed, doing his best to sound calm, "what is Miss Sofia to you?"

He expected the reply, *owner*, in some form. The unit surprised him when she said, "She is my best friend."

"You did it, sir," Mordred said at the bottom of his voice range. "Miss Sofia will be so pleased."

"She will." Still hanging on fiercely to his own excitement, Lionel took Verna through a number of other questions. How long had she belonged to Miss Sofia? Where did they live? Did she remember what happened to her?

It occurred to him Verna might be able to implicate Starr and Williams, but it did not prove so.

"I had been operating poorly for some time. My components—my components were very old. I believe something broke, and I fell down the stairs. That is all I recall."

"Miss Gregory took you for repair, somewhere other than here. They were unable to complete the job. You ended up here with us."

Mordred spoke up. "Master Lionel has saved your life. He is a genius with steam, especially when it comes to units of our vintage." The two units exchanged a look, impossible as that seemed.

Verna turned back to Lionel. "I am very grateful, sir."

A startling pronouncement, withal. But Verna went on, "When I felt myself descending into disrepair, I worried. Not for me, you understand, but for Miss Sofia. We have always been together, and it is not good for her to be alone."

A unit, worried.

Mordred rejoined, "I understand. Master Lionel does not do well while lacking my presence, either."

"Miss Sofia did not have the means to give me expensive maintenance. Things have not been easy for us these past few years."

Mordred assured her gravely, "It will be much better now."

"Sir," Verna turned to Lionel, "where is Miss Sofia? Not here?"

"She was. She's been helping out here in order to be near you. But she's gone home for the day."

"I do not like the idea of her being in that house alone."

Neither did Lionel, truth be told.

Mordred offered, "Miss Sofia will be very happy to see Verna when she arrives tomorrow morning."

"Yes." Only Lionel didn't intend to wait that long. He'd take Verna to Sofia's house tonight, and perhaps stay a while. Maybe stay all night, if Sofia liked the idea.

His pulse leaped at the prospect. "I think I'll take Verna back tonight," he told Mordred.

"Tonight, sir?"

"Will you be all right looking after Sammy and Damian? You'll have to make sure Sammy gets to school in the morning."

"You will...stay there all night?"

Lionel didn't answer. At the sound of his name, Damian jerked to life and rolled forward, his wheels squeaking. He'd been watching all that happened carefully. Now, though, Verna focused on him for the first time.

"Who is that?"

"I am Dammit Twelve. These people call me Damian."

"Hello, Dammit Twelve."

Lionel blinked. Had these two steam units just shared a moment? Ah—it was late and he'd clearly been working much too long.

"Come on," he told Verna. "We don't want to frighten Miss Sofia by arriving too late, do we? We'd best go now."

****

The alley lay dark and silent, full of shadows from one end to the other. Out on Niagara Street, steam lamps burned. All the businesses lay shuttered and quiet.

Lionel had intended to hail a cab and whisk Verna over to the east side, with a flourish. He'd donned his good coat and stocked his pocket for the fare.

But it must be later than he thought. No cabs appeared, and after a few minutes, he decided they might as well walk.

He never noticed the shadows that flowed out from the alley behind them.

Sofia made this journey on foot every day and, he told himself, Verna's wheels were now in excellent condition. She squeaked a bit and puffed steam as they turned up West Ferry, headed for Main. Lionel thought only about the joy he'd soon see in Sofia's eyes.

It happened in a dark block of West Ferry, between two streetlamps. Lionel heard the sound of running feet—slapping against the bricks—and suddenly he and the steam unit were surrounded.

Aw, shit, he thought before the first blow came. They must be robbers. And far more than one or two.

He stepped out in front of Verna, seized by the desire to protect her. No stranger, as a youth, to scraps on Buffalo's streets, he intended to fight back. But this proved no scrap.

Their assailants came armed with clubs. A solid blow to Lionel's right arm fairly numbed it. Another to his head made the dark street swim. He heard Verna rattle forward as if she would defend him in turn, and fear for her rose to his throat.

No, not that. Please don't let her get wrecked again.

Hard hands seized him. Still harder fists pummeled him, kidneys and chest. Just before everything went dark, he heard a hiss of steam.

Chapter Twenty-Four

Sofia jerked awake as a hiss of steam sounded in her mind, and lay in the bed gasping. A terrible dream that had been, though so close to the ones she usually endured, at first she couldn't tell the difference.

She'd been running through the dark streets of Riga, her skirts tangling maddeningly around her legs, and a sense of wild urgency in her heart. As always, she needed to reach him. Danger lurked everywhere, and he must be warned.

She'd pattered up a cobblestone walkway and over a bridge that showed church spires beyond. And then, and then—

Something that had never happened before, not in all the years she'd experienced these dreams.

She reached him.

At first, she thought him nothing but a pile of clothing tossed on the pavement. A black coat perhaps abandoned. But the coat had legs, and shoes, and a hand splayed against the stones.

It had blood beneath its head.

With a cry, she fell to her knees, no thought for her own safety, or whether his assailants lingered close at hand.

He might be dead. This man she loved, the center of her world. He whom she needed as dearly as her own breath.

She turned him over with careful hands. His arms flew wide, as if he asked or pleaded for something. Blood clotted in his dark hair and below it she saw—

Lionel's face.

She'd wakened then, with a pain in her chest that made her think of death.

Lionel.

A warning. Those words echoed in her mind. She didn't know what they meant, but they had her up on her feet, there in her dark bedroom, tossing on clothing with desperate haste.

Was he out there?

Had it been just a dream?

She carried the lamp from the bedroom downstairs. Shadows leaped before and after her as she went. The house felt cold and impossibly empty. Even alone, she rarely felt uneasy here, but now the threat had her on a ragged edge.

Somehow, she found her coat. With trembling hands, she locked the door. Then she stood on her own doorstep and closed her eyes.

Where is he? Where?

This way.

Without hesitation, she followed the call. Certainty gathered strength inside her as she realized she followed a route that would take her to the shop. She saw no one till she passed Main Street, unnaturally quiet at this hour, and there ahead spotted a cluster of figures and a police paddy wagon drawn up.

Her breath came in gasps when she reached the cluster of uniforms, gathered around a figure sprawled on its back.

"Lionel!"

Everyone except the man on the ground turned to stare at her. Four police officers, none of whom she recognized.

One hastily stepped to her side. "Ma'am, do you know this man?"

"What's happened to him?"

"Attacked."

It was only then, incredibly, Sofia caught sight of the second figure, half concealed behind two policemen. It lay on its side in a pool of steamy water.

"My steam unit!"

"Yours, ma'am?" The officer, a man of middle height and middle years, drew a notebook from his pocket. "And what's your name?"

"Is he dead?"

"No, ma'am, but they did a job on him. What is your name, please, and how do you know this man?"

Sofia told him. "And that's my steam unit, the one I took to him for repair." She bit her lip. "He must have been returning her to me."

"At this hour, ma'am?"

"Yes."

"And how did you know he'd be here? Was the meeting arranged?"

"No." *I had a dream*— But she couldn't claim that. They'd never believe her. Swiftly she altered what she meant to say. "I was waiting for Mr. Pike to bring the unit to me."

"I see."

"He looks dead." All this while, Lionel hadn't moved. A thin line of blood ran from one temple. She couldn't see him breathing.

"He is unconscious, ma'am. We're waiting for the

198

ambulance, so—ah, here they come now."

The ambulance proved to be one of the new steam-powered models. It had lamps that lit its way in garish red.

"I want to go with him. To the hospital."

"No, ma'am. If that's your steam unit, you have to take charge of it."

"But—"

"We're taking him to General Hospital. You can call there in the morning."

He made sure he had her name and address before he stepped away. They all stepped away. Sofia watched, agonized, while Lionel was placed on a stretcher and swallowed up by the ambulance. It pulled off in a wreath of steam.

One of the other policemen approached her, a younger fellow. She thought he might be hybrid. "Ma'am, do you need help with your unit?"

"I—yes, please."

Together they righted Verna and got her steady on her wheels.

"The spilled water put the fire out," the officer said. "I doubt it will refire here."

"I need to get her home."

"How far?"

Between them, they towed Verna back to Woodlawn Avenue. Once there, the young officer helped Sofia get her up the stairs.

"Heavy unit," he grated, which made her think he wasn't hybrid after all.

"She's quite old. Just repaired. I hope she hasn't been damaged again." Sofia wanted to sob; she wanted to wail. But not in front of the young police officer.

"She should refire for you without much difficulty. I don't see any other damage."

"Thank you. You've been very kind."

Inside the house, Sofia struggled to relight the lamp. Her hands shook almost too badly to accomplish the task.

Lionel had been coming to her. Bringing Verna. He must have resurrected her.

Why had he been attacked? A simple robbery?

Was it her fault?

When at last she succeeded in lighting the lamp, she inspected Verna. New scrapes showed on one side, but that appeared to be the only harm. The robbers had attacked Lionel and left her alone.

Good thing she was too old to be valuable to anyone but Sofia.

She towed Verna to the kitchen, where she refilled the boiler and, after no less than six failed attempts, fired the burner. She'd done this thousands of times, but never with so much at stake.

Sitting on a kitchen chair beside Verna, she flipped the on switch.

And waited.

"Miss Sofia?"

When the words came from Verna's voice box, Sofia wept in earnest. Verna, distressed, waved her hands and trundled off for a linen napkin, with which she tried to dry Sofia's face.

"Miss Sofia is distressed."

"It's been a very difficult night. And I'm so very happy to see you."

Sofia seized the unit in a fierce hug. Heat from Verna's boiler seeped into her, providing familiar comfort. She pulled herself together as swiftly as she could. "I can't believe he did it—Mr. Pike got you running. He worked so hard on you. And it's so, so good to have you back again."

"I agree, it is good to be with you. Is Mr. Pike the same person as Mr. Lionel?"

"Lionel Pike, yes."

"He did get me running, but I'm afraid I cannot tell you how. I returned to my senses earlier this evening."

"And what happened out on the street?"

"Lionel Pike was bringing me home. We were surrounded by a number of men, and Mr. Lionel was attacked. I tried to intervene, but the men were armed with clubs, and I was knocked over."

"Did you see what happened to Mr. Lionel?"

"Only some of it. I could hear blows landing before, so I believe, my burner flooded, and I went out."

"Oh, God, why would anyone attack him? Did they say anything? Do you think they were thieves?"

"The men shouted at Mr. Lionel. Asked him if he was the Steam Tinker. Said they'd teach him to interfere. Mr. Lionel tried to fight back, but I suppose his assailants were too numerous."

"And then you went out?"

"Yes, Miss Sofia."

"Not a simple robbery, then. We need to get word to the police. Lionel—" Her throat closed. In what had he interfered? Did his attackers refer to his visit to the police station, where they'd met?

What if he died at the hospital? If she went there now, would they let her see him?

Verna watched her carefully. "This Lionel Pike, he

is important to you."

"Yes. Yes, Verna, very important. I think…" Sofia confided in her best friend, "I think I've fallen in love with him."

Verna's expression, of course, did not change. But she emitted a puff of steam. "It is as humans say, high time. I began to despair you would ever wish to marry."

"I am a long way from marriage," Sofia objected. "But he did spend a night and an afternoon here." She clarified, "In my bed." Would Verna be shocked? "So we have a—a connection."

"It is my understanding that often happens."

"Yes, mine too."

"They say humans grow to need each other."

"Some automatons, too."

"Yes. In the shop where I was—where I returned to myself—there were two very handsome steam units of approximately my vintage."

"Two?" Sofia thought of Mordred. "Mr. Pike's assistant is very nice. He's called Mordred."

"A fine name. There was another. Large, with a wide frame and a quiet demeanor."

"You must mean Damian."

"He called himself Dammit Twelve."

"Yes, but that's no fit name."

"Why not?"

"Dammit is considered a curse word. And he's not a bad individual, so it doesn't fit."

"I understand."

"Oh, Verna, I'm so grateful to Lionel for restoring you to me." Sofia's eyes again filled with tears. "And I'm so worried about him."

"Then you had better go to the hospital as soon as

you can."

"I agree. And thence, to the police station."

Chapter Twenty-Five

"You will, of course, be coming back to my house with me, in order to recover." Half giddy with relief, Sofia had barely stopped talking since, directed to Lionel's bed in the ward, she'd found him awake. Awake, and suffering.

He looked a mess, the flesh around one eye swelled and his head swathed in bandages. Both his hands, limp on the starched sheet, had raw knuckles, and Sofia saw red patches on his jaw.

But he would recover, and he was the best thing she'd ever seen.

"I will, will I?" he wheezed.

"Well, you certainly can't go back to the shop the way you are, with only Mordred and—worse—Sammy to look after you."

He groaned.

"If you come to my house, I can put you in my parents' old room and tend you properly."

Their eyes met, and Sofia flushed.

"No, I didn't mean—" Except, she had meant that they could be together. Not right away, obviously, but eventually. She wanted this man in her life the way she'd never wanted anything.

She asked, "What's the internal damage?"

"Just bruised ribs. The bastards kicked me after I went down. I'm tougher than I look."

"Verna said they spoke to you before her boiler went out." Sofia had told him how she'd got Verna back to her house, and shared the unit was still operational. Confused and in obvious pain, he hadn't thought to ask what she'd been doing out on the street in the middle of the night. But he no doubt would, soon enough.

He narrowed his eyes. His voice came in a hollow whine. "I think they're connected with the fighting pit. Somehow they must have found out I've been helping the police."

"You don't think they'll try and harm Damian, do you? If he can testify against them—"

Lionel scowled. "I hope not. Sofia, can you send a message to the shop for me? Warn Mordred."

"Yes, and you have to report all this to the police."

"The coppers were there, weren't they?"

"Yes, but I'm not sure they're aware of the connection between your attack and everything else that's going on."

"All right."

"Once you're at my house, we can send for an officer to come."

She broke off because of a stir at the door of the ward. The large and extremely handsome police officer who entered paused to look around, with his helmet in his hands.

When his gaze fell on Lionel, he moved forward. He gave Sofia a single appraising look before he said, "Captain Fagan here, Mr. Pike. You remember me? I just learned what happened. Do you feel up to giving a report?"

Lionel nodded feebly. "Of course, I remember you,

Captain. Is it common for a captain to go out taking reports?"

Fagan fixed him with bright blue eyes. "This isn't an ordinary case, and I'm not an ordinary captain." He gave a tight smile. "My lady—I believe you know Miss Ginny Landry? She says I'm too hands-on to be a captain, but when advancement's offered, it's hard to turn down."

Lionel nodded. "It's a bit hard for me to talk. Jaw hurts."

"I'm very sorry to hear that, Mr. Pike. I'll make it as brief as possible. Can you tell me what happened?"

In fits and starts, with much wheezing, Lionel told him. The police captain's expression grew more and more grim as the account progressed.

"I'm very sorry, sir. I didn't think there would be any danger attached to you assisting us with our inquiries."

Sofia said, "This seems like more than just a fighting ring, doesn't it?"

"Depends on who's involved and who's at the top. There's a lot of money to be made in a fighting pit. That's why they persist. There's also an element of—" Captain Fagan hesitated.

"Yes?" Lionel prompted.

Fagan said, "I don't like using the word 'hatred,' but I'm afraid it fits. There's a faction in this city up in arms because the automatons are seeking their rights, and even more that they've gained some."

"Humans," Sofia stated.

"Yes, miss. They strike back by abusing units, especially the older ones—merely to prove they can."

"Like poor Damian," Sofia said.

"Yes, miss, and from what we've uncovered, hundreds if not thousands of others."

"But—that defeats the purpose of them gaining their rights."

"It does." Fagan looked disgusted. "Owners don't want to pay their units salaries as well as maintain them, so they turn them out. Those units fall prey to folks like these running the fighting pit."

Lionel wheezed, "You closed that down."

"And quite likely two more promptly opened elsewhere. I'll have to ask you, sir, once you're back at work, to keep your ears pricked for news of dirty dealings."

"I will."

"And, sir, I also have to ask, in light of what's happened, are you still willing to testify?"

Lionel tightened his fists, which also hurt. "More than ever, now."

"But," Sofia objected, "they've given you a warning."

"I'm not about to let them get away with intimidation, on top of what they're doing."

"Hate has no place in my city," Fagan agreed. "And I happen to believe if we don't all stand together—automatons and decent people alike—we've no chance."

"I agree," Lionel said.

"Thank you, Mr. Pike. When are you getting out of here?"

"I'm not sure."

"If I need to contact you, I'll call at your shop, will I?"

"No," Sofia said. "He won't be going back there

for a time. I'm taking him back to my house, to heal up."

Fagan gave her a big smile and an electric blue stare. "Mr. Pike is a fortunate man."

Sofia blushed. "I don't think he feels very fortunate, at the moment."

"I do," Lionel corrected. "Captain Fagan, could I ask a favor?"

"Name it, sir."

"Could you have your officers keep an eye on my shop and make sure Damian—the unit from the fighting pit—stays safe?"

"I'll put someone on it. You just concentrate on your recovery."

Fagan went out and left Sofia and Lionel gazing at one another.

"So," Lionel wheezed at last, "you're determined to look after me, are you?"

"I am, so do not try to argue with me."

"I wouldn't dare."

****

The room looked gloomy, and the bed felt damp, even though Sofia had gone out of her way to stuff it with brass warming pans. In truth, she'd gone out of her way to make Lionel comfortable ever since he'd arrived at her house this morning, following a three-night hospital stay.

But he remained uncomfortable and uneasy, and far from well. In a way, he'd have been happier in his own cramped rooms over the shop.

On the other hand, here came Sofia carrying a tray, her dark eyes glowing upon his face. And every time he saw her for any reason, his heart took flight.

Beautiful woman, with her ginger hair piled atop her head and that look on her face—the one he'd never received from anyone else.

She placed the tray over his knees and asked, "Hungry?"

He was now, though maybe not for food. He groaned inwardly. It would take him some time to be up to much.

Eyeing the tray, he asked, "Where did you get all this?" He hesitated to insult her by insinuating her purse didn't stretch to what he saw on the tray—delicacies that included white bread and an orange. Yet Sofia never made bones about her financial position.

"Folks have been dropping things off, mostly automaton folks. Most of them I don't know, but that nice Officer Greely was among them. He said they're all sorry about the attack and wish you well soon."

"That's kind."

She settled on the edge of the bed. "I find automatons are very kind, by and large. Often far kinder than humans."

"Especially considering the way they're all too often treated."

Her dark eyes grew serious. "Maybe that's why. I've discovered it's those who have experienced pain that are most sympathetic to others who are hurting."

Lionel nodded.

"How do you feel?" she asked, and cupped his cheek in her hand. "How's the headache?"

Lionel's bruised ribs hurt like a bugger, but the doctors had been more concerned with the blow he had taken to the head.

"I'm all right," he lied.

"Then eat. There's more downstairs. They sent a whole sack of oranges. Can you imagine?" Her eyes went wide.

He caught her hand in his. "I hope you'll have some."

"Oh, I couldn't. They're meant for you."

"How can I enjoy them if I know you're going without? Here, have some of this one." He picked up a section of orange, which she'd peeled and separated, from the tray and offered it to her in his fingers.

She leaned forward and took it from his fingers in a long, luxurious caress, closing her eyes in bliss.

Suddenly, Lionel's head didn't hurt so much after all.

"That's delicious," she murmured. "Want to taste?" She leaned over the tray and kissed him. The bright flavor of orange burst upon his tongue, followed by the deeper, duskier flavor of Sofia.

"Um," she said then, "you taste better than the fruit."

He released her hand, but only to cup her face between his palms, the better to kiss her. Eventually the tray dug into his ribs, and he gasped and ended the kiss.

"Get rid of the tray," he suggested.

"No, you need to eat."

"I know what I need. Come here."

He set the tray aside. It hurt when she climbed into the bed and cuddled up on him, but only in the most marvelous way.

Long moments passed. Suddenly Lionel thought he knew how it felt when an automaton came off shutdown and built a fine head of steam. Forget the medicine and all the doctors' cautions. Sofia was the cure he needed.

Before things could go too far, she withdrew a few inches and looked at him. Her dark eyes danced with mischief, or desire.

"Now aren't you glad you came here to recover, where I am able to look after you?"

"I am."

"Of course, 'looking after you' includes making certain you eat this wonderful food your friends have dropped off. And"—she dropped a quick kiss on one side of his mouth—"making sure you get enough rest. Everything else must wait."

"Must it?"

"For a very short while."

And then? Lionel read the promise in her eyes, and his pulse leaped.

Had a man ever been given a better motivation for getting well?

Chapter Twenty-Six

Lionel dozed most of that afternoon, until the need to relieve himself had him struggling to get up out of the bed. The pain nearly put him right down on his back again.

When Sofia came running, he refused to allow her to help him with such a personal matter, and she in turn called Verna.

The unit, expressionless and having escorted Sofia from the room, provided a chamber pot, which Lionel found acceptable.

"Sorry for making you come all the way upstairs to help me," he told the unit.

"Nonsense, sir. After all you did for me, I am eager to help as I can. Besides, you did such a wonderful job on my wheels, the stairs present no obstacle."

"I'm glad."

"Before your repairs, I used to struggle my way up. Going down was even more perilous. It had got so Miss Sofia forbade the attempt."

"Your extenders were shot," said Lionel, thinking how odd it was to be discussing a machine's repairs with it.

"Indeed, they were. Do you realize, sir, how troubling it is to know what is wrong with oneself, but be unable to mend it?"

"It must be."

"You see, sir, I will be forever grateful. You have repaired my innermost workings. So you need feel no embarrassment over me helping you with intimate matters, in turn."

"Well, when you put it like that—"

"Besides, Miss Sofia cares for you, a great deal."

That stopped Lionel cold. He knew he should let the comment pass. It could not be right to, in essence, pump Sofia's best friend for information given in confidence. Yet the temptation proved too great to resist.

"Does she?"

"Oh, yes, sir. I was forced to watch her weep when you were injured. And even now she agonizes over your care."

"She shouldn't. She really shouldn't." All Sofia need do, in order to make him feel better, was kiss him.

Or perhaps all he needed was her company.

"Something's been troubling me, Verna."

"Yes, sir?"

"Do you know how it is Sofia thought to go looking for me the night I was attacked? I mean, it was very late. And she didn't know I'd be returning you to her."

Verna withdrew a few inches. "You will have to ask her that, sir. Now, allow me to go dispose of the contents of this pot, yes?"

Lionel decided to ask Sofia about it when she brought his supper, but no sooner had he been presented with his tray than the Kellys arrived.

Patrick—out of uniform and clearly off duty— brought his wife, Rose, and little Kiera who, seen close up, proved an exquisite child. She smiled at Lionel, revealing sweet dimples, and Pat chatted with Lionel while he ate, only leaving when Lionel's eyelids began sinking shut.

By the time Sofia showed the little family out, he must have been asleep.

He woke some time later from the murky depths of a dream in which fists crashed into his face and chest. He tumbled to the hard pavement, and a flurry of kicks followed. Trying to defend himself, he grunted and flailed.

"Hush, it's all right."

A warm body pressed against his, and fingers encircled his wrists. For an instant, he thought his assailants had hold of him. He stiffened.

The pressure on his body lessened, and light blossomed in the darkness. He lay in bed at Sofia's house. Moreover, she lay in the bed beside him.

Having lit the lamp, she turned to him in concern. She wore a modest, white nightgown with lace around the high collar, but she'd left the top buttons undone. Lionel glimpsed a delicate collarbone and the swell of one breast as she leaned toward him. Her hair hung loose around her shoulders, and she gave off a soothing warmth.

"Sofia? Should you be here?"

"Yes, quite evidently. Were I not here, you could have hurt yourself." She added with certainty, "You were having a bad dream."

He dragged a hand over his face. "Yes. They were all around me."

"Your attackers? Those cowardly bastards." The word sounded shocking, coming from her well-bred lips. The same lips that had been all over him.

"Just a dream," he breathed. "I'm sorry I woke you."

"It's all right." Leaving the lamp burning, she eased back down onto the pillow beside him and curled an arm across his stomach.

"You are safe now."

He smiled faintly. "I was here with you all the while."

She snuggled closer and laid her cheek against his shoulder. "About that, I am not so certain. Oh, your body was here, yes. But your spirit? I think our spirits travel when we dream, sometimes far distances."

"What makes you say that?"

"I told you, since I was young, I have had such dreams of Riga, though I've never been there. And—" She caught her words.

Lionel stirred, and looked at her. "Yes?"

"The night you were attacked, I saw you in just such a dream."

"Ah. I wanted to ask you about that. You didn't say."

"I feared you wouldn't believe me. That you'd think me mad."

"Not that. But how—"

"It's as if my awareness travels even though my body remains in my bed. I inhabit another body, perhaps a spectral one. That night, I ran to you through the streets, following a path my spirit knew."

"Well, I can't argue with that, can I?"

"I suppose not."

"But," he reflected, "it's a bit—frightening. There are places I wouldn't want to go in dreams."

"I'm not sure whether they are dreams or

215

memories."

"How can you have memories of a place you've never been?"

"It's possible the spirit endures beyond death." Her dark eyes met his. "It's possible we knew each other before this lifetime."

"You're talking about in a past life or something? I'm not sure I believe in all that. Sofia, I'm a practical man. I deal in nuts and bolts, in circuits and steam. All those things can be explained."

"Perhaps the rest can also be explained. We just don't have the answers yet. Did you know steamies dream?"

"They do not. If they did, I'd know about it. When they're shut down, they're shut down."

"They don't dream on shut down, no. It's like death to them. But Verna told me, on standby sometimes memories replay through her thought center. If dreams are memories—"

"That's a stretch, Sofia."

"Maybe. Maybe not. Now, go back to sleep. Would you like me to leave the light burning?"

"No need." With her there, he had every possible comfort.

****

"What's all this, son? Still laid up in bed, are you? I heard about what happened. A dirty shame."

Bruce Buchanan bustled into Lionel's sick room like a freight train under a full head of steam. Sofia, who answered the door to him, had hesitated to let him upstairs, but she decided all that energy might do Lionel good.

She felt a bit worried about Lionel. Though he did

his best to hide it from her, she could tell he still experienced a considerable amount of pain. And being an adept at gleaning the emotions of others, she sensed a great deal of anger lurking inside him.

Well, he would be angry. He'd been attacked without provocation and delivered a threat. Not a man who angered easily, the emotion had its claws well into him.

Perhaps, or so she hoped, Mr. Buchanan could help. His presence would at least provide a distraction.

"I'm coming along, Mr. Buchanan." Lionel pushed himself up higher on the pillows, at visible cost.

Buchanan examined him closely. "Well, they did a job on you, and no mistake. Have the police caught the miscreants?"

"Not yet." Now-familiar anger brightened Lionel's eyes.

Buchanan drew up a chair and sat beside the bed. "It took me some doing to find you. I went to your shop, where a young boy told me what had happened."

"Is all well there?"

"So far as I could see. I spoke with your man— Mordred—and persuaded him to tell me where you were."

"I hope you won't tell anyone else." Lionel's gaze moved to Sofia who stood, fingers twisted in the apron she wore. "I would not like to place Miss Gregory in any danger."

"Mum's the word." Buchanan's bright blue eyes narrowed. "Do you think this is connected to the work you're doing on behalf of automatons?"

"I've had little to do but lie here and think, and I suspect so. My attackers warned me off sticking my nose in and going to the police again."

"They don't want you involved because you have too much knowledge and can implicate them. To many in this city, an old steam unit is just scrap—junk. You know what can be done with them. What's being done."

Buchanan leaned forward in the chair. "I suggest we beat these fellows at their own game."

Lionel's gaze searched the rosy, seemingly innocent face in front of him. "How?"

"Remember I said I'd come up with a scheme to expose them? Well, I have. Are you in?"

"Not till you tell me how."

"Gladiators."

"What?" Lionel gaped.

"These bastards—forgive my language, Miss Gregory—they like to put on a show, and they love a fight. I say, give them a challenge. I will announce a contest, backed by a huge prize. One they can't resist."

"A contest."

"Listen, you suspect who may be behind these fighting rings, right? But you're not sure. There may be others in the city like you—not as talented, of course— slapping together steam units. This could bring them out of the woodwork. We know somebody's putting old units together—like poor Dammit—for fights. Let's bait 'em."

"This prize you're suggesting—how much?"

"I was thinking a thousand dollars."

Lionel and Sofia both gasped.

Sofia found her voice first. "That's an enormous sum."

Buchanan shrugged. "It is, Miss Gregory, but means little enough to me. As I told Mr. Pike when we met, I possess a fortune. My one wish is to use it for good, in this case to assist abused automatons."

"If," Sofia began, "they are abused."

Lionel spoke from the bed. "Sofia, you didn't see the aftermath at the fighting pit."

"All right. But gladiators? That sounds—well, brutal."

Buchanan gazed at her. "Yes, it will be—unfortunately, it has to be. We need to capture the attention of men like the ones running those pits."

Lionel, a new gleam in his eyes, asked, "What, exactly, do you have in mind?"

"I announce a competition. Anyone can enter. Entrants are to build one gladiator, but all from used parts, and built from the ground up. There will be guidelines—of your devising, though no one will know that. One entry per entity. We put on a big show—"

"And the models are fighters? Gladiators?"

"Aye."

"Why that?" Sofia objected. "Why not just models that can do something extraordinary? Sing or—or play a musical instrument."

Both men looked at her pityingly. "Miss Gregory," Bruce Buchanan said, "that would not gaff the fish we need to catch."

"The purse alone should—"

"No," Lionel said. "He's got it right."

Sofia stared at him incredulously. "You agree with this mad idea? But how can it put an end to abuse? It *is* abuse!"

"If I build a unit, a fight unit—" He spoke to Buchanan in an aside, "that is what you're asking me to do?"

"Aye."

"I'll have its agreement to participate."

"What sort of unit would volunteer for such an ordeal? It's possible suicide."

Buchanan said, "You'd be surprised. There are many older units willing to sacrifice in order to advance their fellows' situations."

"And this would do that, how?"

"By exposing the underbelly. Hopefully fingering those behind the fighting pits."

"Hopefully," Sofia stipulated. "Meanwhile you're exposing Lionel and whatever unit he builds to risk."

"I'm not worried about that," Lionel said, "so much as the chance my unit wouldn't win."

"He will," Buchanan said.

"You don't know that."

"I do, son. You're the best in this city."

Lionel drew a face. "Far from it. The hybrids are."

"I'm going to talk to the hybrids, see if I can't persuade them not to enter the competition. They're sympathetic to our cause."

"They should support our cause," Lionel agreed. "Still, if Starr and Williams enter—"

"They will. If what you and I suspect is true, they won't be able to resist the prize, or the bragging rights."

Lionel huffed "If what you and I suspect is true, they're doing some damn amazing things with old steam units. The ones I saw at the pit—"

"You can beat them," Buchanan said flatly.

"I'm not so sure."

Their eyes met again. "You can."

A breathless moment ensued before Lionel pushed himself still higher in the bed. "I have to get to the shop."

Sofia crossed her arms on her breast. "Absolutely not." She turned on Buchanan. "Now look what you've done."

"Peace!" the older man beseeched her. "You can have him till he heals up. There's plenty of time. I haven't even announced the competition yet. Meanwhile, Lionel, you have my full backing, though we'll have to keep that on the down low. I'll fund your entry—whatever you need."

"I won't need much. The right design, and components."

"Aye," Buchanan said again. "We'll stipulate, as part of the competition, there will be an inspection by a disinterested party. No new components allowed. The competitors are to be built purely out of scrap."

"And steam."

"And steam."

"Where will you find a disinterested party?" Sofia challenged.

"She's right," Lionel agreed. "Once this gets out, people are going to take sides—those who feel old units are expendable, and those who don't."

"A good point." Buchanan rubbed his chin. "Let me ponder it. Meanwhile, I'll send over some drawing pads and pencils. You can get planning."

Enthusiasm fair shone from Lionel. "All right."

Sofia accompanied Bruce Buchanan downstairs, where he nodded politely at Verna. Sofia could fair feel the rage pouring from her ears, and Buchanan must have sensed it.

When she opened the front door for him, he turned to her and said, "Mr. Pike is a fortunate man indeed, having you in his corner. But Miss Gregory, make certain you are in his corner, completely."

"Of course I am. What are you implying?"

"Let him be who—and what—he is. It's damned special. I know he's busted up, and I know you want to coddle him. But don't. He's a man, and one who fights with his brains. You're angry with me at the moment, aren't ye?"

Sofia glared him in the eye. "I am."

"He's angry too, and he wants revenge. This is his shot at it."

Sofia thought about all the dreams she'd endured in the past, running through dark streets to find the man she loved. She thought about the reality of the chase through Buffalo's streets the night Lionel was beaten, a terrible reality.

"You could have waited," she retorted, "could have given him time to heal."

"You want him on his feet?" Bruce grinned. "This is the best way to get him there."

Chapter Twenty-Seven

"I need to get up," Lionel announced. Four days had passed since Bruce Buchanan's visit. The man had kept his word and sent not only paper and pencils but a fine portable drawing board also.

Lionel had sketched and planned and calculated, but now restlessness had him by the throat. He itched to apply some of his ideas, longed for the smell of the shop—hot metal and steam. He wanted out of this bed.

Not that he didn't enjoy Sofia's company. Part of him liked having her fuss over him, and sleeping away the nights with her beside him brought deep pleasure, even if they did no more than cuddle and kiss.

But she had to let him out of the bed.

Now she paused in folding clean linen and looked at him. "Would you like me to call Verna? Do you need the pot?"

Lionel detested the pot. He was done with it. "I'm getting up."

Her eyes brightened. "You must be feeling better."

"I'm feeling stifled."

"But"—she gestured at the bed, which lay littered with papers—"it's not as if you've wasted the time. You've drawn all those designs."

"And now I want to put them into action. How long have I been here?"

"Almost a week."

"My ribs feel better," Lionel lied. In truth, they still hurt like a bugger, but she'd never let him up if he admitted it. By and large, he did feel stronger, and the anger still burned inside him like a coal fire, not quite banked.

"The physician said to give it a full week. Why don't you wait till tomorrow?"

Lionel detested the physician—a supercilious, long-nosed individual—almost as much as he detested the damned pot.

"I don't think so."

"You're just bored. Look, if you're truly feeling better, I can think of something to pass the time."

At first he didn't grasp what she meant. Not until she softly closed the bedroom door and approached the bed, her fingers already working the buttons of her blouse, did the shoe drop.

He said, like an idiot, "But it's the middle of the day."

She smiled. "All the better to see you, my love."

My love. But those were just words. She didn't mean them.

She paused just out of his reach to take down her hair. It fell around her in a silky curtain, and Lionel's fingers itched for a new reason. His mouth went dry. "Uh—"

"Do you know how hard it's been sleeping beside you every night and not being able to do all the things I longed to do?"

"Pretty hard," Lionel could testify.

"So if you're feeling better, this is my chance."

Lionel made a strangled sound.

She sat on the edge of the bed, now well within his

reach, and parted the two halves of her blouse. She wore nothing beneath.

This time he managed to force out a word. "Sofia—"

"I promise, you won't be bored."

Don't say anything stupid, Lionel's body screamed at him. Men pray for this kind of attention. "Uh—"

"You just lie back. I'll be sure not to hurt you."

"Go ahead. Hurt me," Lionel begged.

****

Twilight sifted into the room slowly as the afternoon died. Sofia had left the window open some six inches, and the sweet air flowed in. At length, Lionel's sanity returned, and he stirred reluctantly in the bed.

He lay with his cheek at Sofia's breast, well within reach of one succulent nipple. She'd given him all the comfort a man could wish before pleasing him at length with her mouth, all while insisting he remain flat on his back. After that she'd fallen asleep, cuddled up to him. He must have dozed off also.

In the past, Lionel had never considered himself particularly fortunate. At least, he hadn't had a lot of luck. A lousy education, which was why he wanted better for Sammy. His parents had died from a fever one after the other during his early teens, leaving him with almost nothing. He supposed he could consider it a blessing when he met old Phil, who'd showed him how to take a steam unit apart and put it back together again. And Buchanan's support might well prove fortuitous now.

But in presenting him with Sofia Gregory, fate had gifted him inexplicably. Beautiful, perceptive, and passionate. Lionel knew he didn't deserve her. For some reason, she'd decided to spend all her warmth and generosity on him, in a dizzying manner.

Lionel could not say his heart wasn't involved. How could a man fail to feel something for such a woman? But, as he'd known from the beginning, after that first night they'd spent together, it wasn't about him.

Yes, she deserved better, far better. Even more, he needed to keep her out of this awful stew into which he'd fallen.

Yet here and now her warmth enfolded him and the glorious scent of her teased his senses. He needed to protect her; he also needed to touch her again.

She moaned when he pressed his mouth to her breast. Her eyes came open, and he found himself gazing into forever.

They kissed. She wrapped her arms around his neck and stretched her naked body against his, like a cat. She ran her tongue luxuriantly around the inside of his mouth before she said, "You taste so good."

"So do you."

A spark appeared in her eyes. "May I feast on you again?"

"I might not survive."

"I'll make sure you do."

"Sofia, wait. It's my turn."

"Ah. But—your ribs…"

"Let me worry about that." Best she learn that, enjoy it as he might, she wouldn't always be in charge, here in bed.

He moved down her body. Heaven ensued.

****

"It is so good having you back, Master Lionel," Mordred said, and not for the first time. The unit, clearly overjoyed to see him, had begun fussing over Lionel as soon as he came through the door the following morning.

He groaned inwardly. Almost as bad as Sofia, whom he'd persuaded not to accompany him this morning, for fear she'd be overly protective.

Damned ingrate, he chastised himself. You're lucky they love you so much.

That thought stopped him cold. He and Sofia had already debated the question of whether or not automatons could truly love. Lionel knew very well they experienced other emotions, namely fear, loyalty, and devotion. Mordred did worry about him. Sofia insisted steamies both hoped and believed, two components of faith.

But love? Well, why not? Mordred now bustled around in a convincing parody of Sofia, and she—

He caught himself again. Sofia didn't love him. She'd merely become swept away in her first physical relationship and, being a warm, generous woman, might well think her heart was involved.

But she hadn't spoken the word, except as an endearment.

Still, he must give Mordred the benefit of the doubt. That thought lent him patience when he told the unit, "Thank you for taking care of the shop while I was away. Everything looks great. Were there any problems?"

"No, Master Lionel. We had a police presence. An officer patrolled the alley at most times."

"One's there now." The man, whom Lionel didn't

recognize, had greeted him when he disembarked from the steamcab Sofia insisted he use.

"An officer called several times to make sure we were all right."

"And were you?" Lionel glanced at Damian, who no longer lingered in the corner but moved around the place with a shop broom in his massive hands. The unit had nodded at him when he came in but said nothing. "You two getting along?"

"We have ironed out a few differences. Damian understands that, if you are away, I am in charge. I put him to work. I hope you do not mind the expenditure of coal, sir."

"I don't mind."

"It did not seem right to shut him down."

Lionel addressed Damian. "Running well, are you? Anything I need to adjust or repair?"

"I am functioning in a satisfactory manner, sir."

Lionel had forgotten the unit still contained Wendy's old voice box, which sounded incongruous coming out of such an oversized unit.

"And what about Sammy?" Lionel asked Mordred. He'd seen the boy—who'd given him a big smile in passing—when he came in. "He been going to school?"

Mordred replied, "He goes out and comes in at the prescribed times, Master Lionel. Who can say where he is in between?"

"Who, indeed? I shall have to contact the school, just as soon as I can. Meanwhile, we have a project, a big one."

He spread his sketches out on the main workbench, which had been cleared of all other debris.

"Both of you, come look at these."

Mordred rolled up promptly. Damian obeyed more slowly, the broom still in his hands.

"Now, what I'm about to tell the two of you is top secret. No one else in the city knows yet, and no one is to know until Mr. Buchanan announces it, understood?"

"Yes, sir," Mordred agreed. Damian gave an odd, high grunt of assent.

"There's going to be a contest."

He launched into an explanation. Both units listened, rapt.

When he finished, Mordred said, "But, sir, I thought you were against using steam units in such a fashion."

"I am."

"Why would you build one specifically to—" Mordred waved an arm at the designs.

"In an effort to expose those behind the fight rings. Mr. Buchanan believes they won't be able to resist the prize money and will take the bait."

"But Master Lionel!" Mordred became so agitated, steam poured from his neck joint. "The unit you construct, however well made, may suffer fatal damage."

Lionel told him as gently as possible, "True. Sacrifices may have to be made. In this case, I will need the cooperation of whatever unit I build. I'm hoping, for the cause—"

Damian rolled farther forward. "I will do it."

"Eh?" Startled, Lionel looked at the unit.

"I volunteer to be your fighter."

Lionel experienced a rush of mingled excitement and dismay. "That's a very courageous offer. But as you can see, I was going to build a competitor out of old components, from the ground up."

"I am made of old components," Damian said proudly. "And I am already a fighter."

"Damian, Mordred's right. You could be utterly destroyed."

"I am willing to take that chance. Sir, I was forced to fight before, at their bidding. I had to watch others like myself destroyed in that place. They forced me to participate in their destruction in order to survive." Damian seemed to choose his next words carefully and delivered them in a high whine that raised the hairs on the back of Lionel's neck. "I want revenge."

So did Lionel. He could scarcely blame Damian, but the notion that a similar fire burned in the unit and in his own gut seemed a leap.

"Ah, well—I would need to refit you."

"I do not mind. I have already been rebuilt several times."

"There would have to be considerable changes. The mechanics from the fight pit, if they participate, couldn't be allowed to recognize you."

"I accept that. I have advantages, too." Damian raised his arms. "I have already been reinforced, and I am very strong."

"That's so." Lionel glanced from the unit to the plans on the bench, and back again, torn. He'd have to can a lot of his plans if he went with Damian. On the other hand—

"I am a fighter!" Damian insisted. "Let me fight."

On the other hand, the will to triumph was everything.

Chapter Twenty-Eight

Spring, in its first full flush, arrived in Buffalo. With an abruptness bordering on mania, the trees lining every avenue burst into leaf. The last of the rain and bitter wind fled, and sunshine brightened skies of clean-washed blue. Even the scents of coal smoke and river water retreated beneath the fragrance of the new grass forcing its way between the paving stones.

Amid all this splendor, Sofia's heart grieved. Nearly four weeks had passed since Lionel left her house—her bed—to resume work in the shop.

He hadn't returned. Not once. Not for her cooking and not for her kisses. Not for the searing, heated sessions they'd shared between the sheets. Oh, she'd seen him, of course, but only when she went to the shop. He spent his nights in the upstairs flat and never invited her to stay.

Sofia could draw only one conclusion—he was a steam tinker before all else, including her lover.

Oh, he seemed happy to see her when she showed up at the shop. But not in any way that gladdened her heart in turn. He wanted to share his plans and his work with her, show off Damian who, voluntarily it seemed, underwent astounding changes. Half the time, at the shop, Bruce Buchanan was there, as well as members of the Irish Squad. They had started out, so Lionel said, standing guard and got so interested in the project they

Laura Strickland

migrated inside.

The contest had been announced by now, amid much fanfare and emphasis on the prize. So far, as Sofia well knew, there were ten entries—more than Mr. Buchanan had anticipated. And the deadline to sign up wasn't till the end of May.

The shop of Starr and Williams had entered. So had a number of independents, like Lionel, and one or two bigger manufacturers. The hybrids, of course, remained out of the competition.

But no one could deny their interest. Patrick Kelly haunted the shop, as did Dennis Greely. And difficult-to-find parts tended to magically appear on Lionel's doorstep.

Lionel, completely immersed in his project, showed no real signs of missing Sofia beyond his pleasure when she arrived. That despite her bone-deep longing for him, like a sickness that rode her blood.

She missed everything about him—the smile that hovered in his eyes, the careful way he touched her, the taste of him, those deep, near-endless kisses. She missed his warmth in her bed and the way she lost herself when he slid into her.

She'd stopped dreaming of Riga and dreamed of him instead, and the streets of Buffalo. She relived over and over the memory of running to find him the night he'd been attacked. But a new dream joined that one. Sometimes she pelted through the streets at random, searching for him while knowing he was in terrible danger, and that she would not reach him in time.

She'd tried filling up her days with other things. Good works with the Freedom of Faith for All movement. Meetings with Jane Pyatt and Ogilvie.

She'd focused on her gratitude at having Verna back in her life. All those things helped, but none answered the ache.

On this particular morning, she went to the shop just in order to lay eyes on the man she loved. Oh, yes, she loved him—she'd admitted that to herself some time back, if not to him. A woman did not feel this way about someone she didn't love, didn't desire nor fantasize about acts they had and might again perform together.

Though odds of that last seemed dismal in the extreme.

Verna had insisted on accompanying her to the shop, as she usually did these days. Verna seemed as fascinated as everyone else with the progress being made on Damian.

The hybrid police officer standing just outside the shop door nodded to them when they went in. Sofia's heart sank. She'd hoped for a word alone with Lionel, but the shop appeared overly full of visitors.

Bruce Buchanan, of course, held sway at the head of the main workbench. The man spent more and more time here, and aggravated Sofia no end.

In addition, Pat Kelly and several older-model automatons she didn't know were in attendance. All seemed to be engaged in a friendly argument.

"What's all this?" she asked, joining Lionel beside the bench.

"Oh, hello. We're just discussing what Damian's ring name should be."

"Ring name? What's wrong with Damian?"

"Doesn't sound much like a gladiator, does it?" Buchanan demanded.

Sofia planted her hands on her hips. "So, what's a suitable gladiator name?"

"We're debating Mauler, Incinerator," Buchanan said with relish, "or maybe something like Destroyer."

"Oooh," Verna squeaked, gazing at Damian who stood poised, polished and gleaming.

Sofia glanced at Lionel. He flashed her a wide grin.

"How about just calling him Intimidator?" Sofia asked sarcastically.

"Not bad," Buchanan declared.

The hybrids nodded.

"Magnificent," Verna suggested, and Mordred seemed to sag where he stood.

"I was being sarcastic," Sofia admitted.

"An unattractive behavior, in a beautiful young woman," declared Buchanan.

Sofia bit her lip in vexation. "Lionel? Might I have a word with you?"

"Sure. Go ahead."

"In private."

"Oh." He looked startled, as if he couldn't imagine what they might have to discuss. She towed him to the room behind the shop, that contained a tiny kitchen. The shadows there swaddled them.

She'd meant to ask him back to her house for the night, to confess how she craved the taste of him and longed to feel the heat of his body covering hers.

Now, though, he spoke before she could. "I'm glad you're here. I want to ask you a question."

Her pulse leaped. Maybe he would ask before she could. Maybe—

"Bruce has advanced me some money for living expenses. More than I can use. I mean, I don't spend a lot on myself. And—"

Her heart sped double time. He wanted to ask her to marry him. He found himself flush, and able to provide, so he meant to confess his feelings.

Her lips parted. "Yes?"

"I wondered how you felt about—"

Her gaze clung to his. "Yes?"

"—getting Verna's face painted. I know how much you liked Miss Kormish's work. And I know how much Verna means to you."

"Verna." The word nearly stuck in Sofia's throat, a direct result of her heart dropping in proportion to her disappointment.

"Yeah. I know she'd have to be away from you for a time, while the work was done, but it would be worth it."

"You're asking me about Verna's face."

"Yes." For the first time he looked troubled. "She'd be beautiful. For you."

Coldly, Sofia told him, "You'd need to ask Verna about that. It's her face, after all."

"Sofia." He seized her hands. "What's the matter? What have I said? I thought—"

"You think," she told him, "about steam units morning, noon, and night. That's all your head—and heart—contain."

"That's who I am. That's what I am." He gave her a hard look. "Is it a problem?"

Yes, quite possibly it was. He was a practical man, one who—as he'd said—dealt in nuts and bolts. He lived very much in the moment. Why hadn't she seen that? When he was with her, Sofia—say, in her bed— he might be there completely, devoting the whole of his energy and attention to their pleasure. But most of his moments would be spent here amid the metal and steam.

She'd given her body and her heart to a man, and he did not find her all that important—merely a momentary distraction. She drew away from him. "I have to leave."

"Why? You just got here. Wait—Sofia!"

"Let me go."

He did. She pressed her way through the shop, past the huge figure of Damian, between the hybrids and around Buchanan, who gave her an impatient look.

Behind her, as she went out, she hard Buchanan say, "Lionel, lad, I hope that woman's not going to prove a distraction."

She didn't pause for Lionel's reply.

She walked. For blocks and blocks, while the sweet, warm air turned to ashes around her. Unshed tears blurred her vision and kept her from seeing the bustling streets, as the denizens of Buffalo streamed forth to enjoy the fine weather. She tramped until her feet hurt and she didn't know where she was. Regret possessed her heart.

She'd been raised a decent and well-bred young woman, circumspect and retiring, certainly not meant to throw herself at the first steam tinker who came along and spoke to her kindly. And she now saw she'd done precisely that. Persuaded him into her bed, taking off her clothes for him. Pleasured him in ways only a woman of the streets might.

Yet it had felt so natural, so heady and empowering. So fated, somehow. The ties between them were not all just physical. Sofia had felt convinced she'd known him in a past life, that he'd meant everything to her then, and they were destined to meet again.

Fool.

Ah, well, if she meant anything to him, and if he'd sensed how upset she was back there at the shop, he'd be waiting for her when she got home. If only she could figure out how to get home.

She did at last, weary and footsore. She found only Verna, who'd returned home on her own, waiting.

Chapter Twenty-Nine

"I'd say he's about ready, lad. And he's magnificent." Buchanan clapped Lionel on the back. "By heaven, son, what an achievement."

Lionel regarded his creation through blurry, sleep-deprived eyes. Damian stood before him, a gladiator in truth, and unrecognizable as his former self.

But the unit's heart—if such it could be called—remained the same, stout and strong. As did his will.

He stood six and a half feet tall, with a double-reinforced skin protecting his boiler and giving him a barrel chest. Lionel had built the shoulders wide to deflect any blows from more vulnerable areas. In fact, every component within the unit was reinforced and protected; each ancient piece had been cleaned, sanded, and buffed, and put together with care. From his head to his wheels, he was as impervious as Lionel could make him.

And he appeared every bit as intimidating. He dwarfed poor Mordred, who'd labored so hard on his construction, and had a hatchet face with a jaw like a sledgehammer. Lionel had replaced his blue glass eyes with similar ones, nearly black, that reflected a little of the fire that burned inside him—and it was a great fire, capable of industrial temperatures. He wore a kind of helmet, vaguely reminiscent of an ancient warrior, and across his massive shoulders and body was draped a curtain of chain mail. His oversize hands could grasp any weapon, from a sword to a mace.

Even to Lionel's eyes—which had inspected every bolt and spring—he looked impressive.

The others crowding the shop seemed to agree. Pat Kelly had come with several members of the Irish Squad—they hovered near the door—and Sammy had skived off school for the occasion. Buchanan, as always, held sway at the forefront.

Only one person was missing.

Sofia should be here, she really should. But Lionel had not seen her in more days than he could count.

Not that he hadn't tried to talk to her. He'd been aware, that day she marched out of the shop, something had gone quite wrong. He just wasn't sure what.

She hadn't been back to the shop since, and when he went to her house, she refused to see him. Verna answered the door and made excuses. She claimed Sofia wasn't there, off about business for the Freedom of Faith movement, and Lionel couldn't tell if the unit lied.

In truth, he'd lost track—immersed here—of how many days had slipped by. He struggled now to count back and realized with vague horror it must be a couple of weeks. Because the deadline for entries approached.

Had she broken things off with him?

She should be here for this, damn it. Whether she realized it or not, she was part of the project. Anyway, he ached for her, longed to catch her smile, hear her voice, take her in his arms and kiss her.

Damian spoke through his reconditioned voice box, a booming bass. "Thank you, sir, for restoring me to such condition."

Everyone there cheered, including the hybrids. A moment, and no mistake, if unquestionably dimmed for Lionel.

"Thank you," he told the unit, "for volunteering so bravely."

Damian examined his own arms, holding them up in turn, and flexed his massive legs. "I am—proud. Who would not be proud to become this? And I hope I do you proud, in turn."

Another cheer. Sofia missed something really special, hearing a steamie speak about hope. In that regard, Damian had proved a wonder. He'd had faith in his transformation from the start, and his belief had in large part fueled the project.

"Now"—Buchanan dusted his palms off, one against the other—"just one piece of business left. A name."

"We've been calling him Damian," Mordred spoke up.

Buchanan drew a sour face. "Yes, but I'm talking of a ring name. We've debated this before."

"I was Dammit," Damian said. "Then Damian."

"What about Driver," one of the hybrids suggested, "in keeping, so to speak, with his other names."

A slow smile spread across Lionel's face. "Pile Driver. You know—like the fellows who make a path for the steam trains. Powerful, determined, and can work all day."

Buchanan's eyes lit. "I like it. And, lad, since you created him, it's only fitting you should name him."

"No." Lionel looked at the unit. "It's fitting he should approve his own name."

"I will be Pile Driver," the unit declared. A third

cheer split the room.

"Wait—wait!" Lionel, now wholly inspired, dashed to the rear of the shop where he hurriedly unearthed a heavy-headed, long-handled hammer. "This was here when we moved in. It'll need to be shined up to match you, Damian, but—" He placed the hammer in the unit's hand. "There's your weapon of choice."

Damian inspected the hammer, hefted it, and settled into a stance. "I shall, sir, drive the competition into the rails!"

****

The ceremony on North Street lasted too long, and the bright afternoon sun had given Sofia a headache. She wished she'd worn a different hat, one with a wider brim to block the glare, so she might better enjoy this victory.

An amazing victory it was.

Amid a crowd of more than a hundred, automaton and human alike, the cornerstone for the First Automaton Church of Buffalo had just been laid.

It had taken some doing, and Sofia had been deeply involved. Truth was, she needed distraction from what she mentally termed her *situation with Lionel*, and had thrown herself into the cause wholeheartedly, spending her days with Misses Pyatt and Rumple, and even going to see the mayor in their company.

The mayor—a man called Abrams, elected after the former mayor had been ousted, following last year's riot in Niagara Square—proved most reasonable and in the end could not think of a cause to deny the automatons permission to build as they wished on land bought with funds raised from their own community. So the stone, today, had been placed with great ceremony.

Automatons, as Sofia had discovered, loved ceremony.

A pity Sofia could not feel more elated about it. She stood with Jane Pyatt on one side of her and Verna, who'd insisted she should be there, on the other.

Jane, with wide eyes, enthused, "Sofia, aren't you glad you came? You simply could not miss this, after all your devoted work."

And, Sofia wondered, was that what her life was to be in the future? That of a spinster of limited means, who proved instrumental in varied causes?

Could she bear it?

An image of Lionel appeared before her eyes, lying sprawled on her bed, drunk with pleasure. It swiftly turned into a far darker image—Lionel lying bloodied and broken, lost to her forever.

Panic clawed at her throat. That could not happen, could it? He remained busy at his shop, not in danger.

Verna turned to her. "Miss, are you unwell?"

"I am—"

Jane turned also, wearing a look of concern. "Come, Verna, let's find a place for her to sit down. There is a café up on Delaware."

But Sofia didn't want to sit. She wanted—no, needed—to see Lionel with her own eyes. Cursed if she'd go running to him, though. No Gregorovich woman had ever chased a man. If he wanted her, let him come to her.

He hasn't, a small voice inside her whispered.

As she stood hesitating, a cry came from across the street. A metallic clang sounded close beside her, and Verna jerked back a few steps.

Jane cried out. "My God, they're attacking!"

Sofia spun. All the while the ceremony had been taking place, dissenters had gathered on the south side of North Street. Now they'd grown angry enough to do something about it. Even as Sofia watched, a fellow at the front of the crowd whipped his arm. A missile flew toward them.

"They're throwing rocks." Jane sounded outraged rather than fearful.

Not exactly the attack she'd imagined, but still— Sofia never finished that thought. Another man whipped his arm and seconds later, pain exploded through her head.

The crowd around the church site seemed to expand. The hybrid automatons there surrounded Sofia, Jane, and Verna like two wings. Even as Sofia's legs failed beneath her, she felt herself lifted against a rough uniform that exuded warmth.

"I have her," a rich Irish voice declared. "Clear 'em out, lads!"

****

This time, Sofia could find no way out of the dreams that possessed her. Usually, the terror and distress brought her awake and she fought her way free from the darkness, gasping. Now she ran and ran with dread in her heart and pain in her soul, feet stumbling over cobblestones, through streets of a city where she'd never been. A refrain played over and over in her head.

Where is he? Where is he?

The cobbles beneath her feet changed to bricks, and the streets became those she knew. Not Riga but Buffalo. The scent of coal smoke and river water filled the air. But the fear remained the same, as did the refrain.

Where is he? I must reach him. The man I love—

"Shh, Sofia. It's all right."

A hand touched her hand, and the darkness shattered into a thousand pieces. Bright sunlight came streaming in. It half-blinded her when she opened her eyes.

Where was she? Lying in a bed, in a bright room, with a man sitting beside her. A window, behind him, emitted all that brightness and kept her from seeing him properly.

But she knew him. Knew that voice and that touch. Her whole body relaxed.

She spoke in a croak. "What are you doing here?"

"Pat Kelly sent word you were hurt. Some degenerate started throwing stones at that ceremony you attended." His fingers tightened on hers. "You were struck in the head."

"Where is here?"

"Hospital."

"Oh, God, I can't afford a stay in a hospital. I—"

"Hush," he bade again. "Don't worry about that now."

Someone stirred on the other side of the bed. Sofia caught a glimpse of Verna's worn, worried face.

"Your stay is paid for, miss. By the Automaton Liberation League."

"That's mad." Sofia focused her attention on Lionel with difficulty, struggling to read his expression. "Why are you here?"

"Why wouldn't I be? Sofia, when Pat brought word—well, he said it was pretty bad. I thought I was going to lose you."

"You were struck in the head," Verna explained. "There was much blood."

"Scared the living life out of me," Lionel confessed.

Sofia gave him a tight smile. "Not a good feeling, is it?"

He leaned forward in his chair so she could see his expression. Worry filled his eyes, and grim lines bracketed his mouth. "No."

They gazed at one another for several seconds before Verna said, "I will leave you alone, to speak."

"No," Sofia objected.

"No," Lionel said an instant later. "I can't stay. I need to get back."

"Of course you do," Sofia said, not without bitterness.

"Sofia, the competition starts in two days."

"And that's more important than anything."

"No, I didn't say that. But at the moment, well—there are so many other people involved, besides me. There's Bruce, and all the hybrids who've backed us, Damian himself, and the whole automaton community."

And who was she, compared with all that? Just a random woman, who loved him. Who'd thrown herself at him.

She said nothing.

He went on talking, "This competition could save a lot of lives, automaton lives. It will prove the value of the older units we love. To say nothing of exposing those behind the fighting pit. If it is Starr and Williams, as I suspect—well, they've taken the bait. Their entry will be our main competition. If Damian—or Pile Driver, as we're calling him—can defeat their unit, it will be like a victory of light over darkness. Don't you see that?"

"Pile Driver," Verna echoed with undisguised approval.

But Sofia said, "No, I don't see. How will having Starr and Williams there expose them as being behind the fight ring?"

"It will show they can fit an older unit to fight."

"So can you. Are you behind the ring?"

"No, of course not. But whoever is has rebuilt dozens of units, over and over again. There are few men in this city capable of that. I believe we'll have them all there, in two days' time—with a vast audience of interested spectators."

Sofia bit her lip.

Impulsively, Lionel said, "When you get out of here, come to the shop and see Damian. Come before the match—both of you. I know it would mean the world to him. Here, I'll give you fare for a cab."

He dug in his pocket and extended the coins on his palm.

Sofia stared at them. Was that all she meant to him? Did he value what they'd shared at no more than a few coins?

When she didn't take the money, his hand trembled. He gave the coins to Verna.

"Come," he urged Verna. "Damian's being so brave. And it might be your last chance to see him in one piece."

Ah, Sofia thought, but she'd finished with last chances.

Chapter Thirty

Sofia seldom saw Verna weep. Not that the unit shed tears, as such. But she did upon rare occasions collapse into a state where she covered her face with her apron, or whatever other garment she wore, and keened.

It had happened after the deaths of Sofia's parents. Once, when Sofia began selling their beautiful possessions.

It happened after Lionel walked out of the hospital room.

For an instant Sofia, consumed with her own grief and disappointment, failed to recognize it as a repeat of those former times. But the high wail punctuated her defenses.

"Goodness, Verna, what is it?"

"He is going to die. And I will never see him again."

"Lionel?" But no, that was ridiculous. The truth came crashing in. "You mean, Damian?"

Verna uncovered her face, which remained unchanged. Other faces, as if on cue, appeared at the door of the ward, and Sofia's fellow roommates stared.

A nurse called, "What was that sound? Are you in pain?"

"No," Sofia assured her.

"Yes," Verna cried.

"It's all right," Sofia said quickly. "My steam unit is—er—experiencing a crisis."

"Well, make it quiet or it will have to leave."

The faces withdrew. Sofia looked at Verna searchingly. "Are you saying—"

"I am in love with him. Dammit. Damian. Pile Driver. I do not care what he is called."

No. Nor, Sofia thought, in what lifetime they met.

A steamie in love? Why not? She'd be the first to acknowledge Verna had strong emotions. Verna loved her, and she loved Verna. And hybrids were marrying right and left.

"But," she objected, "you scarcely know him."

"It did not take long. We used to talk, back when we went to the shop, before you and Master Lionel had your falling out."

"I see."

"He is an automaton of few words but deep feelings."

Courage. Loyalty, presumably. "Yes."

"I have not seen much of him since he was made magnificent. Now I may not, before he is destroyed in the fight ring."

"Listen to me, Verna. Lionel won't let anything happen to him. Even if he's badly damaged, Lionel will resurrect him, as he did before."

"But his intelligence may be lost."

Just like Lionel's. His memory of Sofia had been left in a past life, though she recalled him.

"My goodness," she said. "Is there anything else you need to tell me?"

"Yes. Mr. Lionel's assistant, Mordred—I believe he is in love with me."

"Yes, well." No use denying Mordred's intelligence. Sofia had seen the way he looked at Verna.

"It is a conundrum," Verna declared.

"It certainly is."

"Mordred would make for me a very good and safe life companion. But there is something about Dammit's courageous spirit—"

"I understand."

"When the new church is built, I would like to go there and marry him."

"Really?"

"Yes. I would like to—to—to—" Verna stuttered, apparently stalled in her reach for expression, "to claim that for myself."

For an instant, Sofia went breathless. This ancient, battered unit, oft repaired and continually in service, devoted to her, Sofia, and never asking more than a bit of water and coal, wanted something for herself. For the first time in her existence.

"Then," she said determinedly, "that is what you shall do. Here, help me up."

"Miss, no. You should not get up yet. You have a large bandage on your head. You are attached to that tube—"

"Then go find a doctor, so he can release me."

****

"How are you feeling? Nervous?" Lionel asked the enormous unit. It towered over him by a good eight inches, Lionel standing only about five foot ten, and would make two of him in girth. But at the moment it did not seem like a ridiculous question.

Lionel had lived among automatons a long time. He'd worked on them, taken them apart and rebuilt them, made vital repairs that extended their lives. In the course of doing so, he talked to them, suffered with them, and listened to their various voices, be they squeaks or rasps, or mere puffs of steam. In truth, he'd spent more time in the company of steamies than people. And he could virtually feel Damian vibrating with emotion.

"No," the unit replied. Its ebony marble eyes seemed to focus on Lionel. "You have built me too well to allow for fear. I am nigh to indestructible."

"Yes, well." No one was indestructible, but Lionel did not want to say so. Deep in his piping, in his fire chamber, Damian knew that.

"You have made me so."

"I've done my best."

"And you and I, Master Lionel, are linked. When I go into that ring, you will go with me."

What an idea for the unit to express! Almost philosophical, and completely true. "I'll be with you in spirit, that's for sure." He clapped the unit's cool outer skin. "You have one big advantage. You're the only one of the entries with experience in the ring. Unless Starr and Williams have revamped one of their old fight models."

"If they have, he will be unrecognizable. Like me."

"Yes."

"All in all, Master Lionel, I feel excited. If I could ask but one thing—"

Damian stopped speaking and gazed toward the shop door. The shop had become a hangout for hybrids, and three of them had to move aside now as Mordred admitted someone.

Lionel turned and froze, much as Damian had.

Verna came in. The unit possessed a wardrobe—Sofia seemed to prefer her clad—and this day wore a gown of soft pink that cast a rosy glow on her polished surfaces. Her painted hair and features still looked worn, but stealing a glance at Damian, Lionel saw it didn't matter. The unit stood rapt.

Behind Verna came Sofia, and response to her presence swept through Lionel in a powerful wave. She looked like what she was—delicate, well-bred, and beautiful—and he hadn't expected such a response to her arrival.

Gladness, desire, and wariness churned together inside him, an unsettling brew. Her dark eyes met his for only an instant before they fled. She drew off her gloves, focusing only on them.

Verna rolled directly to where Damian and Lionel stood. She faced the resurrected unit. "Hello, Dammit."

"Hello, Miss Verna."

"I wanted very much to see you before your match. To—to wish you luck."

"I wanted very much to see you also."

"You look very impressive, Dammit."

"I am glad to know you approve of my finished appearance."

"You are utterly magnificent."

Lionel heard the rattle and squeak of wheels as Mordred took himself into the back room. A hand snagged his own.

"Let's give them some privacy, please."

Sofia had tagged Lionel. He turned to her, his gut still churning with emotions.

"Privacy?"

"Surely even you can see they need a moment

alone," she remarked tersely.

Ah, so she remained angry with him. Indeed, he could fairly feel the emotions flying from her like prickles on a weed.

He should clear the air with her, yes. But not here where everyone could hear.

"Let's go outside," he suggested. "I need air."

Out in the alley, it smelled little better. But spring sunshine did stream down. It lent warmth to Sofia's ginger hair, even if it did fail to brighten her dark eyes.

Be a man, Lionel told himself. Take the bull by the horns. Before he could produce another lame platitude, he said, "Tomorrow's the match."

"I know. That's why we're here. She wanted to see him now, in case she doesn't have a chance later."

Lionel nodded as if he understood, though he didn't, entirely.

Apparently reading his expression, Sofia engaged his eyes. "She says she's in love with him. An inconvenient truth, but you know, a woman can't always choose where her heart bestows itself."

Lionel might have objected, Verna not being a woman, but even he realized they no longer spoke of the automatons.

"No matter," Sofia added deliberately, "how she might regret it."

"Don't say that."

"Why not? You treated me shabbily. Used me for sexual release, then set me aside." Sudden tears filled her eyes and trickled over. "The only thing that could possibly make it worse is having my heart involved."

"I didn't. Sofia, listen to me." He caught her elbows in his hands.

Almost fastidiously, she freed herself. "What would you call it?"

Lionel's mind flapped like a bird with one foot caught in quicksand. "I'd call it necessity."

"Necessity?"

"I understand you're angry—"

"Do you?"

"Yes. But it's not the way you put it. I care for you."

"Do you?" she asked again, in clear disbelief.

"Yes. Very much. But—then all this came up." He waved a hand toward the shop. "I had to get Damian ready. An awful lot rides on it; stopping the abuse at the fight pits, not letting Bruce down. Not letting Damian down."

"So you dropped me." She swiped angrily at the tears.

"I did not. I've wanted to see you. Just—look, after the match tomorrow, there'll be time."

"So…what? You'll return to my bed when you have time?"

Now Lionel flushed, beginning to grow angry.

She went on, "Make me a priority? Do me the honor of letting me pleasure you again?"

"It's not like that, Sofia. I care for you and want to be with you. My feelings for you are—well, I don't even have words to express them. I'm not a man who finds words easily for my feelings. I feel for you as for nobody else, but a man has his responsibilities."

"I see. Whereas a woman can just wait until he casts her a few scraps of time."

Lionel drew himself up. "There's nothing I can say that will make a difference to what you think."

"Nothing?"

He shook his head. "Right now, I have to concentrate on the match. We're sure whoever's behind the fight pit has taken the bait." He said without conceit, "There aren't that many men in the city capable of building units like Damian. Even if it's not Starr and Williams, Damian might recognize someone." He touched her hand. "Will you be there?"

"Me? At the match? Why should I?"

"It would mean a lot." Seeing refusal in her eyes, he added, "Surely Verna will want to come."

"I'm not sure I want her to see the unit she loves being destroyed."

"He won't be. He's going to win."

"Then you don't need me there, do you? Please tell Verna I'm waiting for her at the café up on Niagara Street. She can take as long with Damian as she likes."

"Sofia, please—"

But she walked away from him. Not till she'd gone did he realize she carried his peace of mind in her hands.

Chapter Thirty-One

The Great Automaton Match, as it was being called, would be held in the open at Prospect Park. Other venues had been proposed, first the Automaton Center farther down Niagara, and then Mick's Gym—a boxing arena—on Franklin Street. None, it was decided, offered enough room. Interest in the match had exploded, and hundreds were expected to attend.

Of course, with the competition being held in the open, weather presented a factor. Some proponents suggested a canopy should be set up over the ring. Others argued the chance of rain merely offered the builders another opportunity to prove their expertise: Could they construct a unit that would continue to function in a downpour?

Fortunately, the day dawned beautiful, with bird song and a sweet mildness to the air. Lionel, a mass of nerves and unable to shrug off yesterday's quarrel with Sofia, had managed no sleep.

It being a Saturday, the match would begin at three p.m. because they needed the daylight. He arrived at the venue early, with his entourage. They traveled in an enclosed wagon Bruce provided so—he said—no one could gawk at Pile Driver betimes.

Mordred, somewhat to Lionel's surprise, chose not to come, volunteering to stay back and mind the shop. But Bruce put himself in charge of the transport, and a phalanx of hybrids flanked them upon arrival.

Once Pile Driver had been unloaded, one of the hybrids told Lionel, "Pat said we'd better distance ourselves while the match is going on, just to keep things on an even keel. But if there's any trouble, buddy, we'll be here."

The hybrids had taken to calling him "buddy." He didn't mind having them for friends, but the name sounded strange.

He could see Pat's point. This event focused on older mechanical units, which were often regarded far differently than hybrids by the general public.

Already, a human audience had begun to gather in the park. This event had garnered a lot of interest and, so Bruce said, more than a few bets. Even now, men in flat caps with narrowed eyes circulated among the members of the crowd, most of whom gawped at Pile Driver with open curiosity.

Bruce, early in attendance, clapped Lionel on the back. "Only two other entries are here ahead of us. One's been put up by another independent, Tom Elliot. I've just been talking to him. He calls his Destroyer. The other early arrival—you can see over there—is put up by the boiler maker's union."

"They're the ones who backed the hockey team last winter, aren't they?" Lionel asked.

"Aye, lad."

"They might prove some competition." Hastily, Lionel looked around. The unit in question, all black with a dull finish, stood being fussed over by a throng of men in workers' garb.

"I've just had a look at it. You can bet the core's solid, but they haven't spent a lot of time on the finishing. Can it fight? That's the question."

"What is his name?" Pile Driver asked in his deep rumble.

"Incinerator." Bruce grinned. "I have to say, lad, this is more fun than I've had in a month o' Sundays. But we canna forget 'tis serious business at the root."

"Starr and Williams aren't here yet?" Lionel asked, edgy.

"No. Rumor has it they're calling their entry Pulverizer." Bruce looked at Pile Driver. "You good, lad?"

"I can quite honestly say I have never been better."

"Glad to hear it."

Bruce bustled off. Lionel and Pile Driver looked at each other.

"I was hoping Miss Verna might come."

"Did she say she would?" Lionel's heart leaped. If Verna came, Sofia might also. Despite their disagreement.

Tomorrow, when all this was over, he'd make it up to her. Somehow, he'd make things right.

"She said she would try. Master Lionel, if I win—"

"Yes, Damian?"

"I would like to ask her to marry me. If I lose and am damaged beyond repair, I would like you to do something in my memory."

"Steady on, Damian. Beyond repair means—"

"Pulverized," Damian supplied the word. "By the Pulverizer, I expect."

Lionel swallowed hard. This unit had come to mean a great deal to him. As Damian had said, they were linked on a level that bore no regard for metal or flesh.

"I vow to you, Damian, if things go badly, I will do everything in my power to rebuild you and retrieve your—well, personality. If that can't be done, what do you ask of me?"

"Melt me down. Release me back to the elements that came before the metal, so my essence can be returned into the Great Furnace beyond."

Lionel stared, speechless.

"And then," Damian went on, "try and persuade Miss Verna to bond with Mordred. He loves her, I know, as much as I do. And a unit so lovely as she should not be alone."

"I will," Lionel agreed, his throat tight. "But that won't happen, hear me?" The black marble eyes focused on his face, and he repeated it like a promise: "It won't."

****

"Miss, you need not come. I will attend on my own." Verna emitted the words almost serenely as she placed the pink hat on her painted hair.

Sofia, standing with her own hat in her hands, ached with indecision. "I don't think that's a good idea. Jane says anything might happen in the city this afternoon. This competition has stirred up a lot of ill feeling among people who oppose the automatons gaining stature. The police are warning units to take care and remain off the streets."

Verna said, "Many of us will be there in spite of the warnings. The units are fighting to prove our worth, despite age and wear. Even if outdated, we deserve to live."

"But, Verna, what if you're attacked on the streets? Remember what happened in Niagara Square last year, and all over the city. Units were destroyed without mercy, bashed and—and killed. What if you're attacked on the way? It's so far."

Verna faced her. "No fear, Miss. I have been given fare for a cab."

"You have? By whom?"

"One of Dammit's friends."

"Which one?"

"His name is Officer Greely. He is a hybrid."

"Oh. Oh, I see."

"Miss, Dammit is my man. My mate. I will be there to see him fight." She added with quaint dignity, "You may ride with me, if you like."

Sofia hesitated. Should she? She'd as good as told Lionel she would not be there. Yet how could she let Verna go alone?

She set her hat on her head. "I would appreciate that."

****

Starr and Williams' entry arrived amid bustle and fanfare. By then—only half an hour before start time—nearly all the other competitors stood in their assigned stations around the ring. Lionel and Damian had been assessing them avidly while, at least in Lionel's case, trying to appear as if he didn't.

They ranged widely in quality and appearance from the crude to what he intuitively classed as the dangerous. Damian would have to watch out for the boilermakers' entry, who looked like he'd been put together completely from boiler plate. In contrast, the unit built by the Dillon Steam Works shone green, and had a lantern jaw and a huge shamrock painted on his hopper.

His name was Fenian, which Bruce said was some kind of ancient Irish warrior.

"Gates Brothers have dropped out, laddie," Bruce added during one of his eternal rounds. The Scotsman, clearly nervous, had been nipping from a flask he kept in his vest pocket. "Couldn't get their man finished in time, apparently."

"Good," Lionel replied. The competitors he could see looked plenty intimidating.

But when Starr and Williams arrived and unloaded their entry, all the bustle momentarily stopped.

Lionel knew both Elijah Starr and Lloyd Williams by sight, though he had no real acquaintance with them. Their shop was bigger and newer than his, and probably far better equipped. They also charged a lot more for their work than he did. Among other steam shops, they had a reputation for taking advantage of their customers, but no one could doubt their skill.

Elijah Starr made up in girth what he lacked in height. Perhaps thirty years old, he had a bald head and a clever face complemented by watchful eyes. Williams, a few years older, and probably pushing forty, looked like an assassin. Lionel had never seen him smile, and wasn't sure he wanted to.

Now, however, all Lionel's attention centered on their entry. They unloaded him down a ramp from the back of a covered wagon, and he emerged like a king from his throne.

Or, no—maybe more like a marauder descending on a hapless village, Lionel thought. For though the unit appeared well finished, it had a raw and brutal aspect.

"Oooh," said the crowd in a collective gasp.

The newcomer stood, like Pile Driver, at over six

feet tall. He had a face of sculped metal, apparently beaten out of used plate, that quite disquietingly included a wide, bloodthirsty grin. Someone had fashioned teeth out of what looked like small pieces of pipe, not all the same size, so his mouth bristled like that of a shark.

His body, too, had been sculpted. The hammer marks were still visible all over the tortured skin. Muscles stood out on his chest and arms, and his legs, in contrast, were constructed from steel ingots. He carried a club in one hand.

"My God," Bruce breathed, turning up beside Lionel and Damian as if by magic. "Will you look at that?"

"I'm looking."

"What's its name?" called someone in the crowd, and Lloyd provided an answer. Previous rumors proved confirmed as the name was taken up and passed around.

Pulverizer.

Lionel glanced at Damian, who shifted the hammer he held from one hand to the other. The sledge had been cleaned and polished to within an inch of its life and now gleamed wickedly.

"I am not afraid," Damian said.

"Good lad." Bruce clapped the unit on the shoulder. "Do you—er—recognize anyone? From the fight pit, I mean."

"Yes," Damian confirmed, "and that is why I am not afraid." He raised his hammer. "The time for revenge has come."

Chapter Thirty-Two

"Those men," Lionel spoke to Damian in a low voice, "they're the ones? You're sure?"

Damian emitted a strange sound, like a groan. "The one with no hair—"

"That's Elijah Starr."

"He refitted me. He refitted all of us and was in charge of taking us to the fight pits. The other man appeared at the pits sometimes."

Lionel turned to Bruce. "Go find Pat Kelly, or any other member of the Irish Squad. They need to hear this."

Before the fight. Lionel didn't add that, though it sounded aloud in his head. In case Damian didn't survive and couldn't give evidence later. Lionel didn't like the look of Pulverizer, not one bit.

Bruce hared off, and Lionel asked Damian, "What about the fight unit? Do you recognize him?"

"It is difficult to tell what is under his armor."

"Yes."

"They had a favorite unit, often repaired. He frequently proved victorious for them and in fact won the night you found me. That may be him, refitted."

"You all right about bashing him in?"

"I am."

Pat Kelly strode up, trailed by not only Bruce but Terry Greely. Both hybrids listened with inhuman attention while Damian repeated his information.

Pat turned to Terry. "Set up a cordon around the park. Be discreet, mind. We don't want to tip anyone off. Let folks in, but try not to let anyone from the competitors' camps out."

He looked at Damian. "Good luck, son. We're all behind you."

"Thank you, sir."

"And good work identifying the buggers. I hope we can stop them hurting any more of us."

"I am happy to be of help."

Once Kelly and Greely left, Lionel forced himself to turn to Damian. "You know, if you want to withdraw now—well, the trap's been sprung. And you could still testify."

Bruce groaned. "Pull out? What about our reputation?"

"I care far more about Damian's welfare than our reputation."

But Damian drew himself up. "I want to fight. I have a score to settle."

"Good man!" Bruce declared. "Lionel, come with me. They're about to draw numbers for the matchups. Oh, and you have to paste this on him."

He thrust a placard emblazoned with a number into Lionel's hands.

"Forty-nine?" Lionel questioned. "But there aren't that many competitors."

Bruce shrugged. "Some kind of unique description. Pulverizer, over there, got HO."

"All right. Let's go see about the matchups."

A large board had been erected, and the number draw was already underway beneath it when Bruce and

Lionel arrived. Two human police officers were in charge. As he walked up, Lionel thought he saw Williams, there ahead of him, pass paper money to one of the officers.

"Hey!" he cried.

No one paid him any heed. Voices resounded on every side, and bets were still being taken.

The officer who had received the payment drew the numbers while the other placed them on the board in opposing rows.

"First match—Dillon Steam Works' Fenian, number 17, against Bob and Ed's Boiler Repair's Smasher, description KO!"

Smasher looked like one of the cruder models. Bob and Ed's was a small shop, like Lionel's. They'd built their model with oversized fists.

"Second match—Boyd Steam Cabs' Shifter, marked CME, against Monroe Castings' Crusher, number 422. Third match, Starr and Williams' Pulverizer, HO, against"—there came a dramatic pause—"Tom Elliot's Destroyer, 888."

The crowd gave a loud, disappointed hiss.

"Fourth round, Pike's Steam Repair's Pile Driver, 49, against Erie Steel Works' Exterminator, 77."

Lionel shuddered. Exterminator looked like one of the better entries, and so it should be. The fellows at Erie Steel Works knew their stuff.

"Boiler Maker Union's entry, Incinerator, will go in the next round."

"That's an advantage for them," Bruce complained in Lionel's ear. "He won't be all bashed about."

"And Starr and Williams got an easy opponent in the first round," Lionel returned. "Easier than ours."

Bruce narrowed his eyes. "I think Pile Driver can take Exterminator. Don't you?"

Lionel shrugged. He felt quietly confident in the unit he'd built, but he was no braggart. "I think he can best anyone." He eyed Pulverizer unhappily. "I'm just not sure about the damages."

"The rules!" roared Harold Carruthers from Burke's Gym, Master of Ceremonies. "Rounds will continue until one competitor is knocked down and cannot get up, or its fire is extinguished. Or until one unit is damaged too heavily to continue the fight. Other than that, no holds are barred. No weapon is excluded. Competitors may change weapons during a bout if they can reach their seconds to retrieve them."

Everyone there—machine and human alike—now listened as if spellbound. Even the birds stopped chirping.

"I shall declare the winner of a bout, and that unit will advance to the next round, until only one victor is left.

"Repairs are allowed to be performed between rounds, but only with used parts, and machines may not leave the park and teams may not send runners to fetch parts not brought in with them."

Lionel exchanged a look with Bruce. Had he brought everything he might need?

Carruthers held up a beefy hand. "Above all! If at any time before, during, or after this competition it's discovered that new parts have been used in the construction or repair of these units, the competitor and its makers shall be disqualified. Are there any questions?"

"Yeah!" A member of the Boiler Maker's Union

called out. "How long between rounds?"

"Fifteen minutes."

"And," asked Bob of Bob and Ed's Repair, "can we work on our units during other matches?"

"You can tinker, yes."

That, Lionel told himself, was what he did best.

"First match begins in ten minutes," Carruthers cried. "If a competitor is not here on time, it forfeits its match."

"Come on," Bruce said. "Our man's waiting."

Pile Driver had been inspected on arrival for new components. Of course, not everything could be seen during a cursory inspection. Lionel wondered if anybody would be foolish enough to cheat.

As if the thought prompted his presence, a man stepped out to bar their way. Elijah Starr made two of Lionel in girth and carried himself with the cockiness Lionel lacked. He had small, careful eyes of muddy brown that examined Lionel with cold dispassion.

"Pike, is it?" he demanded.

Starr was well aware of Lionel's identity. If he wanted to play games, Lionel would go along with it. "Yeah."

"Heard a lot about you, we have, over at S. and W."

"Heard a lot about you too," Lionel returned with some weight.

"Hear you're in tight with the hybrids." Starr's lip curled back like that of a pit bull. "And the cops."

"I wouldn't say that."

"I would. See, maybe there's something you don't understand, pal. We're a brotherhood, us men."

"We?"

"Us fellows who work with steam. The mechanics, the tinkers. We're supposed to stand together no matter what."

"Are we? But I think sometimes the *what* matters."

"That's where you're wrong. We need to have each other's backs. That means not running off to the damned hybrid coppers like a little girl snitch, and not making stupid accusations."

Bruce bristled. "Now you listen here—"

Lionel touched him on the arm. "Men like us," he repeated, "are supposed to love what we do, and care about the units we repair. Not abuse them for a buck."

A brutal expression crossed Starr's face. "Not a buck, pal. A whole cartload of bucks. And they're God-damned machines. It's not like we're hurting anyone."

"You've worked on 'em, rebuilt 'em, and you can say that?"

"Oh, so you're one of those," Starr sneered.

"One of what?"

Starr's cold eyes turned cunning. "I hear your lady friend thinks the mechanicals deserve a *church*. She's a sympathizer. Does that mean you are too?"

Lionel's heart skipped a beat. "You leave her out of it."

"Listen to me, pal—nothing gets left out of it here, today. The prize money would have been enough, but then you went and made it personal."

Abruptly, he seemed to change the subject. "What do you think of the competition?"

"Pretty good."

"Maybe. Some of 'em. But the way I've got it figured, it's between our entry and yours. And it's time for some payback."

Lionel grew cold with anger. "I agree completely."

"Well, get ready. We're going to Pulverize you."

Chapter Thirty-Three

"He's on to us," Lionel told Bruce unhappily as they walked back to Damian's station. "He knows I'm working with the police. I only wish he hadn't dragged Sofia into it."

For the first time, he felt glad Sofia remained so angry with him that she'd stayed away.

Only—she hadn't. When they arrived at their station, he saw that Verna, complete with her pink dress and a matching hat, stood toe to toe with the towering Damian. And behind her, doing her best to appear casual, stood Sofia.

"Aw, hell," Lionel said.

Bruce gave him a sharp glance. "You two have a falling out, did ye?"

"Yes."

"Why is that, then?"

"I'm not sure." Sickness churned in Lionel's gut. He didn't need this, not now. He needed to concentrate on Damian.

"Women, eh? Still and all, it will be good for Pile Driver to have his lady here."

"No doubt." And he, Lionel should have a word with Sofia, warn her that Elijah Starr had made veiled threats.

Bad enough he had to watch Pile Driver go into harm's way. The idea of Sofia at risk made him sweat.

With that thought in mind, he walked up to her and, far more abruptly than he intended, said, "I thought you weren't coming."

She turned those incredible dark eyes on him. When she did, he could feel all the ties that had been formed between them during their intimate moments together come alive inside him, stir, and tighten. For an instant he went breathless.

But the look she gave him held more anger than welcome. "I couldn't keep Verna away. And I didn't want to let her come alone."

"It's not safe for you to be here." Lionel glanced around the park, which now teemed with humans and mechanicals. Onlookers were supposed to remain behind a cordon, but clearly were not. Even Verna and Sofia had got through.

Where was Pat Kelly? Lionel would feel safer leaving Sofia in his care.

But amid the milling and roiling bodies, he couldn't see the tall hybrid anywhere.

"Look," he told Sofia, "the matches are about to begin. I'll have to be ringside."

"Don't let me stop you."

"Stay near Bruce, all right? Promise me?"

Sofia gave him a searching glance. "Why?"

"Because things here could turn ugly. Not everybody in this crowd's a supporter. All right? Remember what happened when you were struck in the head."

She nodded. Then she touched his hand. "Good luck. Really." Some of the anger left her face. "I know how hard you've worked."

"Thanks." He kissed her quick and hard, and hoped

it would tell her what he felt inside.

****

"He asked me to marry him, if he wins the contest."

"What?" Lost in her own thoughts, Sofia almost failed to heed Verna's words. The feel of Lionel's lips on hers. The scent of him surrounding her. How much she wanted him.

"Dammit has asked me to marry him."

Sofia stopped walking and stared at her steam unit, as a hundred emotions tumbled through her. Gladness emerged on top. "That's wonderful. Did you say yes?"

"I did."

"Oh, Verna, I'm so happy for you."

"He must first survive the bout. If he does not survive, he thinks the chances of a successful repair are remote."

"We've been over this. Lionel can fix him."

"I do hope so. Dammit does not seem certain. And while I must admit he looks very, very impressive with his hammer, I also harbor some doubt."

"Well, don't doubt him. A woman," Sofia drew a breath, "must believe in the man she loves."

But did she believe in Lionel? In the clever competence of his mind, yes, and the quick skill in his hands. Of his feelings for her, she remained less certain.

He'd kissed her. That had been for luck. The way another man might rub a rabbit's foot.

"I think," Verna said, "Dammit is the most impressive of all the entries."

"I agree."

"He is one hot piece of metal."

For the first time in days, Sofia dissolved in

laughter.

****

Sofia and Verna had trouble getting close enough to see, because the ring area had observers three deep or more on all sides. Shoulders blocked the way, and elbows protruded like bony fencing. When Sofia tried to push her way through, she received nothing but glares and a few curse words.

Finally, a group of mechanicals, seeing Verna, let them in. The match had already started by then. The big, green mechanical fought with what some observers nearby called a shillelagh and had a near-hysterical group of supporters who shouted encouragement in a foreign tongue.

His opponent, a somewhat smaller unit of pale gray worked metal, had oversized fists which he used to good advantage, being able to extend the length of his arms and reach the top of the green unit's head.

The match proved appalling and hideously noisy. Sofia wanted to leave after the first few minutes, longed to slip back into the crowd, but Verna watched avidly, and the bout continued for what seemed like an age.

Standing with her hands over her ears, Sofia decided that, had they been human, both combatants would now be dead. Was that what attracted people to these matches? The units could take so much more punishment than humans.

In the end, even though the top of his head was beaten to a flattened surface, the green unit toppled the other with a blow from his club that leveled him onto his back. He lay in a gout of steam and failed to get up again.

"Oh, my," Verna said.

The green unit lifted its arms in victory.

"The unit wearing the shamrock won, but can he fight in the next round? Look at his head," Sofia protested.

"Fortunately for him, his brain center is not located in his head but lower down. He will fight on. Perhaps not fortunate for my Dammit. He is a tough opponent."

Sofia glanced at her friend. Didn't it affect her to see metal skin bashed and torn this way? If that were Lionel going into the ring…

But, no. She couldn't let herself think about it. She still loved the man, though obviously he didn't love her in return. And she retained some pride, didn't she?

The green unit's supporters had gone wild. Apparently they'd bet heavily on him to advance. He was escorted from the ring, and the next two competitors went in.

"When is Dammit's bout?" Verna asked.

"I'm not sure."

By the time the second bout, between a competitor who had a grin like the grille on a steamcab and one armed with an oversized metal wrench, Sofia had a screaming headache. The grinning unit defeated the other by knocking both its arms off—something that seemed to please the crowd very much and had them chanting, "Shif-ter! Shif-ter!" The grinning unit then knocked the other onto his side with a spectacular crash that disconnected his head.

While he was being carted away, Lionel appeared at Sofia's side.

"Well, what do you think?"

So he had remembered she existed! "It's awful. All that damage and—and waste."

He looked surprised. "I think most the damage we've seen can be repaired."

Verna asked Lionel, "When does Dammit fight?"

"After the next round." Suddenly Lionel looked nervous. "If you have good thoughts, think 'em."

"I will be praying hard," Verna assured him.

Lionel turned back to Sofia. "I'm glad you came. I was afraid—well, you were done with me."

Sofia assured herself she was done with him, quite done, though it might not be a good idea to announce it now when he needed all his confidence.

"We'll talk later," she said.

He looked uneasy, but nodded. "You'll be here after the last match? You'll wait?"

"I'm sure Verna will want to stay and see her hero." In whatever condition he might be.

"If he is her hero. He'd have to win for that."

"No." Sofia looked Lionel in the eye. "That's where you're wrong. She'll love him no matter what."

The next bout started then, between a unit called Destroyer and a huge, wide unit called Pulverizer. Lionel, who remained beside them for the duration of the match, seemed terribly interested in Pulverizer, who, so it was announced, had been put up by Starr and Williams Repair.

The men who'd damaged and stolen from Verna. Those who were probably behind the horrible fight pits.

Sofia leveled a look of malevolence upon the unit, which fought with gusto. Despite her ill will, it defeated its opponent handily with a series of blows so brutal even the crowd seemed shocked.

"I do not like him," Verna declared after Pulverizer won by bashing in his opponent's thorax and causing his boiler to burst. Hot water gushed forth, and his opponent fell to his knees in his own liquid.

"He's brutal. This whole thing is brutal."

"I have to go—we're next." Before Sofia could react, Lionel placed another of those hard kisses on her lips. "For luck."

And he left, the crowd closing back up as if he'd never been there.

Chapter Thirty-Four

Pile Driver looked magnificent when he rolled out into the ring. His shoulders gleamed, and his chain mail glittered in the sun. The sledgehammer gripped in his fist appeared a formidable weapon.

His opponent, Exterminator, was taller, but not as wide. Even to Sofia's inexperienced eyes he looked well made. He had a short sword in his hand.

"Oh, my, oh, my, oh, my," Verna moaned.

As if he heard her, though he couldn't possibly, Pile Driver swept the crowd with his black marble eyes, which now carried a reddish gleam. When he located Verna, he gave her a slight bow, and the crowd went wild.

"Oh!" Verna puffed a little gout of steam.

Sofia squeezed her eyes shut. She didn't want to watch this. She couldn't bear to see Damian get hurt.

"Remember the rules," the master of ceremonies called. "Let the fight begin!"

It didn't help Sofia to have her eyes shut, after all. She could hear far too much, and that made her need to see what was happening. Her eyes flew open, and she stood clutching Verna's arm.

Lionel, with Bruce at his side, stood almost directly opposite her and Verna. She caught glimpses of him through the battling units, his expression stark, his eyes wide.

The match seemed to happen far too slowly, as if the units swam through molasses, yet with horrendous violence. Sofia hadn't enjoyed the first two matches. This experience proved ten times more terrible with a personal acquaintance of one of the combatants.

Though she had to admit Pile Driver seemed to be getting the better of his opponent. Ponderous and powerful, he moved in on Intimidator, delivering first one blow and then another with his long-handled hammer. Intimidator retaliated with his sword, repeatedly scratching Pile Driver's surface, but couldn't get through the draped chain mail to hit anything vital. Pile Driver's eyes began to glow deep red as his steam built up. He looked unstoppable.

The crowd now hollered so deafeningly, their voices muted the clang of the combat. Red-faced men waved arms and betting slips, and Sofia's very soul quailed.

Oh, why had she come?

Pile Driver delivered a hammer blow that dented Intimidator's left shoulder, and one that staved in the side of the unit's face. Intimidator responded by stabbing at Pile Driver's elbow joints where, presumably, he was most vulnerable, before going for his neck. The tip of the sword skittered off, though Pile Driver paused for a moment as if he felt pain.

Impossible. He didn't, he couldn't. But Sofia began to pray.

Pile Driver jerked back into motion and delivered a blow that knocked Intimidator's arm off from the elbow down. The screams around Sofia became deafening. Intimidator responded with a sword thrust that got in under Pile Driver's chain mail and pierced his thorax.

A howl arose. Intimidator withdrew his blade and a gout of steam came with it from Pile Driver's chest.

Verna made a sound like a kettle boiling, and Lionel, across the way, appeared ready to climb into the ring, his face a rictus of horror.

Pile Driver paused again. He seemed to gather himself before he shunted his hammer from his right hand to his left, and swung at Intimidator's other arm—the one with the sword. With a loud crash, the arm fell off and, in one mighty hammer blow, Pile Driver smashed the top of Intimidator's head flat.

Intimidator tottered. With his face now nothing more than crumpled, eyeless metal, he swayed violently before Pile Driver sent him over backward, employing a nudge to his chest. The unit crashed down, and his fire went out in a gout of mingled smoke and steam.

Steam still flowed from Pile Driver's thorax, a steady wisp barely discernable in the sunlight.

The master of ceremonies declared him victor, and Lionel rushed inside the ring to his side.

"Damaged, he is damaged," Verna lamented.

"Yes."

"Do you think he will be able to continue fighting?"

Fairly sickened by what she'd seen, Sofia asked, "Do you want him to?"

"Yes. He wants to prove our worth. He wants to prove he has the right to choose his fate. He wants to stop others being forced to do this against their will."

Lionel escorted Pile Driver from the ring. Intimidator's owners gathered around to collect him.

"Come on," Sofia told Verna. "Let's go see about Damian's damages."

****

"How bad is it?" Lionel asked Damian the question even as he unfastened the chain mail curtain that draped over Damian's shoulder. He needed to get a better look at the damaged thorax. Lionel's heart beat double time, and he had to force his fingers to steady as he examined the wound that pierced Pile Driver's skin.

"I am still functional."

The hybrids had all gathered round, screening Pile Driver from other eyes. Pile Driver was clearly their champion, and Lionel wondered madly if they'd bet on him.

Bruce came pushing in. "Well, laddie? Can he make the next round?"

"I don't know yet," Lionel replied. "I have to see how bad this rupture is."

"I am still retaining water," Pile Driver said. "The stroke was above my water line."

Lionel ran his hand over the pierced outer skin and pictured what lay beneath. He frowned. "It won't be, once I refill you. Which I'll need to do before the next match." He looked into the unit's face. "Plus, with a steam leak, you'll be down on power. Depending on who you have to face—"

"I have fought with much worse injuries in the past. I am still able."

Regretfully, Lionel said, "I don't know if I can let you continue on. A breached boiler has a risk of explosion under pressure—like during a match. If that happens, well, it will probably destroy your impulse center. I can't guarantee I could put you back together."

Pile Driver stared into Lionel's eyes. "I have faith in you."

Pat Kelly pushed in between the other hybrids and close beside them. "How bad is it?"

"That stroke went through three levels of sheeting—the outer skin, the reinforcement, and the boiler itself."

"How big is the split?"

Looking into Kelly's very human green eyes, Lionel needed to remind himself this individual, too, possessed a boiler deep in his barrel chest.

"Not bad," Pile Driver replied. "Only the tip of the blade has penetrated. The steam makes it look worse than it is."

Kelly leveled a look at Pile Driver. "Sounds like you want to fight on."

"Yes, sir, I very much do."

"Good man. Just remember, we're going to need you to testify against Starr and Williams in court after all's said and done, for that's where this is going. I have three other units and two humans standing by who've recognized our Mr. Starr from the fight pits. It just took getting the right people together at the right time. But Pile Driver, you'll be our star witness."

Lionel stirred. "Can a steam unit testify in court?"

"It's never been done," Kelly admitted. "But life's full of firsts."

Lionel looked at Pile Driver. "Maybe you should withdraw from the match. You're far too important to risk."

Pile Driver lifted his head. "I am glad to be important. But I fight for revenge. If I am to be given a choice—"

"Of course you have a choice."

"I will fight on."

"Good for you," Kelly said, and clapped Pile Driver on the arm. "There'll be a break now before the second rounds begin. Those will be tough matches too. Lionel, I suggest you complete what repairs you can, as quick as you can. We're hoping to make an arrest at the end of the competition."

"What charges?" Lionel asked.

"Well, that's the thing. There's actually no law against abuse of steam units. There is, however, a law stating we must be paid. Were you ever paid for your matches, my man?"

"No, sir," Pile Driver said.

"You can arrest Starr for that?" Lionel asked.

"Aye, and then there is the wee matter of theft. They've been stealing components, from units like your Verna, to keep their fighters going."

"Doesn't seem like much," Lionel said.

"Baby steps, sir. I swear we'll get them. Above all, they mustn't be allowed to profit here today." Kelly looked at Pile Driver. "Right?"

"You are right, sir." Pile Driver fixed his dark, marble gaze on Lionel. "Master Lionel, can you patch me up?"

"I have boiler patch. It might not hold up."

"Or it just might, sir. It just might."

The fifteen minutes between rounds seemed to pass by far too quickly. By the time Lionel completed his hasty repairs, Verna had arrived and stood distracting Pile Driver while Lionel replaced his outer skin.

"Here," he bade Bruce, "help me drape the chain mail."

A dozen hands, many of them belonging to hybrids, reached out to help. Pile Driver's head was rubbed—for luck, the hybrids said. Lionel no longer even paused to question the fact that hybrid steam units believed in luck.

These were people, supporters. Friends. It didn't matter if they were shiny steel or pockmarked by rust, or if the steel lay beneath a layer of living skin. He couldn't deny they cared.

And what about Sofia? Did she care too? She'd accompanied Verna to their assigned area, but hung back, keeping away from him. Had he killed any feelings she had for him, lost all that warmth and intimacy?

Ah, hell. He couldn't think about it now. He had to get Damian through this in one piece.

The only untested unit was now Incinerator, the coal black model put up by the Boiler Makers' Union. Bruce, who'd run off to view the standings, came bustling back to say Incinerator would go next, against Fenian.

Lionel glanced at Pile Driver. He stood toe to toe with Verna, his hands cradling her upper arms, and they spoke softly together.

Of what?

He couldn't tell, but he could guess by the tenderness between them. Suddenly he ached for Sofia. He wanted that connection with her, to ground himself in her presence.

But this wasn't the place or the time. Already, he could hear the howls from where Incinerator and Fenian's match was set to begin.

There'd be an opportunity to talk to Sofia later. He hoped.

Chapter Thirty-Five

In the end, Lionel just couldn't keep from walking over to watch the match between Incinerator and Fenian. The thunderous crashes coming from the ring, as well as the howls of the crowd, drew him against his will.

The Boiler Makers Union—as might be expected—had done a magnificent job with their entry. He came equipped with a rattling roar, and emitted a gout of steam each time he let loose with it. Fenian, however—the wounds from his previous match pounded out—proved a dynamo with his shillelagh. By the time Lionel got there, Incinerator had several significant dents in his outer skin, and Fenian kept trying to go for the unit's knees.

Smart, as well as powerful.

It proved a close match. When Fenian finally went down in a cloud of billowing steam, the Irishmen in the crowd cried foul, saying it wasn't fair for their man to have to fight a fresh unit.

The boiler makers responded, saying if their entry wasn't durable enough to fight a second round, he shouldn't be in the competition. An impromptu fist fight broke out inside the ring and added considerably to the entertainment until members of the Irish Squad broke it up.

The next rounds were then announced. To make it

fair, Incinerator would face Pile Driver in the final match of that round, in order to give the boiler makers a chance to make repairs. Before that, Shifter would fight Pulverizer.

Lionel hurried back to give Pile Driver the word. Verna and Sofia had gone to observe, he supposed.

"If Pulverizer wins his match," Pile Driver said, "and I win mine, I will then face him in the final round."

"Yes."

"Master Lionel, I do think I know him. I suspect he is one of the units I fought before, who defeated me. He is the one the promoters favored. Now I will have to try and defeat him."

"Are you all right with that?"

"I will do what I must. For the Greater Good."

"How's your leak?" Lionel had topped him up and, in essence, now held his breath.

"Not presently leaking."

"That's good." Of course, Pile Driver had to get through two more bouts to win. A good bash to the thorax could open that wound up again or cause it to rupture completely. Not, Lionel told himself hastily, that they had to win. Pile Driver had already accomplished the purpose for which he'd been built. Arrests would be made and the value of older units proven. In fact, it would be best to keep Pile Driver in one piece, to make sure he could testify.

"Look," Lionel said, stepping closer to the huge unit. "You and I both know how risky it is for you to keep fighting. If you want to withdraw—"

"Withdraw?"

"There'd be no shame in it. You could have a life

with Verna."

"I want a life with Verna."

"Well, then." Despite his offer, Lionel's heart sank. What did that say about him?

"I also want revenge against those who made us fight. You are a good man, Master Lionel. You let me choose. They are not good men."

"You'll still have your revenge, in court."

"I want to stand above their defeated unit."

"I have to admit, I'd like that too."

A howl went up from the ring.

Lionel said, "How about a compromise? If Shifter beats Pulverizer, we call it quits and let Incinerator fight him for the championship."

Pile Drive contemplated that. "Agreed."

"And in any case, Damian, it's been an honor knowing you. Best of luck."

"Thank you, sir."

Another roar went up from the ring. The crowd began to chant, "Pulverizer! Pulverizer!" as the fatal cloud of steam arose in a cloud.

Lionel's gaze met Damian's.

"That did not take long," Pile Driver said. "Let us see if I can dispose of Incinerator as handily."

The match between Pile Driver and Incinerator took far longer than the one before it, and had Lionel sweating bullets. The big, black unit came in hard from the start, emitting its gnawing rattle and puffing dark steam. Powerful and ponderous, he clearly intended to take Pile Driver out one limb at a time.

Despite his weight and injured boiler, Pile Driver had speed as well as experience in the ring, both of which now stood him in good stead. He managed to sidestep most of Incinerator's blows, though he took glancing hits to both shoulders, that left dents. And he swung his hammer in great, swooping arcs that did damage with nearly every blow.

When, in the end, he took out first one of Incinerator's knees and then the other, both cheers and groans came from the onlookers. It had not taken long for the crowd to choose favorites. Incinerator tottered on his broken knees until Pile Driver delivered an almost delicate blow to the back of his head. Incinerator went down with a great gush of boiler water, and the master of ceremonies announced Pile Driver's victory.

"Final round will be between Pile Driver and Pulverizer for the championship! Fifteen minutes for repairs."

"Good job," Lionel told Pile Driver, whose eyes had returned to black after glowing red through most the match. "You managed to avoid even one blow to your thorax."

"Yes. Pulverizer is smarter. He will go for me there."

"Good luck in the next match, Pike." A voice spoke from behind Lionel. He spun around and saw Elijah Starr, sleeves rolled up and a grease-stained shop apron covering his barrel chest. The man wore a smile that revealed gapped teeth, like little tombstones, but it didn't reach his cold eyes. "Looks like it's us fighting out the championship."

"Yeah."

"Hope your unit knows how to fight dirty. Mine does."

"He'll do whatever he needs to in order to win."

"You've built a good unit." Starr eyed Pile Driver

up and down. "But I'm sure it has its weaknesses."

"Everybody does."

"That's so true." The tombstone smile grew wider. "And we don't like squealers. Like I told you before, men like us should stick together. But lily-livered pansies go running to the police."

"We don't like abusers," Lionel returned steadily.

"Abusers? Of what? Roosters fight, dogs fight, men fight. You can see how these people love it. Machines are just machines."

"You can work with 'em and say that?"

"You can work with 'em and not say it? I've taken these units apart and put them back together again. Just like a steamcar."

"Not quite."

"That's right, I forgot—you're one of those," Starr accused.

"Those?"

"Touchy-feely. I suppose you think they warrant a damned church, too. Well, Pike, let me tell you something. If they have a god, I'm him—'cause I hold the power of life and death over my units, right?"

"If that's how you look at it."

"And I'll tell you another thing. You'd better prepare yourself. Because we always go for that weak spot."

"My man's ready to fight," Lionel insisted.

"It damn well better be."

****

"Excuse me, miss. Have you placed a bet yet on the final round?"

Sofia turned to face a quiet man in a flat cap, who looked vaguely familiar. Of medium height and with a thin, ordinary face, she couldn't immediately say why he set her inner alarm bells ringing.

She and Verna, who said she couldn't bear to watch, had fallen back to Pile Driver's staging area, quiet now as everyone attended his match with Incinerator. A few minutes ago, a great cry had gone up. At this point, Sofia just wanted all the crashing, hollering, and violence to end, but she knew Verna would want to visit Damian after the match.

If he won—or even more likely, if he didn't.

"No," she told the man. Had she seen him when she took Verna in for repairs? "I'm not betting."

"You must be the only one here who isn't. Who's your favorite? Pile Driver just defeated Incinerator, there. I can let you in on some good odds."

"No, thank you."

"Final round's between the two favorites—Pile Driver and Pulverizer. Which one are you backing?"

Verna rolled to Sofia's shoulder. Sofia expected a request from her to bet. Instead, Verna hissed into her ear, "He is Lloyd Williams, from Pulverizer's crew."

Sofia understood the warning bells then. She glanced around, looking for Lionel, Bruce, or a stray member of the Irish Squad, but all remained at the ring. Two large brutes, however, did lurk at a short distance, pretending not to watch them.

Her alarm turned to fear. "No. Please leave us alone."

The man—Williams—stepped closer. "'Fraid not. Your man's Lionel Pike, right?"

Her man. She might be angry with him, and hurt, but yes, he was her man, for good or ill.

But she wasn't about to admit it to Williams.

Instead she looked him in the eye and said, "I asked you to leave us alone."

"Sorry, miss, I can't do that. I have to insist you come along with me."

"What? Why?"

"Pike needs to learn a lesson."

"I'll scream."

"You won't." Williams seized Sofia brutally, even as his two men closed in. Verna moved closer also, and began to fight, delivering a lucky blow to Williams' cheekbone.

He thrust Sofia into the hands of one of his men before locating Verna's off switch, and powering her down.

Terrified, Sofia stared into his cold, gray eyes. How could this happen in the middle of a crush of people, and no one noticed?

"Come with us," Williams repeated. "Don't struggle, and no one will get hurt."

Chapter Thirty-Six

"Where is Verna?" Pile Driver asked as Lionel hastily peeled back his layers to inspect the patch on his boiler. Without any direct hits to the thorax, it had held. But a fine, hairline crack marked the surface of the dried tar, and he asked himself if he should apply another layer.

The fifteen minutes allowed for repair wouldn't give it long to dry. A good move, or a bad one? Starr had no doubt caught those wisps of steam in the first round and, as he said, Pulverizer would go for that vulnerable spot.

"Let me get you fastened back down," he said. "I want to move that chain mail so it provides more protection across this area."

"I thought she would be waiting here to congratulate me."

"Eh? Yeah, well they're probably watching from farther off. Giving us some room here. We don't have much time."

"I would like to see her before the final bout."

"I know, pal."

"I am fighting for her, for justice, and for our future together."

"You just hold those thoughts. They're inspiring." Lionel gestured to one of the hybrids, who came hurrying. "Can you help me reposition this chain mail?"

Shifted and refastened, Lionel hoped the mail would help deflect any direct blows. He checked all Pile Driver's vitals. His fire burned low and steady with intense, yellow-white flame. His water stood at the correct level, and would unfortunately be enough to put that fire out if he went down.

"One minute." The signal came in relay around the ring.

Lionel looked his man in the face. "You ready for this?"

Pile Driver's eyes began to glow. "I am."

"Then go get 'im. Remember, you're fighting for all those units who didn't have a say and were destroyed."

"And for Verna."

"And for Verna."

A great cry went up when Pile Driver entered the ring. It came mostly from the voice boxes of the hybrids and automatons, but plenty of humans hollered for him too, and a wave of awe struck Lionel, making him feel humble. What had he done, in building Pile Driver? Perhaps built a few bridges also? Lowered a few barriers? Created a hero for whom all could root?

He hoped so. He also hoped, for far less altruistic reasons, Pile Driver might win this match. The police would move in and make their arrests, the case would go to trial, and it would all be over.

He swept the crowd, searching for Sofia. When this was over, he would need to talk with her, try to make matters between them right. She felt angry now, but could she stay that way?

He wanted her in his life.

Yet he didn't see her anywhere, and he decided she

and Verna must be lost back in the crush.

Then the match started, and he couldn't think at all.

Pile Driver looked fine, wading in against his opponent, swinging his hammer. His eyes glowed with banked fire, and he emitted confidence. Pulverizer also put on a grand show, the dents inflicted by his last opponent casting glints of light. Starr had exchanged his former weapon, a bludgeon, for an axe which he held almost loosely, blunt side forward.

As if he'd use it to pulverize.

An axe, Lionel knew, made a particularly dangerous weapon against a steam automaton. But he hoped Pile Driver's mail coat would deflect most of the strokes.

They went in flailing at each other, axe against hammer, and the noise in the crowd immediately ramped up to deafening. Lionel heard whines and mechanical rasps, clicks, and rumbles, as well as human voices, and a chill raced up his spine.

Pile Driver understood why he fought: The value of those in this crowd, constructed of components as old as his own; The right to choose his fate, and to survive.

Blam, blam, blam. So far, each blow had been blocked, axe on hammer and hammer on axe. Slowly at first, and then more swiftly, the two units pressed their attack, and the clamor of it increased.

Pulverizer assumed a crouch and swung his axe, blade circling. Pile Driver might be quick, but Pulverizer's ponderous bulk made him hard to push over.

A flurry, and a clanging strike. Pulverizer's left arm broke at the elbow, and hung useless, connected by merely a few wires. The crowd's approval and dissent rose to the skies.

Pulverizer grunted and huffed. He assumed a crouch and swung his axe—blade forward this time—for Pile Driver's knees.

The edge of the blade connected and skittered off the heavy plating, leaving a deep gouge on the right side. Lionel knew the units did not feel pain as such—not physical pain anyway. But experiencing destruction on the wheel would be shattering.

Pile Driver shifted his hammer into his left hand and struck for Pulverizer's unhinged arm. The unit sprang back just in time to avoid more than a glancing blow.

Raising the hammer in both hands, Pile Driver swung for Pulverizer's head. Lesson learned, Pulverizer did not try to crouch again.

The pace of the battle increased. The crowd now verged on the edge of hysteria, and Lionel felt pressed on all sides. He hoped Sofia remained safe.

Clang, clang, clang!

One of Pulverizer's blows, blade foremost, dodged Pile Driver's hammer and struck the chain mail, just over the place where Lionel had laid the patch. For the first time, Pile Driver faltered and stumbled backward, his wheels jerking.

Lionel strained his eyes for any hint of steam. Elijah Starr, across the ring, hollered something to his unit. Pulverizer struck again.

And again.

Three blows, the axe delivered before Pile Driver successfully blocked any more. By then, the mail hung split, rent clear through.

And the metal beneath?

The units moved too quickly. Lionel could not see. But he feared his eye did catch a faint wisp of steam coming from Pile Driver's chest.

Another blow, and he might rupture.

Lionel knew that. Elijah Starr would know it also. He hollered at his unit again.

Starr was bent not only on victory but destruction.

And upon what was Pile Driver now bent? He must realize his own danger, but his eyes glowed red and, since his single stumble, he advanced courageously.

The hammer came up and, winking wickedly in the bright sunlight, swung sideways in a big, thunderous arc, connecting with Pulverizer's left shoulder and staving it in. The joint held, but the impact crumped the mechanism and froze the arm in place, as if fused.

Pulverizer retaliated with a solid strike from the axe—gripped in his other hand—that connected with Pile Driver's skin just above the patched seam and rattled Pile Driver from head to wheels. Steam began to gush from his thorax, clear for all to see.

But he kept moving.

The crowd reacted with roars of disapproval, or perhaps approbation. Once more, Pile Driver transferred the hammer from hand to hand. Those who had seen his last bout expected him to go after Pulverizer's other arm in an attempt to disable him. Pulverizer himself might well have expected it, for he rolled backward a foot as if preparing to maneuver out of the way.

He never had the chance. Instead, Pile Driver swung the hammer overhead and, with steam pouring from his chest as from an overheated steam kettle, brought it crashing down on the top of Pulverizer's head.

The crowd went silent for an instant. Everyone stared as Pulverizer's head crumpled. A second blow crunched the metal down over his eyes, a third drove him to his knees, and flattened his head to a quarter of its former height.

Pile Driver did not stop there. Both hands now swinging the hammer, eyes glowing red and with steam pouring from his chest, he pounded his opponent down to the ground.

Shock kept the onlookers silent one moment longer, before a mighty cheer arose. It came first from the voice boxes of the assembled automatons, echoed by not a few human throats. The uncanny howl of it exploded up from the park and floated out over the river.

To be heard in Canada, no doubt.

Lionel snapped to life even as the master of ceremonies raised one of Pile Driver's arms and declared him the winner. Quickly, he ducked into the ring. How long could his man keep operating while losing steam at such a rate?

But Pile Driver surprised everyone by lifting his voice.

"Hear me, please!" One by one, the other voices fell silent. Everyone stilled in place. "I would like to say, I did not fight this match for glory or to entertain any of you. I fought for a Cause and a Greater Good.

"I hope my victory here today will prove that older steam units such as I, those so often tossed aside in our world, declared useless and scrapped, have value. We have worth!"

Another cheer arose, this one strictly from the automatons, a rattling wail.

"I hope this will put an end to forced matches, to units being poorly maintained, patched, and driven into slavery. To abuse that makes them nothing more than this."

Dramatically, he gestured with his hammer to the pile of rubble that had been Pulverizer.

"Let this end the dirty matches in back alleys and warehouses, where there is no hope."

A chill chased its way over Lionel's skin, and he broke out in a sweat. At that instant, he knew Sofia had been right. If automatons could hope, they could believe. In whatever they chose.

Pile Driver threw down his hammer. "I will never fight again, never help to destroy one of my fellows or further the fortunes of our oppressors. Let this city be a place of freedom for all!"

He staggered then. The light in his eyes dimmed, and the amount of steam issuing from his chest abruptly lessened.

The steamies in the crowd stared in respectful silence. Some of the humans appeared angry. Elijah Starr, still across the way, looked like he could spit nails.

Disregarding them all, Lionel ran to his man.

"You're a hero," he told Damian. "A God-damned, first-class hero."

Damian regarded him, and two sparks of light flared in his eyes before quickly dying away.

"I wanted them to hear. We are so seldom heard."

"Well, you're heard now. How bad is it?"

"No power left. Shutting—"

The unit stilled. Laying his palm against the hot metal, Lionel said, "It's all right. We'll get you back to the shop. I'll have you up and running again in no time."

Focused on Damian, Lionel barely noticed that members of the Irish Squad, in uniform and accompanied by regular police, had moved in. But he heard Starr's bellow and looked up in time to see him surrounded and being arrested. He began to struggle, and chaos broke out.

Pat Kelly and Bruce appeared at Lionel's side.

"Help me get Damian away out of here," Lionel asked. "I don't want him damaged any further."

"That might be difficult, laddie." Bruce said. "A full-on fist fight's broken out."

Yet as they slowly rolled Pile Driver from the ring, leaving behind a trail of boiling water like blood, a phalanx of automatons formed around them. Mostly old units, rusted and worn, they coalesced into a living shield that moved with him, protecting their hero and his helpers. Their bodies took every glancing blow until they reached the staging area, and the wagon.

Lionel had hoped Sofia and Verna might be there. They weren't, but Lionel told himself he couldn't worry about that now. Hopefully they'd seen the victory and Sofia had possessed the sense to get them out of harm's way.

Not until they loaded Pile Driver and prepared to leave did Terry Greely come running.

"Mr. Pike, you must see this."

"Not now, Terry. I need to get Pile Driver to safety."

"Sir, I must insist."

Impatient, Lionel followed where the hybrid led, Pat Kelly coming along behind. They found her lying amid a small group of automatons, her pink dress soiled with hot water, and her painted eyes staring at the sky.

Heart in his mouth, Lionel hunkered down beside her.

"Verna? Are you with us?"

"Sir," Terry said, "I don't think she's operational."

Ignoring him, Lionel asked Verna, "Where's Sofia?"

No reply.

"Verna, has something happened to her?"

Desperate, Lionel looked around. This area of the park had already cleared out. No sign of anyone who might have seen a single woman.

A single woman who meant everything to him.

"Damn it," he muttered as his fear ramped up considerably.

Terry suggested, "Perhaps Miss Gregory returned home."

"Perhaps." But she wouldn't leave Verna. Not voluntarily.

Pat said, "Best to take Miss Verna back to the shop with Pile Driver. If you can get her running, she may be able to tell you what's happened."

"Yes."

"Terry, lad, go ask them to bring the wagon round here, aye?"

Terry pelted off. A hand touched Lionel's shoulder. "Sir, it will be all right."

But fear had Lionel by the throat, and he couldn't agree.

Chapter Thirty-Seven

Even before they got Verna restarted, back at the shop, Lionel feared the worst. By then, word came that though Elijah Starr and some of his known organizers had been arrested, Lloyd Williams was nowhere to be found. And the sick feeling in the pit of Lionel's stomach told him the truth.

They placed Damian on the main workbench and Verna on the other, where Lionel at once began checking her over. Immediately, he found she'd been powered down. It was the work of an instant to set her on her feet and restart her.

The first word to issue from her voice box came in a wail that raised the hairs all over Lionel's body.

"Taken!"

"Calm down, Verna, tell me."

"Miss Sofia!"

"Where is she?"

Distraught, the unit could only wail. Everyone there, human and metal alike, stood about helplessly; a weeping woman, it seemed, was a weeping woman.

At last Lionel seized hold of her. "Verna, you have to tell me what happened to Sofia. Is she in danger?"

"Men. Humans. Took her."

"Where? When? During the match?"

"Yes, at the park. She was very frightened."

"Who?"

"Mr. Williams, from where I was taken for repair."

The sickness in Lionel's gut spread outward. He should have known. Hell, he had known.

"Where? Where did he take her?"

"I do not know. they powered me down."

"I will put out the word on the street." Pat Kelly sprang into action. "There are a thousand eyes. Someone will have seen."

"It's my fault." Verna wept. "I should have defended her."

"No." Lionel tasted bitter gall in his mouth. "It's my fault." Why hadn't he kept her close to him, made sure she was safe?

"You sit tight," Pat told him. "Get our hero's repairs underway."

"Dammit!" Verna cried, and rolled to the workbench. "What happened to him?"

"He won the match." Lionel joined her. And yes, that had been of major importance at the time. Now, it paled in comparison with Sofia, alone and frightened in the hands of his enemies. "He has a ruptured boiler."

"Can you save him, Master Lionel?"

"I believe I can."

One had to keep believing.

****

The gag smelled like oil and tasted worse. It had been made out of a shop rag like the ones Lionel used, and tied far too tightly around Sofia's head. Lloyd Williams—he with the cold eyes—had forced it upon her before bundling her into the back of a delivery wagon, like so much cargo.

She choked back waves of sickness caused by the motion of the vehicle, and fought to control her terror.

To think she'd brought her damaged steam unit to this man's shop, had trusted him—at least in the beginning—with Verna's welfare. Was that what had touched off all this trouble? Tossed around in the back of the wagon, she tried to think. Starr and Williams had stolen Verna's components to feed their underground fight pit. She'd met Lionel, and—

Lionel.

At the thought of him, an ache started, one of such proportions it dwarfed even the fear. Despite her anger over the way he'd treated her, she loved him. She believed she'd loved him through at least one other life, and those bonds had strengthened between them when they made love. They held still, and she longed for him. She probably always would.

However long she lived—and at the moment, she feared for the length of her continued existence.

She wept silently, and gained a whole set of bruises, tossed as the wagon traversed a number of streets. At length the vehicle slowed. A man's voice called instructions, and the wheels rumbled over an uneven surface.

When the back doors of the enclosed wagon opened, Sofia saw Williams and one of the hulking brutes who'd helped seize her. She stiffened in every limb as they dragged her out with little regard to her welfare. She left some skin on the bed of the wagon, and heard her dress tear.

"Get her inside, then set up the pit."

Pit? Sofia's heart pounded so she barely heard the words. They appeared to be in a good-sized open area steeped in gloom, through which she was dragged by the brute, without ceremony. Thrust into a tiny office furnished with a rough wooden desk and chair, she sought for inner strength.

"Tie her up."

Williams had followed Sofia and the brute into the room. He now dragged the workman's cap from his head and, even as Sofia was bullied into the chair and tied there, he stared her in the face.

What terrifying eyes he had! Sofia had seen more warmth in the molded metal visage of an automaton.

"So," Williams said, "you belong to Pike, do you?"

Sofia's every protective instinct sprang to life. She shook her head. "No."

"Don't lie to me. You won't like the consequences."

"I barely know him. I took my unit to him for repair, the one you failed to fix—"

Williams stepped forward and, with calm deliberation, struck Sofia across the face. The slap jerked her head around, and the sharp sting brought involuntary tears to her eyes.

"I said, don't lie."

"It's the truth." Sofia could feel her lip swelling. "Ours is a business relationship."

"So he paid you to tumble him?"

The blood drained from Sofia's face. "I don't understand what you mean."

"You know, I hate women like you. You look all prissy and play at being the lady, but then you lie. He spent at least one night at your house. Am I supposed to believe you sat around drinking tea?"

"Why do you care?"

"He ratted us out to the police. To the hybrids. He's a God-damned steam lover. There's a brotherhood among the tinkers in this city. He betrayed it."

"He's working for the good of—"

Williams raised his hand and Sofia silenced.

"For the good of a few piles of metal and wire, screws and rusted wheels? Don't make me laugh."

"They're more than that," Sofia said, arguing it against her better judgment.

"They're really not, you know. I've taken them apart—down to nothing. I've seen."

"And what happens when you take us apart? What are we, when it comes down to it?"

"Bones and lumps of flesh and blood vessels, I'd imagine. Might be interesting to find out. Maybe I'll take you apart, and see. Bit by bit."

Sofia closed her eyes against that image, but it endured. "What do you want?"

"Pike ruined a lucrative business of ours. So now I've taken something he values."

"He doesn't. Value me, I mean. He doesn't love me." Sofia stated it with absolute conviction. "He cares more about his steam units."

"Well, that's a damn shame."

"Why? Just let me go. I'll say nothing."

"You'll go running to those God-damned hybrids. They've already arrested my partner. I'll have my revenge before they come for me."

He called through the open door behind him, into the bigger room beyond. "Set up the pit as quick as you can. Are the units here?"

That word again—pit. Sofia's blood chilled to ice.

When Williams turned back to her, she said, "Pit? You're going to make me fight?"

"No, my dear, not you." His face cracked in a stern

smile. "You're merely going to watch."

Chapter Thirty-Eight

"Here, Mr. Lionel. It's a note. For you."

"Eh?" Lionel stared without real comprehension at the folded piece of paper Sammy held out to him. They'd been back at the shop for an hour, and he'd spent that time talking to members of the Irish Squad and trying to figure out where Sofia might be. A thousand scenarios flashed through his head—everything from her suffering abuse at Williams' hands to outright murder.

Pat Kelly, still present and directing the search along with Bruce, stepped to Lionel's side as he snatched the paper from Sammy's hand and unfolded it.

It read, *A tit for a tat. You took from me, now I've taken from you. If you want to save her, come to William and Babcock Streets. Wait there. Come alone or you'll never find her.*

"What does it say, sir?" Pat asked.

Shocked to silence, Lionel handed over the note.

"Ah, hell," Kelly said after he'd scanned it. He tipped his head to one side as if consulting his artificial intelligence. "William and Babcock, on the East Side. Nothing there but the stockyards and train yard."

"They've grabbed her and must have her at a warehouse or some such place," Bruce said, reading the note in turn, while pain and horror crashed through Lionel in waves.

Bruce turned to him. "Laddie, you can't go. It's a trap. They'll get you alone and murder you."

"If I don't go, he'll murder her. Drop her body somewhere. I'll never know."

And Sofia would never know how he felt about her. He hadn't known himself, till this moment. But the prospect of losing her—of any harm coming to her, especially on his account—felt like a blow to the gut from Pile Driver's hammer.

Verna rolled over to him. "Is that about my mistress? Can you find her?"

Pat said, "Lionel, I do not think it a good idea for you to respond to this missive. Let us move in and observe the site. The regular police are already involved. They'll set up a cordon and do a search."

"He said to come alone." Lionel glanced through the open door of the shop. Already, the alley grew dark as the spring day progressed to a close.

Had he the courage for this? Had he the courage to try and live without Sofia?

No.

"I have to go," he told Kelly. "Alone."

Kelly's expression, of course, didn't change but he emitted dissatisfaction with Lionel's decision.

"I think—"

"Pat, if something happens to her because of me, how will I live with it?"

Pat relented. "I understand. I have a wife. Give me a minute to talk to the lads and formulate a plan."

Kelly moved off. Lionel found himself looking into Verna's painted eyes.

"Bring her back to me, sir, please," the unit begged. "She—"

"I know, Verna, she's your best friend."

"She is my *sister*. Please bring her home."

"Verna, I'll do my best."

****

He took a cab to William and Babcock Streets, disembarked, and walked up William a short distance. By then, the early dark held sway over the area, which opened out into the vast rifts of the stockyards, backed by a branch of the Erie Railroad line. Some traffic rattled by down William, but the homes across the street seemed eerily quiet and well-shuttered. The paving bricks gleamed in the light of the streetlamps.

He knew members of the Irish Squad must be nearby, though he couldn't see them. Pat had promised as much. They meant to surround the area, and the place—possibly one of these houses or a warehouse beyond—where Sofia was being held.

Before anything could go too badly wrong, they would close in and make some arrests.

"We'll grab Williams," Pat assured him, "and rescue Miss Sofia."

But no one was here. Nothing moved except a crumpled piece of newsprint, driven along by a rogue breeze. Not sure what to do, Lionel turned in a slow circle.

A steam-powered panel truck careened out of Henrick Street and screeched to a halt behind him. Before he could turn, three men leaped out. A sack was drawn over his head, and he was bundled into the back of the truck, a large and heavy body sitting atop him. The back doors slammed. The truck jerked into rapid motion.

Damn, damn, damn. A trap. Well, he'd known that,

and so had Kelly. But he'd swallowed the hook to this trap whole. Had the Irish Squad seen what happened? Would they follow?

The sack smelled like moldy onions, and his captor's weight on his chest made it hard to breathe. He tried to keep track of the turns the truck made and thought they were headed east, but after a dozen or more turns he became convinced they were merely driving in circles.

Trying to lose any followers.

Steady on, he told himself. Wherever you're going, Sofia will be there. That's all that matters.

The wheels of the van rumbled over a very rough surface before it stopped. Hard hands hauled Lionel up and, nearly smothered, he was dragged into a building.

The place smelled like sand and rust and, above all, heated metal, a scent with which Lionel was well acquainted. With his elbows clamped to his sides by his captor, he stumbled forward. The sack was pulled from his head.

A pit.

It had been roughly made amid a wreck of a building—a disused factory floor, perhaps—cordoned with rope and full of smoothed sand. But Lionel could not mistake it for anything but what it was, a killing ground.

What the hell? Alarm mixed with the apprehension in his gut. Why a pit? One secreted away, no less, where no one could find it.

Like the impromptu venues where the steamies had been forced to fight.

And, where was Williams? Lionel turned and, upon the thought, saw the man come striding out from the back of the building. Was that where he had Sofia hidden?

With a flood of determination, he demanded, "Where is she?"

Williams' thin face remained inscrutable, but malice shone in his eyes. "Oh, she's here. For the show."

"What show?"

Williams swept the ring with an arm. "Here. And now. A private presentation for my satisfaction, and hers."

"Where is she?" Lionel demanded again. "If you've hurt her—"

"If I've hurt her, what?"

"I'll make you pay."

Williams swept him with a look. "Big talk, from a man of your ilk."

What was that supposed to mean?

"Nobody's going to disturb us here, Pike. No one knows where you are—or she is."

Lionel didn't bother to argue it.

"We have some time. Not long, but enough. Will you fight for her?"

"Fight?"

"Battle. Gladiators, like back in the park."

"Fight who, you? Sure."

Williams laughed softly. "Not me. My fighters. Carl, bring 'em in."

A unit rolled up from the shadows. It looked like one of the repaired fighters Lionel had seen the night he'd met Damian, constructed from old parts, reinforced with steel plating.

Behind it came another. And another.

Lionel grunted. "You can't be serious."

"Oh, I am. They say three's a lucky number. It will be, for you, if you can defeat each of my fighters in turn. In the ring."

"You're crazy."

"Quite possibly. But I'm giving you a fair chance to win the freedom of your lady. If you win all three matches, the two of you walk out of here, free and clear."

Big if.

"Are you scared? Then you don't deserve her. Maybe I'll keep her. She'd be better off with me."

Lionel's throat went dry, and he eyed the three units, each puffing steam.

He was no fighter. He was a steam tinker, plain and simple. As such, did he possess any skills that might help him win?

His eyes narrowed. "What weapons?"

"Each of them fights with what it's holding. You can choose from anything here." Williams indicated a pile of weapons to one side.

"Anything here?"

Williams gave a sly smile. "Sure."

"Then I accept your challenge. But I want to see Sofia first and make sure she's all right."

Williams signaled to someone behind Lionel. "Bring her in."

Lionel spun. Through a doorway in back came two goons carrying a wooden chair. To the chair was strapped Sofia.

Her hair had partially fallen down and lay in bright ginger locks all around her shoulders. Her dress had torn at shoulder and knee. Her eyes looked huge, dark and burning with anguish. A gag covered her mouth.

Emotions rose inside Lionel, a staggering wave of anger, outrage, and love. He'd never considered himself an emotional man. He tended to keep his head and rely on his common sense. But now he felt as close to a wild man as he'd ever been.

"Sofia," he said hoarsely. "Have they hurt you? Are you—"

"She can't answer you, Pike."

"I'll get you out of here, I swear." Lionel wanted to tell her how he loved her, how he'd do anything for her. Sacrifice himself, if necessary.

His spine stiffened. Williams no doubt meant to demoralize him, but by showing him Sofia, helpless and frightened, all he'd done was lend Lionel steel.

He turned to Williams. "Let's do this." He'd forgotten the Irish Squad. He'd dismissed, for the moment, chances of rescue. There remained only his love for Sofia, and the skill in his hands.

Sofia made a strangled sound around the gag, one of protest. But Williams gave Lionel a look of satisfaction.

"Choose your weapon, Pike."

"I want that." Lionel pointed to a hefty crowbar propped against the wall.

"That's not a weapon, it's a tool."

"My tools are my weapons."

Did a flash of alarm pass through Williams' eyes? If so, it faded swiftly.

To his men he called, "Keep watch outside. If you see anyone, give the signal."

Lionel directed a long look at Sofia, one he hoped conveyed everything he felt. Then he walked over and picked up the crowbar.

****

The weapon felt good in Lionel's hand—sure and strong. He balanced it across his palm as the first of the three units rolled into the ring and faced him, its wheels making lines in the freshly spread sand. Sand on the floor of a pit, as Lionel knew, absorbed blood—or other bodily fluids such as hot water and oil.

He thrust all that out of his mind and regarded his opponent. It stood about six feet high and was no polished specimen such as had appeared at the match in the park. Instead, it appeared to have been put together from other wrecked units. Part of its torso shone sculpted silver, and part was rusted plate.

But even from where he stood, Lionel could see that the outer skin had been reinforced. The unit made two of Lionel in width and probably tripled him in weight.

Don't think about that either. Don't think about Sofia or how frightened she must be, or whether Williams will really let her go.

Concentrate.

With a squeak and a rumble, the unit rolled toward him, a club in its hand. Lionel remained where he was, heart pounding and thoughts racing. How fast could the unit maneuver? For certain, he, Lionel, could not withstand a blow.

The unit raised its club as it came, rattling like a wall of iron. For an instant, doubt paralyzed Lionel's brain. *I'm no warrior. But at this moment in time, I'm all she has.*

When the unit bore down on him, he sidestepped and delivered a blow from the crowbar that resounded on the unit's right arm and made Lionel clench his teeth. Not pretty, no, but the unit had strength.

It absorbed the blow and turned more quickly than Lionel expected. Lionel saw the club raise again, and his mind screamed at him.

Think. Think!

He turned the crowbar in his hands and, using the curved end, slashed at the unit's wrist above the hand holding the club. He heard a snap, and the weapon froze in place.

He might be no warrior, but he certainly knew what powered a steamie's appendages.

And how to take one apart.

Chapter Thirty-Nine

Sofia gasped through the filthy gag when the terrible unit's wrist gave way and the hand holding the club froze in place. Her terror—much of which centered on her own plight—had shifted as soon as she saw Lionel and amped impossibly when he ducked into the ring and she grasped what must happen next.

She'd wanted to protest, to call to him, but the damned gag prevented it. She could only watch and pray.

Verna prayed frequently. Sofia, not so much since her parents died and her life began to crumble. But now, belief came surging.

All for Lionel.

Only ten people occupied the room for this private match, including Williams and his muscle. No screaming crowd like at the park. The crash of metal on metal sounded terribly loud as Lionel, moving lightly on his feet, struck the disarmed unit again and again, smashing the joints, breaking both knees and, eventually, sending it onto its back with a mighty push.

Feet braced and the long iron bar in his hands, he turned to face Williams, who stood beside Sofia's chair. Lionel's dark hair tumbled over his forehead, and his eyes glowed.

He looked…magnificent.

"One!" he called.

Sofia glanced at Williams and wondered what he thought. His expression remained closed, his face inscrutable.

And then—

Sofia wanted to cry out, for the next opponent approached from behind Lionel. It carried a spear—a spear!—and rolled on silent wheels.

She wailed around the gag and tried to signal Lionel with her eyes. He turned.

Just as a thrust of the spear took him in the right shoulder.

He raised the bar in his hands and the tip of the spear disengaged from his flesh. He shuffled to one side as the unit—this one much taller than the first—stabbed at him again.

The first opponent still lay where he had fallen, blocking Lionel's retreat. He bounded up and over the defeated automaton and used his bar to knock the spear away.

Red blossomed high on the sleeve of his shirt. He gave no sign he felt any pain.

What if she, Sofia, had to sit here, helpless, and watch him killed? What would happen after? Williams couldn't possibly let her go, having witnessed this.

If Lionel died, did she care what happened to her?

No.

She remembered her dreams of running through darkened streets to find the man she loved, how desperate she'd felt. This felt like that, only she couldn't run.

The unit with the silent wheels had to roll around his comrade, and Lionel swiftly made use of the obstruction to keep a distance from it. He too circled, swinging his bar before the unit drew near enough for him to attack. Dealing a number of measured blows, he dented the metal, which flaked off in rust.

The unit apparently lacked the imagination to change direction and attempt another flank attack. Instead, it struck across its fallen fellow, the barbed tip of the spear coming heart-stoppingly close to Lionel's flesh.

Just in time, Lionel reversed the bar in his hands. Using the curved end, he hooked the spear out of the unit's hand before disabling it by stabbing it in both shoulders. A final blow to the neck joint set its head askew. It powered down.

A victory, but it had come at a price. Blood soaked the arm of Lionel's shirt, and he breathed heavily, sweat standing out all over his face.

But he called, "Two."

Williams did not look happy. He signaled to his men and called, "Get those units out of there."

Lionel stood with his chest heaving while the two defeated units were towed out, the downed unit leaving a dark stain in the sand.

He had to be tired and in pain, but it didn't show. He still stood balanced lightly, the bar clenched in the hand of his injured arm.

Sofia felt his gaze touch her like an assurance, or a caress.

She turned her gaze on the third and final unit, which stood unmoving at the entrance to the pit. It looked huge in the glaring light, and wore a kind of metal jacket over its wide thorax. Following her gaze, Lionel also turned and eyed it. Sofia wondered if he already searched out its weak spots.

If it had any.

"This is Smasher," Williams called when the other units had been towed away. "It's triple reinforced and made out of components from units that have survived many a match. I don't think you'll defeat this one so easily."

Lionel stared as the unit jerked into movement and started toward him. It came with a squeal of its wheels and, Sofia saw to her wonder, bore no weapon.

Nothing to knock out of its hands. How did it fight?

Lionel backed off a few steps, perhaps contemplating the same question. The answer came swiftly enough. When it came within reach, Smasher raised both arms. With a sound like that of a coiled spring letting go, its oversized fists extended, becoming solid steel weapons.

Lionel barely reacted in time. He stumbled back, nearly losing his footing, and Williams made a sound of satisfaction.

"This one," he said to Sofia almost pleasantly, "won't break."

So it seemed. Lionel, regaining his balance, began to aim crashing blows upon first one fist and then the other, to no avail. Backing, ever backing, he retreated around the pit while Smasher punched out with those fists, which withdrew and drove forward like pistons, seemingly inexorable.

The breath caught in Sofia's throat. If one of those blows, just one, landed—

No sooner had that thought appeared in her mind than one did. The fist—nearly as big as Lionel's head—took him in the left shoulder and sent him spinning.

He fell to one knee. The iron bar dropped from his hands.

For an instant he remained there, as the unit advanced, and Sofia screamed in her head.

Get up! Up!

If that fist connected with Lionel's skull, it would be over. No human could endure such a blow.

Lionel scrabbled blindly for the bar. He picked it up, but instead of running, he dropped to one side before the unit's advance, and rolled. The terrible fist raised high, and descended upon him.

No!

Williams' men all murmured now, and Williams lifted onto the toes of his boots in eagerness. Sofia wanted to close her eyes. She didn't want to see that blow connect, but to save her life she couldn't look away.

Prone on his back, Lionel twisted out from under the descending fist and swung the bar, all in one motion. The bar crashed into the automaton's left wheel assembly, and the wheels exploded. The unit listed to its left, and Lionel sprang nimbly to his feet behind it.

Crash, crash. The bar connected with the backs of the unit's legs at the knees. Wobbling perilously, it shuffled and turned. It raised its fist in a mighty blur.

Lionel tried to respond by hooking the extender just behind the fist, but his injured right arm failed him. He stumbled back and shifted the bar to his left hand.

Sofia expected him to swing for the unit's extended arm—no doubt everyone there did. Instead, he swung the bar in a great, shining arc that terminated at the unit's neck joint. Its head flew off and rattled across the sand to a sudden stop.

The observers exclaimed. Lionel drew a breath and, deliberately now, attacked the body of the unit, delivering a series of blows so hard they lifted his feet off the sand. Striking joint after joint in turn, he knocked the downed unit apart.

Then he turned and, the bar still in his hands, faced Williams. His eyes glowed, and his breath came in gasps, but he looked steady and competent, the way he did back in the shop.

"Well, Williams? You a man of your word?"

Williams looked at the rubble that had once been his unit.

"Let her go," Lionel demanded.

"I don't think so. Get him!"

Even as Sofia's heart protested, all hell broke loose. Williams' men jerked into motion, and Lionel leaped directly at Williams, the bar raised high in his hands. The factory doors broke open, and in poured a small army of police officers.

Sofia, her head spinning, recognized Pat Kelly and other members of the Irish Squad. Two of them dragged Lionel off Williams, with some difficulty, and took Williams in charge. Others swiftly corralled Williams' men.

"Mr. Pike, see to your lady," Pat Kelly urged.

And then Lionel was there, hunkered down in front of Sofia's chair, plucking at the knot on the gag with desperate fingers. His eyes gazed into hers ardently.

"Are you all right? Sofia?"

The gag came away. Sofia had barely enough time to drag in a breath before he kissed her.

A kiss in a thousand. The kiss of a champion who'd won his lady's freedom. The kiss of a steam tinker who'd found his way home.

The strength of it crested inside Sofia, a powerful wave. On the heels of the stark terror, it overwhelmed her. Tears flooded her eyes and, when he drew away, spilled over.

"Oh, sweetheart," he said, "I'm so sorry." He put his arms around her, chair and all, and just held her. It was one of the best feelings she'd ever known.

"Mr. Pike?" Pat Kelly appeared at their sides. "Is Miss Gregory hurt?"

Sofia answered somehow, through her emotion. "I'm all right."

"Then," Pat sounded kind, "I suggest Mr. Pike untie you."

"I'm really sorry." Lionel kissed the tears from Sofia's cheeks. "I wasn't thinking. And—my hand's a bit numb."

In the end, Pat picked apart Sofia's bonds, using his mechanical fingers that looked so very human. But it was on Lionel she leaned when the police officers escorted them from the building.

"How did you manage to turn up when you did?" Lionel asked Kelly on their way out.

"We followed you."

"But how? That truck took more turns than a corkscrew."

"Terry, there, ran after the truck."

"Ran? But," Lionel protested, "it was blocks and blocks."

"Sometimes, Mr. Pike, it pays to be steam-powered. After he located you, it took a while to relay a message to the rest of us, and for the squad to move into position. We arrived in time to see the end of your match."

"Oh." Lionel raised a brow. "I'm sorry you had to witness that—me smashing apart that unit, I mean."

"Not at all, sir. I thought you went about it very intelligently. I surmise that sometimes it is also good to be a steam tinker. Anyway, what will a man not do, for the woman he loves?"

Chapter Forty

Lionel did his best to persuade the police officers to take them home. They refused, Pat Kelly citing the wound to Lionel's shoulder and his blood-soaked sleeve.

He also mentioned the ordeal through which Sofia had passed, and her need to visit the hospital, where they were instead conveyed.

Sofia could not rightly say how she felt. Shattered, as when she awoke from one of her dreams set in Riga. Euphoric over the kiss Lionel had given her. Full of pride for him, and thrilled by the way he'd fought for her. So relieved at it being over, she could barely speak.

In fact, on the way to the hospital, they didn't speak much, though Pat Kelly's words played over and over in Sofia's mind. *What will a man not do for the woman he loves?*

But, did Lionel love her? That kiss seemed to argue so, but he'd never said it, and she couldn't bring herself to ask.

A woman shouldn't have to ask.

At the hospital, they were separated. Sofia, asked to wait in a barren room, was at length seen by a long-faced physician who pronounced her suffering from bruises and a few scrapes taken in the back of Williams' wagon, as well as nervous exhaustion. He gave her a packet of sleeping powders and told her to go home.

Fortunately, Verna arrived then, escorted by a member of the Irish Squad called Tim Murphy. Murphy told the physician they'd wait a while until Lionel's condition was ascertained. Verna attempted to comfort Sofia.

"What was Mr. Lionel's condition when he went in to see the physician?"

"I'm not sure." Sofia mopped tears from her face, using the heels of her palms. The darned tears just kept coming without her permission. "Not good. He was stabbed in the shoulder during the combat, by this terrible, rusty spear. There was so much blood."

Verna produced a handkerchief from the pocket of her pink dress and wiped Sofia's face tenderly. "He is young and strong. I am sure he will recover."

"Are you?"

"Oh, yes."

"How is Damian?"

Verna hesitated. "He too is strong. But damaged. The partial rupture of his boiler has made it necessary to place him on standby. The hybrids have been topping him up regularly."

"That's good of them."

"Yes, it is. But a temporary measure, I fear. Dammit will need Master Lionel in order to recover fully."

"Oh, dear." The damned tears started up again.

"Do not worry, Miss Sofia. I have prayed on it. I am assured all will be well."

Sofia stared. "You're assured?"

"Yes, miss."

"By whom?" Sofia could not help but ask.

"Why, by the powers to which I pray. The steam that rushes through me, the water that produces it, the fire in my belly, and the metal that holds it all."

"Oh!"

"I believe, Miss Sofia. And you must believe also."

Sofia stared into Verna's painted eyes. "Must I?"

"Yes. Because you love Master Lionel just as I love Dammit. And because—"

Here, Verna paused.

Sofia caught her breath. "Yes?"

Softly, Verna concluded, "I rather think *love* is the reason for everything."

****

Bruce Buchanan arrived some short while later, crashing into the waiting room with Sammy in tow. Buchanan looked harried and overwrought, and his fair hair stood on end.

"Miss Gregory, what is the word? How is our hero?"

Distraught, Sofia answered, "I have no idea. I've been waiting and waiting."

"It's all right, my dearie. I'm here now, and I'll get some answers."

He stormed off in search of a nurse. Sammy sat on the edge of a chair and gazed at Sofia unhappily.

"Mr. Lionel is gonna be all right, isn't he?"

"I hope so, Sammy."

"Only—he's looked after me, see, for a long while now. Took me in off the streets, and gave me a place to live. Don't know where I'd be if something happened to him. Back on the street, probably."

"I'm sure that won't happen."

Sammy's customary tough exterior crumbled a bit.

"I guess I haven't always done right by him, in return. Gave him a hard time about my chores and going to school."

"I think he understands how you feel."

"If he gets better, I'll do better."

A brief silence fell, after which Sammy slanted a look at Sofia and asked, "So the hybrids said he fought in the pit."

"Yes."

"Three steam units."

"Yes."

"Destroyed them all."

"He did."

"Shiiit," Sammy drew the word out. "Who'd have thought? Speared in the shoulder, Terry Greely said. But he'll get better, right?"

Sofia thought of the blood soaking through Lionel's shirt. "I hope so. But if there are any prayers in you, Sammy, better start saying them."

****

A physician turned up some two hours later and escorted Sofia to the ward where Lionel had been placed. Bruce Buchanan, who'd returned from his inquiries quite frustrated, had spent the intervening time pacing the waiting room. He nevertheless sent her off to see Lionel on her own, with a gruff, "Give the laddie our best, eh, lass?"

Even Verna stayed behind, so Sofia was alone, save for the physician, when she entered the shadowy ward. Night had long since fallen. Most of the patients appeared to be asleep, including Lionel, when she reached him.

The physician placed a chair beside the bed and

said, "We had to perform surgery to repair his shoulder and clear it of metal fragments. I'm hopeful he will, in time, regain full use of it."

"Hope is a good thing."

The physician gave her an odd look and left. Sofia sat on the chair, wondering what good a useless arm might be to a steam tinker, and looked at the man she loved.

The lamps in the ward burned low; she couldn't see him very well. But his face looked pale against the pillow, his eyelashes stark and black. That unruly hair of his still tumbled over his forehead, and white bandaging swathed his upper right arm.

She longed to brush the hair back from his face but hesitated to disturb his rest. So she touched him with her eyes, sat back, and let the terrible terror drain from her body, at last.

How long she sat there, and dozed, she couldn't say. She came awake to the movements of a nurse, checking the patients along the far wall, and found Lionel also awake, watching her in turn.

"Hello," she said, with rising delight.

He smiled. Suddenly, everything in Sofia's world came right.

She slid off the chair and, with a glance for the nurse, onto the edge of his bed.

"You all right?" he asked huskily.

She nodded, not trusting her voice.

He tried to reach for her, and winced.

"Your arm—" she croaked.

He flexed the shoulder and looked unhappy. "Will I be able to use it?"

"The physician hopes so. And we have Verna's

prayers on our side."

"Verna's prayers?"

"She believes, apparently, in fire and water, metal and steam."

"That's all right, then." His smile flashed again. "I believe in those things too."

"Lionel, how can I ever thank you for what you did? Fighting to save me that way."

"It's what a man does for—"

The nurse bustled up. "I'm sorry, miss. Visitors aren't allowed to sit on the patients' beds." The nurse glared at Sofia. "You shouldn't even be here after hours. The patient needs to rest."

Sofia stood. "The physician showed me in."

"You can have ten minutes. But you must stay in the chair."

Sofia and Lionel exchanged a guilty look.

After the nurse left, Sofia said, "Bruce and Sammy are here, out in the waiting room. Both of them are very worried. Sammy says he's sorry for the hard time he's given you, and I think he means to change for the better."

Lionel snorted. "Won't last. But it's a nice thought."

"Everyone's quite concerned for you. Verna and the members of the Irish Squad." Sofia hesitated. "Does it hurt very much?"

"Like a bugger."

"I'm sorry."

"So long as they got Williams and can close his operation down, it's worth it. No units should be pitted against each other that way, ever again. It didn't feel nice, beating those steamies apart. I can only imagine them forced to attack each other."

"Oh, yes." Sofia's heart fell.

And here she'd been thinking he fought for her.

A small silence ensued before Sofia asked, "Do you think you can mend Damian?"

"Oh, yeah—if I have the use of my hand."

"Do you think he and Verna will marry?"

"I know it's what he wants."

"He can live with us, at my house, if he likes. I've plenty of room."

"That's a kind offer."

"Not really. Verna's like family." Sofia swallowed. "Oh, Lionel, that contest—I was so scared."

"Me too," Lionel admitted. "And I was angry and indignant and determined that bastard wouldn't win. I knew I couldn't beat his units using force. But I also knew where they were most vulnerable."

"You were magnificent."

"You think so?"

Sofia nodded solemnly.

"You know," Lionel said, "I'd feel a lot better if you were here on the bed, close to me."

"The nurse said—"

"Hang the nurse. She's gone."

Sofia returned to the side of the bed, where she perched carefully. The pose didn't last long. Lionel's good arm snaked out and drew her down to him.

The kiss seared all Sofia's senses, burned away her fear, weariness, and even some of her doubt. Lionel took his time with it, tangling the fingers of his good hand in her hair before wrapping her tight, snuggled against him.

He tucked her face into the crook of his neck, and

bliss flooded through her.

"That's better," he said.

It was. Better than dreams of panicked flight through dark streets. Better than watching him risk his life.

Yet the doubt still nibbled at her mind. Had he fought for her? Or for the greater good?

"We are going to get in such trouble," she whispered, "when that nurse comes back."

"You think I'm afraid of her? Like I said, some things are just worth the risk."

Chapter Forty-One

A crowd awaited them when they disembarked from the steamcab and walked down the alley. Bruce Buchanan, dressed in his finest, rushed forward to meet them, with Sammy close behind. A string of others followed, seeming to unwind from the shop door—hybrids and a veritable conglomeration of ancient mechanicals.

Not till they entered the shop did Lionel, with Sofia close at his side, see Damian—or Dammit as he supposed he should call him. Dented and leaking steam at an alarming rate, the unit was up and running, and stood near the main workbench, with Verna next to him. A banner, nailed across the rear wall of the shop read, *Welcome home!*

Lionel shot a look at Sofia. "Did you know about this?"

She gave a small smile. "Yes."

"It's why you insisted on coming here, rather than your house, isn't it?" That had surprised him. Last time he'd been released from the hospital, she'd taken him home and pampered him. Things had become heated and erotic.

He'd been looking forward to that.

She returned his look. "They've all been so worried about you. Besides, I wasn't sure—"

Bruce seized Lionel's hand—fortunately the good

one—and pumped it. "Come in, come in, laddie. Fellows, bring forward the chair."

Chair? Lionel experienced a prick of alarm. Two of the mechanicals shuffled forward with an upholstered arm chair, adorned with a bow.

"So you can recuperate with all your friends around ye," Bruce explained. "You can be the master tinker and give the rest of us instructions till you're all healed up. We know there's a lot to do, but you ha' many willing volunteers.

"How kind," Lionel managed, thinking he'd rather recuperate all alone, except for Sofia.

"Nothing to concern you," Bruce went on. "Sammy here will be your runner. Even your meals are being provided by certain of the wives."

"Very considerate." Lionel, truly touched, looked around at all the beaming—and impassive—faces. "Thank you all," he said. "A man truly never had better friends."

One of the mechanicals eased Lionel into the chair even as Terry Greely stepped forward. "Pat couldn't be here, Mr. Pike, but he wanted me to tell you both Elijah Starr and Lloyd Williams are in custody and headed for prosecution. Dammit, here, has been able to make a full witness statement, and we have one from Miss Gregory also. It's all in hand."

"That's good." Lionel felt strange seated in the chair, a bit like a king on a throne. "So long as the forced fights stop, and steam units have a say in how they're used, in future."

Terry tipped his head. "I believe the forced fights will stop. Whether a discarded mechanical can earn sufficient, er, autonomy to decide its own destiny, is another matter and, I suspect, will have to be legislated."

"That will take time," Bruce chimed in. "But we can back politicians who lean toward justice for all. I know that's where my money will be."

He snapped his fingers. "Speaking of money, I nearly forgot. You and Dammit won the pot at the gladiator competition. A thousand dollars. I'm ready to pay out whenever you are."

"Yeah?" Lionel slanted a look at Dammit. "I imagine we should split the prize then, half for you and half for me."

Dammit puffed a cloud of steam. "You would share with me?"

"Fair's fair, right? Besides, you're getting married. Five hundred dollars should be enough to set up a household."

Sofia jerked violently, and Lionel looked at her. "Just in case the newlyweds want a place of their own."

"Oh, yes. Right."

"Thank you, sir."

"You've very welcome. And, call me Lionel."

Dammit turned to Verna. "I will be able to buy you that new face you wanted. Though I must admit I find you lovely the way you are."

"Oh, Dammit!"

Everyone laughed. Well, almost everyone.

Lionel looked at Mordred. Was the ancient unit upset by what was taking place between Verna and Dammit? Would he accept their marriage as equably as he'd accepted all else that happened during his years with Lionel? And how did you soothe the feelings of a steamie?

He gestured Mordred closer. "Doing all right, Mordred?"

"Yes, sir. I am very happy to have you home."

"You're still my right-hand man, you know, whatever else happens."

Mordred sighed out a little puff of steam. "I am glad to hear it."

"And you know, I was thinking—as a project, maybe you and I should try to rebuild Wendy. I know we scabbed quite a few vital parts off her, but it would make a challenge, wouldn't it?"

Mordred raised his head interestedly. "A very fine challenge, sir."

"I'm glad you like the idea. Meanwhile, if you could manage to clear everyone out of here, I'd like a word alone with Miss Gregory."

"Of course, Master Lionel."

"And you'd better call me Lionel too. No masters here."

"Yes, Lionel. Thank you." The unit turned to the room at large. "If you will all follow me out back, there is what I understand to be called 'a spread' laid on. And Lionel would like a few minutes alone with his lady."

Grinning, the guests all filed out the back, Sammy the last to leave.

The boy cast a look at Sofia before he went. "I guess you're not so bad. I think I can live with it."

"I should hope so," Lionel said.

****

Sofia watched the lad go thoughtfully. "Whatever did Sammy mean by that?" she asked when the shop emptied out.

"I can't imagine."

"Would you like me to bring you a plate?"

"No, Sofia. I'm not exactly feeble, and my legs work just fine."

Sofia, fighting the damned tears that seemed to come so easily these days, tried to change the subject. "Poor Mordred. It must be hard for him, seeing Dammit and Verna together."

"I mean what I told him—I'll rebuild Wendy as soon as I can. Maybe the two of them can find happiness together."

"That would be wonderful."

"Everybody deserves a chance at love."

"You believe so?"

"I do—whether metal or flesh and blood. It's like the whole religion question. I figure it doesn't matter so much what you believe, but that you do believe."

Sofia's heart swelled with emotion. Before she could speak, he asked, "Will you do something for me?"

"Of course."

He held out his hand. "Come here."

As soon as she drew near enough, he caught her fingers and drew her down across his knees.

"Lionel! I'll hurt you."

"You won't. I told you, I'm not feeble. Everything but my shoulder works just fine."

Sofia gazed into his eyes and suddenly felt as if the bottom had fallen out of her world. She had nowhere to stand except upon her desire for him, and his for her.

"Why did you send everyone away?"

"I wanted to ask you something."

"Go ahead."

A faint flush came to his cheek. "I hope you're not

mad I gave away half the prize money."

"Of course not. It's a fair decision."

"I thought so. I also think five hundred's enough. Plus what I'll be making, refitting more units for jobs at the orphanages. There's a need for units at hospitals, too."

"Enough for what?"

"For us to live on."

Sofia's throat closed. "Us?"

Lionel shut his eyes for an instant. "Sofia, when I found out Williams had snatched you—well, I was never so scared in my life. I knew then how I felt about you. And I kicked myself for failing to let you know when I had the chance. When I went into that ring— well, I knew if anything happened to you, it didn't matter whether I lived or died."

"Oh." The damned tears started flowing again.

"Here, don't cry. Sofia, I love you. I love you so much, I don't have proper words for it. I think if we join forces—you with your house and me with my living and prize money—we'll be all right."

"Join forces?"

"I'm mucking this all up, aren't I? Sweetheart, I'm asking you to marry me."

"Are you? Are you really?"

"Yes. I want to be at home with you. And I want you to be at home with me."

"That's the only place I ever wanted to be."

"Is that a yes?"

For answer, she kissed him. A mighty cheer came from the rear of the shop, and suddenly they were surrounded by friends, flesh and metal, human and automaton, one indistinguishable from the next.

And Dammit, laughing for joy, filled the room with steam.

A word about the author...

Multi-award-winning author Laura Strickland delights in time traveling to the past and searching out settings for her books, be they Historical Romance, Steampunk, or something in between.

Her first Scottish Historical hero, *Devil Black*, battled his way onto the publishing scene in 2013, and the author never looked back. Nor has she tapped the limits of her imagination.

Venturing beyond Historical and Contemporary Romance, she created a new world with her ground-breaking Buffalo Steampunk Adventure series set in her native city in Western New York.

Married and the parent of a grown daughter, Laura has also been privileged to mother a number of very special rescue dogs and is intensely interested in animal welfare. These days while she's writing, you can always find her latest rescue, Lacy, nearby.

Her love of dogs, and her lifelong interest in Celtic history, magic, and music, are all reflected in her writing. Laura's mantra is Lore, Legend, Love, and she wouldn't have it any other way.

Visit her at:

laurastricklandbooks.com

Thank you for purchasing
this publication of The Wild Rose Press, Inc.

For questions or more information
contact us at
info@thewildrosepress.com.

The Wild Rose Press, Inc.
www.thewildrosepress.com